HO

Ruth-Ann slammed on the brakes and we screeched to a halt two feet from the ambulance. I was out of the car without being aware I'd opened the door. A cop emerged from behind a patrol car and grabbed my arm.

"Ma'am, you can't go in there. There's been—"

"This is my house! Let go of me!" I shoved him out of my way and sent him reeling into his rear fender as I took the three brick steps to my porch in one giant leap. The front door was wide open, and I ran smack into two white coats pushing a gurney. A sheet was drawn up over the figure lying on it, concealing the face. Through blinding tears my peripheral vision picked up Jamie and Eve sitting on the couch, their faces pale and drawn. I think I screamed my father's name as I fell to my knees and ripped the sheet from the still form. . . .

Carrie Carlin mysteries by Nancy Tesler

PINK BALLOONS AND OTHER DEADLY THINGS

SHARKS, JELLYFISH AND OTHER DEADLY THINGS

SHOOTING STARS AND OTHER DEADLY THINGS

GOLDEN EGGS AND OTHER DEADLY THINGS

GOLDEN
EGGS
AND
OTHER DEADLY
THINGS

A CARRIE CARLIN MYSTERY

NANCY TESLER

A Dell Book

Published by
Dell Publishing
a division of
Random House, Inc.
1540 Broadway
New York, New York 10036

Dell® is a registered trademark of Random House, Inc., and the colophon is a trademark of Random House, Inc.

ISBN: 0-440-22615-5

Printed in the United States of America

Published simultaneously in Canada

April 2000

10 9 8 7 6 5 4 3 2 1

OPM

For Noah
with love

ACKNOWLEDGMENTS

For their valuable contributions, my thanks to—

Leah Gabriel, for lifelong friendship and for sharing the experience.

Ann Loring and the roundtable writers for their always constructive criticism and on-the-mark suggestions.

Dr. Ruth Tesler for medical information.

David Beckman for his generous sharing of ideas.

Wendy Rickles for her enthusiastic support.

Jessica Knudson, belatedly, for title suggestions.

My editor, Jackie Farber, for her expertise and her insightful recommendations.

My agent, Grace Morgan, for her encouragement, her friendship, and her continuing belief in me.

Michael, for being there.

My sons, Ken, Bob, and Doug, for being.

And special thanks to my readers, whose comments I welcome by e-mail at nanmys@aol.com, or on my Web site, www.nancytesler.com.

"Thinking to get at once all the gold the goose could give, he killed it, and opened it only to find—nothing."

"The Goose With the Golden Eggs"
Aesop's Fables

1

THE CREAM-COLORED ENVELOPE was crammed into my mailbox along with three bills, four solicitations, my professional biofeedback magazine, a sale notice from Loehmann's, and the Public Television Sweepstakes offer. No checks. I tossed the bills onto my desk, dropped the magazine, the ad, and the letter onto the coffee table, dumped two of the solicitations, and put the worthiest causes in a basket to be considered when I win the sweepstakes. Then I opened the sweepstakes offer.

Notice I said *when* I win, not if. Recently, my mind-set regarding easy money has undergone a major transformation. Never again will I carelessly toss one of those fat envelopes into the trash, and every week I blow a buck or two on a lottery ticket. Don't get me wrong. I'm selective. I don't buy into the come-ons (public television being the rare exception), but I diligently fill out the forms and stick the stickers on every ticket that's delivered to my Norwood, New Jersey, home. Not because I'm a candidate for Gamblers' Anonymous, nor have I turned into one of those gullible sweepstakes addicts currently making news, but because, just occasionally, the gods smile and miracles happen. I'm personally acquainted with someone to whom one did. My dad.

It wasn't one of the Massachusetts lottery's biggest pots, but it was the pot of gold at the end of the rainbow for him. Despite gifting me and my children with ten thousand each and curing my insomnia by setting up trusts for their college educations, the windfall has allowed him all sorts of luxuries heretofore out of his reach. At the time it caused quite a stir up in Worcester, where he and his wife live. The kids and I drove up for the celebration. All our pictures were in the papers, we were interviewed on television, and we were wined and dined by the mayor, who threw a gala bash in Dad's honor. It may sound prejudiced coming from me, but it couldn't have happened to a nicer guy.

David Carlin may well be the last of a breed fast becoming extinct. A truly honest human being. A big gentle bear. Like the panda. He brought me up from the age of three without the help of a wife or nanny, on a diet of love and old-fashioned aphorisms, maxims by which he continues to live. *Do unto others, A stitch in time, Don't judge a book by its cover,* and so on. He was never big on the one about sparing the rod and spoiling the child, so I had a pretty happy childhood. It's only since he married Eve—a sixtyish-plus lady whose taste tends to run to pointy bras à la Monroe and skintight sweaters welded onto a body that's more Roseanne than Marilyn—that the last one, that one about the book cover, has been giving me trouble.

Admittedly, my reaction to her has been colored by her habit of thrusting her more than ample bosom, like a giant mother hen, between my father and me in a well-intentioned effort to keep his heart pumping. Also by what I perceive as her minimally disguised disapproval of me.

To be honest, I'm not totally free of blame for this. The conclusions she's drawn have a certain validity when you consider that she and my father had been married only a few years when it was trumpeted all over the media that I was the prime suspect in the murder of my husband's mistress. Granted, I'd committed that particular murder in my head numerous times, but it was more in the way Jimmy Carter lusted in his heart. Anyway, I am only five foot three, weighing a hundred and twelve pounds; as a divorcee I'm raising, pretty much single-handedly, two adolescent kids, Matthew, age eleven, and Alison, thirteen; and I'm a mental-health professional, a biofeedback clinician, whose job it is to teach people how to cope with the more stressful times in their lives without developing holes in their guts or taking a flying leap off the nearest bridge. You'd think it would've crossed her mind that this was hardly the profile of a modern Lucretia Borgia.

My dad's been my hero and my rock since my mother died. My recollection of her is vague, so I was pretty shaken up when he had his heart attack several years back. He was still in the hospital recovering from that event when he and Eve met. She, to give credit where credit's due, was heading up a volunteer army of gray ladies who saved the day and probably not a few lives when a strike had drastically reduced the hospital staff. She takes excellent care of him and he seems to be supremely content eating rabbit food and being clucked over, so I keep my mouth shut and my feelings to myself. It's only by pure chance and unfortunate coincidence that I've compounded the felony in her eyes by continuing to get mixed up in unpleasant situations. Seriously unpleasant. As in homicides. Solving, not committing. If you exclude the mistress, three at last count.

Perhaps because of these experiences and because I'm now living with the detective who investigated the murder of which I was accused, I've developed a keen interest or, as some might say, an obsession with puzzle-solving. Eve, however, views me as trouble and not exactly the medicine a doctor would order for a sixty-eight-year-old man who's had a serious heart attack and, subsequently, open heart surgery. Imagine my surprise, then, when, after I'd filled out the sweepstakes form (my sights firmly set on that trip to Finland, Russia, and Scandinavia) and opened my bills, I got to the linen-textured envelope, glanced at the engraved return address, and realized it was from her. In the very first paragraph she referred to me as her dear daughter and the only person in the world to whom she could turn in her present dilemma. My internal radar began sending out warning signals. I fortified myself with a glass of ice-cold chardonnay and curled up on the couch to peruse the rest of the letter's contents in an atmosphere of relative tranquillity.

It was Friday and I'd arrived home just before six o'clock, allowing myself plenty of time to prepare a gourmet dinner. I'd scheduled my last Attention Deficit Disorder patient for four and had managed to get out of the office by five so I could stop by the market for the ingredients. The children had been picked up after school by their father, who was taking them to Mystic Seaport in Connecticut for the weekend. I'd been looking forward to a quiet, or if all went well, a not so quiet evening with Ted, Lieutenant Ted Brodsky, the detective I mentioned. We've been living together in my three-bedroom fifty-year-old house for just about a month, and I'm still not entirely comfortable with the arrangement. It's as though I've drunk some marvelous exotic wine and I can't help wondering if the flavor I'm enjoying at present isn't going to end up giving me heartburn. You know how some people have trial separations? Well, what we're having is a trial get-together. Ted would like to do the whole bit, with rings and rice and all the trimmings, but I jumped on that bus nineteen years ago and found myself unceremoniously dumped off before the last stop. It's taken some time for the bumps and bruises to heal, and I'm a little leery about another go-round. And there're my children to consider. They like Ted, but I have to be certain it's going to work for them as well as for me.

The second paragraph told me that Eve was planning a visit, length unspecified, without my father. She would be arriving tomorrow, Saturday; would I pick her up at Newark Airport at six twenty-five P.M.; and would I please not call the house. She didn't want to talk about this on the phone. It all had to do with a favor she needed from me having to do with the dilemma, the source of which she didn't explain in the letter.

My first reaction was irritation at her assumption that I would have no plans for the weekend or would be happy to alter them at the delightful prospect of a visit from her. Plus, if she were planning to stay for more than a day or two, I couldn't think where I was going to put her. My second was discomfort, as I remembered that Eve hadn't yet been apprised that Ted had moved in. He still maintains his apartment, and if things got sticky he could always move back for a few days, which he's done on occasion for propriety's sake if one of the kids has a friend sleep over. But I wasn't in the mood for a lecture regarding the unsuitability of my children being exposed to what, to her, would surely seem an illicit arrangement, especially since I was a touch nervous about it myself. Forget the morality issue, which my children and I have discussed and with which we've come to terms. It was the particulars of my divorce. My ex, Rich Burnham, who'd left me because he was having an affair (actually two or three), could, according to the law, live with as many women as he could fit into his bed. I, on the other hand, living with one man but being an alimony recipient for four plus more years, was on shaky legal ground. So far, Rich has been pretty cool—mostly, I think, because he enjoys his bachelor lifestyle, he's not tight for money, and the last thing he would want is a court battle where he might end up with custody of the children.

In frustration I tossed the letter onto the table. What favor could Eve want that she couldn't ask me for over the phone? She had no right to drop in on me unexpectedly. She was simply going to have to go to a hotel. By the time Ted walked into the kitchen–family room at around seven-thirty, I was banging pot covers, scowling at my reflection in the oven door, and talking to the rack of lamb.

"The animal's dead, sweetheart," he said, dropping a kiss on my head. "Let it rest in peace."

I slammed the oven door shut, crossed to the table, and tossed the letter at him. "Guess who's coming to dinner tomorrow."

He draped his jacket over the back of the couch, shed his shoulder holster, and scanned the letter. "What's so terrible? The kids are away for the weekend, and we don't have anything special on. She can sleep in Allie's room."

"For openers, she's probably expecting to sleep in my room. She doesn't know you're living here."

He grinned, pulled me down on his lap, nuzzled my neck, and grabbed both breasts. "So now she will. One picture's worth a thousand words."

One of the things I love about Ted is his sense of humor. Also his cool, which he manages to keep when everyone else—me especially—is losing theirs. It's one of the things that makes him a good cop. I've seen him pissed off, I've seen him exasperated, and once or twice I've seen him glacial, but I've never seen him out of control. My annoyance began to dissipate. He was right. I'm over twenty-one—actually I'm over forty. Just over. I might owe the court, but

I didn't owe this woman any explanations regarding my lifestyle choices. I allowed myself to relax and enjoy the nuzzling, etc., till I heard the rack sizzling.

"Since when did I get to be her dear daughter?" I grumbled during dinner, between mouthfuls. "I thought I was the bane of her existence."

Ted took a sip of wine and peered at me over the top of his glass. "What is it about her that bugs you?" His eyes crinkled at the corners. "It can't be that you're jealous of those Jayne Mansfield hooters."

I snorted derisively, but I thought about it and tried to be objective. When she and Dad first married, I was probably a little jealous. Not of the hooters—I've never aspired to a D cup—but because I'd had him to myself for so long. But he seems happy and not lonely anymore, and I'm really grateful to her for that.

"I suppose it's that holier-than-thou, supercilious attitude she gets when she's around me," I admitted finally. "She always makes me feel like she's caught me with my hand in the cookie jar."

"Your hand frequently is in the cookie jar."

I glared at him.

"I mean figuratively, from her perspective," he amended. "She can't understand why you keep getting into . . . peculiar situations. So why don't you take this opportunity to show her what a nice, quiet existence you lead most of the time? Make friends."

I wrinkled my nose in distaste.

"Do it for your dad. He knows you're not crazy about her."

"He doesn't. I'm always very polite."

"Carrie, my love, don't ever play poker. You're transparent."

I sighed. "What do you suppose she wants? What's going

on that she doesn't want to talk about it in front of Dad?"
My fork stopped halfway to my mouth. "You don't think
there's something wrong with him, do you? Something he
hasn't told me about?"

"No. She mentioned she needs you to do *her* a favor." He
grinned. "Maybe she wants you to have a little daughterly
talk with him. Maybe he's blowing his winnings on wine
and fast women."

"Yeah, my dad and the pope."

"Seriously, from her letter it seems to me that this is
probably about needing your expertise as a professional."
He chuckled. "I can't wait to find out exactly which of your
several areas of expertise she plans to tap into."

We got to the airport fifteen minutes before the plane
was due, parked the car in the short-term lot, and took the
escalator to the waiting area outside the entrance to the
gates. We were turned back at the metal detector, so we wandered into a nearby bookstore and killed time browsing
through the stacks of bestsellers. I was engrossed in the lat-
est Janet Evanovich when I felt Ted tugging at my jacket
sleeve.

"Brace yourself. There she is."

I glanced up to see Eve getting off the moving walkway. She was wearing a fluffy faux-fur jacket of an inde-
scribable color, sort of mottled yellow-brownish-beige.
Whatever animal it was supposed to resemble escaped me,
but it matched her wildly frizzed-out hair perfectly. She
had on high boots, dark tights under a brown skirt, and
a small red hat that looked like it belonged on a bellhop
except it had a bow in the front. I couldn't suppress the
thought that she looked kind of like an oversize organ
grinder's monkey. She was dragging a small suitcase on

wheels and carrying a shopping bag. I took a deep breath, pasted a smile on my face, and marched over to her.

"Hello, Eve," I said trying to sound welcoming as I bent to kiss her cheek. "How are you?"

She dropped her shopping bag and enveloped me in a bear hug. From somewhere around my chin I heard a muffled, "Carrie, Carrie, I'm so glad to see you." Her hair was tickling my nose. I sneezed. Almost everyone, especially Ted, towers over me, but Eve makes me feel like Brooke Shields. It's the one positive thing about our relationship.

Over her head I shot a look of desperation Ted's way. He rescued me, breaking her stranglehold with professional adroitness. Picking up her suitcase and shopping bag with one hand, he put his other arm around her and led her toward the escalator. Mutt and Jeff.

"Is this all your luggage?" I heard him ask.

She gave him a quavery smile and nodded. "How much does one person need?"

Why did it pop into my head that this was a reference to the visit the kids and I had made to Worcester for the lottery party, when we arrived toting five suitcases, a laptop computer, four live animals, and a couple of stuffed ones? I dismissed the thought as paranoid and mean-spirited. Nonetheless, that twinge of annoyance stirred again in my gut.

Despite Ted's assurance to me last night, I had to ask. "Is everything all right with Dad?"

"Yes, yes, he's fine. Pushes himself too hard, cheats on his diet, but he seems to be getting away with it." She heaved one of those sighs usually reserved for me.

"Then what's this about, Eve?"

She glanced uneasily at Ted, took my arm, and we dropped back a few steps. "It's kind of women's talk," she whispered.

Oh, God, she's sick, I thought. *That's why she doesn't want Dad to know.*

"Are you okay?" I asked.

"My blood pressure's up, no wonder, but other than that, I'm fine."

"Well," I said, enormously relieved. "If that's all it is, you've come to the right place. I'm a whiz at reducing blood pressure. Tomorrow we'll take a run over to the office, I'll hook you up to—"

"Oh, heavens, I don't need any of that mumbo jumbo you do."

The twinge became a stab. The woman was barely off the plane and I was on my way to an ulcer, all my biofeedback training forgotten. Well, not quite. I took several deep diaphragmatic breaths and smiled. "What can I do for you, then?"

"Let's wait till after dinner. We'll talk when Ted goes home."

After that mumbo-jumbo crack, I wasn't about to pull any punches. "Ted won't be going home. We live together now." Like Henny Penny, I raised my eyes heavenward, waiting for the sky to fall.

"Oh, really," she murmured, flashing Ted a look that seemed to contain more consternation than condemnation. "Well, maybe he won't mind leaving us alone for a while."

I glanced at Ted from under raised eyebrows. He winked and blew a kiss.

"No," I said. "I'm sure he won't."

What in God's name, I thought, dumbfounded, *could have precipitated such an extraordinary change of attitude?*

2

DINNER WAS a relatively silent affair and over quickly. Eve ate practically nothing, just pushed the Stroganoff I'd fussed over around on her plate. I could see that her loss of appetite wasn't a recent event, because once she'd taken off her coat, it was obvious she'd dropped a couple of pounds since the last time I'd seen her. Her face had lost its apple-cheeked rosiness and she looked pale and tired. I started to feel guilty about my inhospitable attitude, wondering if she'd told me the truth about not being ill. And yet she wasn't dragging—more the opposite, as though whatever was on her mind so consumed her thoughts, she couldn't be bothered to eat. Occasionally, I caught Ted eyeing her and wondered what his diagnosis would be. He tactfully offered to make coffee and do the dishes, which left the way clear for us to talk.

She followed me into the living room. I poured a glass of brandy, placed it on the table beside her, and settled myself next to her on the couch. My strategy was to lead into the heavy stuff gradually.

"So," I said. "How does it feel to be the toast of the town?"

"Not what I expected at all," she responded, her voice taut with tension. "You can't imagine what's it like. People call us—people we haven't seen in years or . . . or people we don't even know."

I thought I'd zeroed in on the problem. "Are you and Dad being hounded by strangers wanting money? Is that what this is about?"

"No. That isn't—"

"Knowing Dad, I'll bet he's giving away the store. You want me to talk to him?"

She shook her head. "That's not why I—that's not it." She took a swallow of the brandy. "I need a favor," she began.

From Calamity Jane?

"Something's happened that . . . I . . . have this friend . . . who . . . who has a . . . situation."

I remembered asking an acquaintance for the name of a divorce lawyer when Rich left—for my "friend." I hadn't fooled her then, and Eve wasn't fooling me now. I'd bet my new Honda that what I was about to hear was going to be all about Eve.

"What kind of situation?"

She held up her hand to silence me. "I told her you've had quite a bit of . . . well, experience dealing with unusual . . . um . . . things, and you might be willing to help."

To which of my *experiences* was she referring? I didn't think motherhood or biofeedback were in the running. What else was I experienced in? Divorce, dealing with the law. And homicide. Oh, boy. "Go on."

"My friend . . . we're extremely . . . close. We . . . we grew up together. Something's come up that she's not sure how to handle." She took another slug of brandy and went on. "A long time ago . . . something happened in her life, something extremely painful. It . . . it was never . . . there was never any closure even though she spent years trying to . . . trying. Finally, she decided she had to get on with her life, close that chapter, you know, and now suddenly, it's . . . someone's . . . someone says he knows where . . . knows something that would give her the answers she's been searching for."

"So what's the problem?"

"This person wants a lot of money for the information."

"Let me understand this. This person, let's call him the extortionist, says he has—"

"I didn't say he was an extortionist."

"You're talking about someone extorting money from someone else for information that may or may not be true. What else should I call him?"

She began twisting the button on her sweater. "It's more of a business transaction. You see, if he's telling the truth, it could be such an important thing to this woman. It . . . it could change her whole life."

Curiouser and curiouser.

"What happened to your friend all those years ago?"

"That's not . . . not the issue. What's important is how she deals with the situation now. If she pays this person what he's asking, do you think that he'll deliver? Do you think he's to be believed?"

I leaned back against the sofa cushions and watched as she nervously twisted that button till it was hanging by a thread. "How can I answer that? I'm not an expert on extortionists, but my guess would be honesty isn't their strong suit. Of course, every situation is different, and I guess a lot would depend on what the information is that he's selling. Is it just valuable to your friend or is it something he could sell elsewhere?"

"Oh, it's only valuable to my friend."

"Is the extortionist someone she knows?"

"He . . . he's someone who she feels could have access to the information she's looking for."

I felt like we were playing twenty questions and I'd used mine up. "Look, why don't we get Ted's input? He'd know much better than I would what—"

"No! No police."

"Ted's not just any cop. He's like—well, you know, family. He could—"

"No! My friend was adamant. You have to promise."

"Why?"

"She . . . . she doesn't want to take any chances that the police might interfere. If this person gets scared off, she might never find out what she needs to know. And she doesn't want any publicity. Her husband is well-to-do and something like this could trigger . . . other attempts."

Translation: My husband just won the lottery. We're minor celebrities, and our pictures have been all over the tube.

"So what is it you and your . . . friend want me to do?"

She flushed and, leaning forward, clutched at my arm. "I'm . . . she's asked me to meet with this person. The meeting is set for tomorrow. I'd rather not go alone. If you would come with me—"

"Hold on. Wait a minute." Warning bells started a cacophony in my head. "She sent you to make the payoff?"

"I'm . . . acting as a sort of intermediary . . . a messenger . . ."

But they kill messengers, don't they?

"Why doesn't she do it herself? Why should she put you in danger?"

"I won't be in any danger."

"Of course you will. What kind of people do you think you're dealing with? Who is this friend?"

She avoided my eyes, kept twisting the button. "It's no one you know."

The button gave up the ghost. I bent down and retrieved it from under the coffee table.

"Don't you think if I go with you, I'm entitled to know what it's about?"

"You needn't worry. You'd be safe. You'd stay in the car."

"Oh, I see. I'm to drive the getaway vehicle."

She shot me an annoyed look. "You're my insurance. I'm not as reckless as you think. He'd know someone knows where I am and is waiting for me. I came to you because you . . . you seem to—well, you seem to know how to handle yourself in these kinds of situations."

Translation: I've always said you have more guts than brains.

I'll concede that I've done some pretty outrageous things in my life—barging in where even cops would fear to tread without backup, as Ted often reminds me—but I've never done it just for the thrill of it. And I'd like to believe I've never deliberately done anything quite so foolish as this plan my stepmother was now proposing. What would make a woman, normally cautious to the extreme, place herself in such a position? Only one thing that I could think of. Desperation.

"When is this meeting supposed to take place?" I asked.

"Tomorrow at noon."

"Where?"

She hesitated. "We're meeting in a little bookstore on the Upper East Side."

Translation: I'm not telling you unless you commit to coming with me.

There was a lot of clatter in the kitchen, Ted letting us know he'd finished the dishes.

"Coffee time," he called out cheerfully.

"Don't say anything to Ted," Eve whispered just before he appeared in the doorway holding two mugs of coffee. "Please."

Ted took in our expressions. "Looks serious. Can I help?"

"Eve needs some time to think about it," I muttered.

"Okay," he said easily. "You two have your coffee. It's de-caf. I'm going to take a shower and catch the news upstairs." He handed us each a mug. "Call me if you change your mind."

"How was your friend contacted? By phone?" I asked, as soon as I heard the bedroom door close.

"Something came in the mail."

"How much money are we talking about?"

"It's . . . a considerable sum."

"And your 'friend' has access to that kind of money?"

"She has some money of her own, and like I told you, her husband is quite well off."

Translation: Good-bye, lottery money.

The thought made me angry. For the first time in his life, my dad was financially secure. He didn't deserve to be robbed, especially by someone he trusts. "Have you dis-cussed this with Dad?" I asked, ice creeping into my voice.

"It doesn't involve him, and in his condition there was no point in upsetting him."

Translation: No point in taking a chance on his turning off the money spigot.

"Tell me about your friend. Give me some background. I need to know more if I'm going to help you."

The hand holding the glass began to tremble. A little splash of liquid spilled onto the table as she set it down. "I've told you all I can."

"Then count me out." I stood up and held out the button.

She snatched it from my hand, stuck her chest out and her nose in the air. "Fine. I don't need you. I'll go myself."

Translation: You're a real bitch, just like I've always thought.

I guess I was acting like one, and if my father knew he really would be disappointed in me. But I let her stew, hop-ing she'd come around. "If that's how you want it. You know your way around the city?"

She gave a little jump to bring her feet in contact with the floor and stood. "I'll take a taxi."

"I'll lend you my pepper spray," I said. "You might need it in case this person's not as cooperative as you expect."

If looks were lasers, I'd've been zapped into oblivion. But I wasn't about to let myself be intimidated. "At breakfast we'll figure out what you're going to say. Who knows, maybe you can bargain him down—save your friend some money. If he doesn't knock you over the head and steal the gold out of your teeth first." I took her arm. "Come on, let's go upstairs."

She stopped by the foot of the steps and regarded me coldly. The cookie-jar Eve. "I never would've thought you had such a mean streak in you, Carrie."

"I wouldn't call it a mean streak," I said lightly. "It's more of a survival mechanism. I've just learned the hard way that you can't stop a speeding train."

She looked so miserable, I softened. "Listen, let's sleep on it and we'll talk in the morning. Maybe we can come up with some solution that will satisfy us both."

Translation: Maybe I can knock some sense into your silly head in the morning.

Ted looked up from the newspaper when I walked into the bedroom. He laid it down on the bed as I closed the door behind me.

"You're as red as the bow on Eve's chapeau," he said. "You have a fight?"

"No." Pulling my sweater over my head, I headed for the bathroom. I glanced in the mirror and was shocked to see that he was right. I was ashamed of myself for bullying Eve, and it showed. I ran the cold water and splashed it over my burning face. He followed me and stood leaning against the doorjamb.

"What's going on?"

"I wish I knew."

"Trouble in the marriage?"

"Not in the sense you mean."

"In what sense?"

"She's working on it," I replied grimly.

"What does that mean?"

"It means she may be getting herself involved in something that'd send my dad over the top."

"Want me to talk to her?"

I squirted face cleanser into my hand, mixed it with water, and applied the foam. "She won't tell me what the problem is, and for sure she won't tell you."

"Who am I, Simon Legree?"

"You're a cop."

"You think she's in trouble with the law?"

"Not yet."

He considered that. "Sounds intriguing. So if she won't tell you anything, what does she want from you? What's the favor?"

Flippantly, I replied, "She wants me to drive the getaway car."

There was a pause. "You *are* joking."

"Don't worry. I haven't committed to anything."

"That's not an answer. You can't solve everybody's problems, Carrie."

"Believe me, I don't want to." I rinsed the water off my face, squeezed a neat roll of toothpaste onto my toothbrush, and began brushing furiously to avoid a discussion.

He handed me a towel. "Insist that she tells you what this is about and don't let her talk you into doing anything stupid."

"*Moi?* Do something stupid?" I tossed the towel back at

him and peeled out of the rest of my clothes. "Perish the thought."

He eyed me appreciatively. "You're cute when you're naked. Come to bed. I've suddenly lost interest in Eve's problems."

I snapped off the light and snaked my arms around his neck. My fingertips brushed the jagged scar that puckered the skin just below his collarbone and just above and to the left of his heart, involuntarily drawn there as if by a magnet. It was almost as though something deep inside me believed if I rubbed hard enough I could rub it away, and along with it the memory of the day the bullet had ripped through his shoulder. He read my mind.

"Ancient history," he murmured, his lips lingering on my throat. "This is now."

I let go of the image, reveling in his warmth, losing myself in the sensuous feeling of his skin against mine. We had the whole day tomorrow to figure out what to do about Eve. I had better plans for tonight.

Much later, unable to fall asleep, I lay in bed listening to the sounds of the night—the soft purr of one of the cats; a grunt from Horty, our monster dog, as he pursued a rabbit in his dreams; the rustle of a tree branch scraping against the window; Ted's even breathing, marked by an occasional snore. All sounds normally more comforting than disturbing. Not tonight. My conversation with Eve played over in my mind. I realized I knew very little about her background, only that she was a widow, had been for several years before she met my father, that she had no children and had been living in Framingham, a small town not far from Worcester. I thought I remembered Dad telling me she was originally from someplace in the midwest, but if she had family there, she certainly never talked about them. Had she lived there when she was married? How long had she been married? What had her husband died of? Did my father know the answers to any of these questions?

Marry in haste, repent at leisure—another of my father's maxims, though to give him credit he'd never rubbed my nose in that one. Had he made any attempt to follow his own advice, find out these things before he'd married Eve? If the friend was an invention and Eve was talking about herself, which I was pretty sure she was, what had happened to her all those years ago that she wouldn't talk about? If the friend existed, why wouldn't Eve tell me what had happened? Because of my involvement with Ted? Knowing of the relationship, why come to me for help, then? Questions without answers tumbled around in my head. Finally, as pinkish dawn crept through the blinds, exhaustion overtook me. Spooning myself around Ted, I fell into an uneasy sleep.

I am sitting alone in my car outside a small bookstore. I keep trying to read the name of the store, but it's raining and a bright neon sign on the side of the building is blinking on and off, on and off, impairing my vision. Through the sheet of rain I see Eve making for the car, her arms filled with books. Then someone is running after her, calling her name, and she drops the books and aims my pepper spray at him. And he grabs his chest and falls and I begin screaming, "You've killed my father, you've killed my father!"

Then Ted was shaking me and his calm voice was whispering, "Wake up, Carrie, wake up. You've been dreaming again." And I fought my way to consciousness and reached for him.

3

WE SLEPT LATE. Ted's beeper went off around nine-thirty, and when I opened my eyes he was sitting on the edge of the bed, pulling on his socks.

"What's going on?" I mumbled. "You're not on today."

"Some psycho on the East Hill in Tenafly plugged his next-door neighbor with a sawed-off shotgun. Said the rain from the guy's lawn was leaking into his billiard room. Can you beat it?" He leaned over and kissed me. "Crazy god-damned people."

"Where's Fowler?" I grumbled. "It's his weekend."

"Took a header down his steps last night, broke his ankle. So I'm it."

I came fully awake and sat up. "You're not going to leave me all alone with Eve for the whole day?"

He grinned. "Weren't you going to take this opportunity to make friends?"

"That was before I found out she was a woman with a past."

He reached for his holster and plucked his jacket off the

chair. "I'll get back as soon as I can. We can decide how to
handle whatever it is then." He dropped a kiss on my head.
"Just keep her here."

But I was too late. I discovered that Eve was gone shortly
after I came down to the kitchen to let Horty out. At first I
thought she was still asleep, but Shadow, our neighbor's
cat, decided to pay us a visit, and the caterwauling that en-
sued in the yard would have awakened half the town if they
weren't already up. Horty's part Lab, part Saint Bernard, and
aptly named after the elephant in *Horton Hears a Who*. Our
three Siamese cats, Luciano, Placido, and José, use him for
a pillow, but Shadow doesn't know that. I got Horty back
inside, dashed upstairs to apologize to Eve, and found a
hastily scrawled note on the pillow.

Carrie, it said. *Borrowed your car. Will leave it at bus station. Saw
you have two sets of keys. Will return these tonight. Sorry to bother
you. My problem. Eve.*

Consumed with guilt, I stared at the note. Reread it ten
times, which didn't enlighten me any further as to where
Eve had gone. Why had she left so early? Because she was
afraid I'd have stopped her. Which I would have. How had I
let this happen? If I'd been more sympathetic, hadn't been
such a smart-alecky pseudopsychologist, she'd still be here.
How would I ever explain it to my dad if something happened to her? And damn, she'd taken my Honda, the first
new car I'd had in years, paid for by insurance after my '89
was totaled on the Tappan Zee Bridge last November. How
had she gotten my keys? Surely, Ted or I would have heard
her if she'd come into my room this morning. Then I remembered I'd left my handbag on the hall table. I scooted
back downstairs, dug around in the outside flap. Of course

the keys were gone. And it was the set with my pepper spray, which I carry on the same key ring. How had she managed to open and close the garage without our hearing? We must've slept like a couple of druggies. I have a one-car garage not attached to the house, and Ted parks in the driveway, so he wouldn't have noticed when he left earlier that my car was gone. I dashed outside, saw the tire depressions on the frozen grass where she'd managed to get around Ted's Miata.

I stood outside in my slippers and robe, letting the icy February wind whip my hair across my eyes and cut through my flannel bathrobe, chilling me to the marrow. What to do? I could call Ted. No. He wouldn't be able to leave a crime scene for this. Freezing, I ran back into the house, aware that the chill I was feeling had as much to do with my culpability and my fear for Eve as with the temperature. I heard the phone ringing as I slammed the door behind me.

Please, let that be her, I prayed as I dashed into the kitchen and grabbed it.

"Hi, honey," my dad's voice boomed.

Oh, hell! "Hi, Dad."

"You sound out of breath."

I tried to keep the panic out of my voice. "I just ran in from the yard."

"Everything okay there? I know you weren't expecting Eve. I would've called and asked if her coming was okay with you, but she only heard from the lawyer in New York a few days ago—something about her late husband's estate—and just decided to go on the spur of the moment yesterday."

So my dad wasn't aware that she'd written to me. And who was the lawyer? "No, it's fine, Dad. The kids are with Rich this weekend, so there's plenty of room."

"Oh, good. How are those monkeys?"

"Wonderful. Everybody's fine." If I had to keep chitchatting, I was going to have a nervous breakdown. "Are you feeling okay?"

"Pretty good for a guy with an unreliable ticker. Bought a new Buick. Eve tell you?"

"No, but we didn't have a chance to talk much. She was tired." I made an effort to generate some enthusiasm. "What color is it?"

"Dark green. Lots of room. Drives like a dream."

"Can't wait to see it." I definitely was going to have a nervous breakdown. "Listen, Dad, I have to—"

"She tell you we're going to Europe?"

"No! When?"

"June. Paris, London, Rome."

"Oh, that's great. I'm so excited for you."

"Where is that lazybones? Still sleeping?"

"Yeah—I think so. Or in the bath. I'll have her call you tonight. We're . . . uh . . . we're going shopping as soon as she's dressed."

To thine own self be true and thou canst not then be false to any man—another of my father's (and Shakespeare's) little axioms, and I was being false to him. But compared to his wife I was George Washington.

"On Sunday?" he asked.

"Yeah, the stores are open in the city." What had Eve said about the meeting place? Upper East Side, at a bookstore. There were about a million bookstores in Manhattan, for God's sake. But she'd said a small bookstore. I moved the phone off the pile of phone books, knocked over my pencil holder, ignored the scattered pens and pencils, pulled out the Bell Atlantic yellow pages, and flipped to "Bookstores."

He laughed. "Well, I'll leave you ladies to it, then," he said. "Have fun and spend some of that money I sent you."

I forced a laugh. "I certainly intend to. Talk to you later, Dad."

"Okay. Glad you and Eve are getting along. Means a lot, your making the effort. Tell her I said to be good and keep out of trouble."

I blanched. "I will. You take care of yourself."

"So long, hon."

"Bye, Dad."

I sank onto the chair, resting my head on the pages of the thick phone book, then lifted it and started running my finger down the list. Hopeless. Even confining myself to the Upper East Side, starting at Sixty-first Street, I found three small bookstores listed just under the *A*'s.

Maybe she'd written down the address somewhere. I imagined she wasn't too familiar with the city, so she probably wouldn't have committed the address to memory. Leaving the phone book open, I dashed upstairs to Allie's room. Eve's suitcase was sitting on the chair by the desk. I lifted it onto the bed. It wasn't locked. Opening the lid, I peered inside. Neatly folded lingerie. A lacy blue nightgown. Two sweaters—one red with spangles, one raspberry with a design outlined in sequins. One navy blue skirt. One green skirt. A red print scarf. Two pairs of panty hose and a pair of black suede shoes. A flat-brimmed blue hat with multi-colored bird feathers growing out of the crown. A cosmetics case containing a couple of jars, two lipsticks, two brushes, rouge, eye shadow, and a bottle of blood-pressure pills. Feeling like a peeping Tom, I fished around in the side compartments and drew out some costume jewelry and two credit cards. No papers, no notebook. No leads.

Think of this as a puzzle, I told myself. *You're pretty good at solving puzzles. Think. Was this all Eve had with her when you picked her up at the airport?* I tried to picture how she'd looked as she

came off the moving walkway. She'd been wearing the vo-
luminous jacket and the silly red hat, pulling this suitcase
and carrying her handbag and something else—a brown
paper shopping bag. The shopping bag. Where was it? Had
she taken it with her this morning? I dashed over to the
closet, opened it. No shopping bag. My eyes darted around
the room, lit on brown paper peeking out from the corner
between Allie's desk and her white-painted dresser. A second later I had the bag in my hand. I reached inside and
took out an unwrapped computer game—obviously a present for Matt. Eve never visits without bringing something
for the kids. Mentally, I gave her points. There was a gift-
wrapped box with Allie's name on it and a paperback novel.
Frustrated, I started to return the bag to its corner when
something—the Curious Georgette, as Ted used to call it—
in me made me want to see what Eve was reading. I drew
out the book. It was a mystery she'd probably picked up to
have something to read on the plane. *Paying the Piper*, by
Sharyn McCrumb. I flipped through the pages, noticed an
inscription on the flyleaf: *For Jamie.* Must be a used book. I
tossed it back into the bag and sat on the edge of the bed,
willing a bolt from heaven to strike. I said a silent prayer,
apologizing to God for my neglecting to keep in touch unless I was, figuratively speaking, in a foxhole. He was unfor-
giving. No bolts. Defeated, I got to my feet, was halfway
out the door, when I gave the room one last look and saw
the bookmark with which Eve had marked the page, lying
half under the bed. In the unlikely event she returned in
one piece, I didn't want her to know I'd been going through
her things, so I walked back and retrieved it. I was about to
drop it in the bag when I noticed the name of the store
where the book had been purchased. Printed in stark black
lettering over the outline of a black orchid: *The Black Orchid
Bookshop, Mysteries, Thrillers, & More, New & Old,* 303 *East* 81st

Street, New York, New York 10028. On the flip side was a se-
ries of handwritten numbers: 2/6 . . . 12. The book had been
sent from New York. *Paying the Piper*. The puzzle pieces
were falling into place. If I was reading the clues correctly,
Eve had gone in to New York to pay the piper—i.e., the
extortionist—and they were meeting at a small bookstore.
On February 6, which was today, at twelve noon! It seemed
that God, knowing how good I am with puzzles and moving in one of His mysterious ways, had indeed come through.

4

GALVANIZED INTO ACTION, I called a taxi to take me to the bus station, took a two-minute shower, threw on a pair of jeans and a sweater, grabbed my jacket, a comb, and my cosmetics case, and did a crash makeup job in the backseat of the cab. My black Accord was parked by the bus shelter, intact, no visible dents or scratches.

A light snow was glossing the blacktop as, just before eleven, I pulled onto the George Washington Bridge. If all went well I'd arrive at the designated block early enough to stop Eve before she went off with the extortionist. But Murphy's Law intruded, and all didn't go well. At a Hundred Twenty-fifth Street a three-car pileup was forcing the traffic off the FDR and onto Second Avenue. By the time I turned onto Eightieth Street, it was twelve-twenty, my nerves were raw, my nails bitten, and I was exercising my divorce-inspired vocabulary at every red light I hit. Hardly the way for a biofeedback professional who teaches self-control in non-life-threatening situations to behave, but I excused myself on the grounds that Eve's life might well be in jeopardy.

I headed east on Eightieth, came around on First, and drove slowly up Eighty-first Street to Second Avenue. It was a quiet, primarily residential street comprised mostly of brownstones. Nothing ominous about it, except that Eve was nowhere to be seen. I searched for a parking space, went around the block three more times till I saw a silver Audi pull out. I gunned the engine and skidded in nose-first before some pushy New York driver beat me out. Even we supposedly laid-back suburbanites drive like Mario Andretti in the city.

The snow had turned to sleet. I pulled the hood of my jacket up over my head, stepped out into the accumulating slush, and slogged up the street. About halfway up the block an off-white awning with black lettering identified the mystery bookshop advertised on the bookmark. It was nestled between a children's clothing resale shop and a brownstone. There was a seafood restaurant on the corner and an Italian restaurant across the street. A nearby toy store enticed customers inside with a happy window overflowing with all manner of colorful dolls.

The entrance to The Black Orchid was up a short flight of stairs. Shouldering the door open, I found myself surrounded by stacks of books in a cozy narrow room. I paused in the doorway, taking in the room, hoping to spot Eve lurking near one of the bookshelves as she waited for her mysterious companion. The store was small, with room only for the shelves of books, a couple of tables, and a few chairs. No place to lurk. A young man, arms loaded with paperbacks, was browsing through the shelves. He moved aside to let me pass. I approached the counter and smiled at the pretty, auburn-haired woman sitting behind it.

"Excuse me . . ."

The woman looked up. "Hi," she said, her manner friendly. "Can I help you?"

"I hope so. I . . . uh . . ." I stopped, not sure how to begin.

"You looking for something in particular?"

Someone in particular.

I fished the bookmark out of my pocket and held it out. "Uh . . . I'm supposed to be meeting someone. She left this bookmark for me, so I'm pretty sure I'm supposed to meet her here. I'm a little late and I was wondering if she's come in yet."

"What's she look like?"

I told her.

The woman grinned. "Oh, yes, she was here. She picked up a book that we'd ordered for her. Left about half an hour ago."

"I don't think she would've ordered a book. She isn't from this area."

"Well, maybe your friend has a clone, because it sure sounds like the same lady."

She was right. There couldn't be two people on this planet who dressed like Eve, or two hats as outrageous as the one she'd been wearing, although the one in her suitcase ran a close second. I'd figured she and the "piper" were going to meet here, but maybe there'd been something in the book that told her where they were to meet. "By any chance was the book *Paying the Piper*, by Sharyn McCrumb?"

"No, but we have that book in stock if you'd—"

"No. Are you sure she ordered the book?"

"Come to think of it, guy came in a few days ago ordered it for her." She flipped through a notebook. "Eve Carlin. That her name?"

"Yes. Do you know the man who ordered it?"

"Uh-uh. He's not a regular."

"What'd he look like?"

She looked at me questioningly, but she answered. "Lemme think. Mid-forties, maybe a little older. Dark eyes and hair. Sorry, I really didn't notice much else."

"You remember the name of the book?"

"Sure. *Children in the Crossfire*. Something about lost children. It's not a mystery. Had to special-order it."

"You don't have another copy, then?"

"It's out of print. Got that one from a used-book dealer. Guy gave me a birthday card to put in the book."

Damn. Like I'd figured, instructions had been left in the book. What to do now?

I thanked her for her help and was on my way out the door when the browser intercepted me. "I think I saw her."

"What'd you say?"

"The lady wearing the funny red hat. She have on a big fluffy jacket?"

I almost grabbed him. "Yes! Did you see where she went?"

"She was walking up the street looking for a number on one of the brownstones when I got here."

I wanted to kiss him. "Which one?"

"Dunno. Maybe the one next to the toy store. Or maybe the cleaner's. I'm not sure."

"When was that?"

"About half, three-quarters of an hour ago. How long I been in here, Bonnie?" he asked the woman behind the counter.

"About that," she agreed.

"Thank you, thank you very much," I said, pumped his hand gratefully, and rushed out.

I canvassed the cleaner's, the resale shop, the toy store, even both restaurants, describing Eve to the waiters and salespeople. No one remembered seeing her. I went back to the car, sat behind the wheel, and did some deep breathing. Eve was here on this block. She was probably fine. Sooner

or later she was going to walk out of one of these brownstones. I convinced myself all I had to do was wait. I tried a
progressive-relaxation exercise, focusing on releasing tension in my back and shoulder muscles. It didn't work. I was
getting more annoyed and colder with each passing minute. What was I doing sitting here, worrying about this
woman I didn't even like who was behaving in a manner I
wouldn't tolerate from my children? Whenever I started the
engine to warm myself, I had to wave off disgruntled would-
be parkers, so through most of my vigil I froze. I thought
about running back to the bookstore and asking to use the
phone to call the police, but Eve wasn't a missing person.
She'd only been gone since early this morning.

The sky had darkened and the sleet had begun making
little pinging noises on my roof and windows. There wasn't
a soul out on the street. I was debating whether to page Ted
just to share my misery, because I knew there was nothing
he could do, when through my rearview mirror I caught
sight of a scene so bizarre, I thought I was hallucinating. A
creature that looked like Sesame Street's Big Bird was standing on the second-floor fire escape of a four-story brownstone. As I watched, I saw it start to scramble down the
slippery metal steps. In New York, people parachute off the
Empire State Building, so you tend to accept unusual sights
with more aplomb than you would in, say, Iowa. Still, it was
the dead of winter and even a thief would have more sense
than to try to make his getaway from an ice-coated fire escape. Maybe they were filming a movie, but, then, where
was the crew? I got out of the car to get a better look and
realized with a start that the apparition was neither a fig-
ment of my imagination nor an escaping burglar. It was Eve.
She was hatless, her coat open and flapping in the wind like
the wings of a wounded ostrich. Her hair was flying in all
directions. I raced across the street, shouting her name, and

got to the building just as she landed on the first-floor grate.
She glanced frantically around as she realized that the steps
had come to an abrupt end. Horrified, I watched as she
teetered on the edge of the platform, peering down into the
void below.

She can't be planning to jump, *I thought in disbelief. It's at least
fifteen feet to the ground.*

"Eve," I yelled. "There's a ladder. Unhook it!"

She stared at me blankly. Either she didn't hear me or she
didn't understand what I meant.

"Above your head. A big metal hook!"

She looked up, saw the hook, struggled with it for a moment, then the ladder came loose and, with a loud thud, hit
the ground.

New York fire escapes seem to be designed more with
Olympian athletes than with buxom senior citizens in mind.
This one was no exception. The ladder was up against the
building, and Eve was forced to swing one leg over the railing, hang on to the rungs with both hands, then attempt to
bring over the other leg. She must've been pumping enough
adrenaline to lift a car, because after several attempts, she
actually managed it. I watched in amazement as her right
leg found purchase on the top rung. For one terrifying
moment she seemed to hang suspended in midair. Then,
miraculously, her left leg followed suit, and she began to
back slowly down to mother earth. I was breathing a sigh of
relief when I saw her feet slip on a patch of ice and slide off
the ladder. Scrambling up several rungs, I caught her around
the waist, clutched wildly for a hold, and missed. We ended
up sprawled on a mound of last week's snowfall, which had
been shoveled onto the side of the walk. Luckily, the snow
cushioned my fall. Not so luckily, my body cushioned Eve's.
It took me a full minute to see if my legs still worked and to
recover the breath that had left my body with an audible

whoosh. By the time I'd managed it, I was startled to see that Eve was unhurt and already on her feet.

"Where's your car?" she gasped, grabbing my arm and yanking me up.

"What?"

Her voice went up a decibel and she started shaking me. "The car! Where'd you park?"

I pointed. "There—at the end of the block, but—"

She took off, running in an awkward lope through the slush. I limped after her, thinking the Big Bird analogy hadn't been that far off, and it was no picnic, being squished by Big Bird.

"Eve, wait," I called. "What happened? What were you—"

"Just unlock the car and let me in!" she shrieked.

And thank you so very much for coming to my rescue.

But her eyes were wild and she was breathing in short gasps, and I was afraid she'd drop at my feet if I didn't move fast, so I opened the passenger door, scurried around to my side, started the motor, and pulled out onto Second Avenue. She didn't question me, didn't ask how I'd known where she was. When I glanced over at her, her head was back against the headrest, her eyes were closed, and her skin had turned the mottled, pasty color of parchment. I drove another few blocks and pulled over to the curb next to a small deli.

"You want me to get you some water?"

She shook her head without opening her eyes. "Just take me home."

"Eve, what happened in there?"

Her voice was barely audible and I had to lean forward to catch the words. "I . . . nothing. Nothing."

"Nothing? You climbed out on the fire escape! You nearly killed yourself!" I didn't add *and me when you landed on me*, but I thought it as I shifted position and my bruised hip and knee screamed in protest.

A minute went by before she spoke. "I . . . had to. The door . . . the door . . . was locked."

"What door?"

"To . . . the apartment."

"You mean, no one answered the door when you got there? That's what you meant about nothing happening? So how did you get out on the fire escape? Why didn't you just go out the way you came in?"

She opened her eyes, and tears started flowing as though some unseen hand had turned on a faucet full blast. "Someone . . . someone locked me in. With . . . the body."

A chill ran through me and I began taking deep breaths to fight the nausea that threatened to do me in. Déjà vu. *Oh, God, let it not be like the time I walked in on a dead body in Key West.* "What do you mean? What . . . what body?"

"He was . . . his head was . . . down on . . . in . . . the soup and—"

"His head was in the *soup?*" I had an insane, terrible urge to laugh. I took another deep breath, struggling to fend off hysterics.

"On the table . . . like he'd been eating lunch when . . . I . . . I never saw a . . . anyone who . . . and I . . . didn't know . . . I thought he was . . . hurt or something and I kind of pushed at . . . and . . . he fell over and all this blood and . . . stuff . . . ran down his face . . ." The words trailed off and she began sobbing, painful, wrenching sobs.

I felt like howling right along with her. "Who was it? Did you know him?"

A whisper. "O-Omar."

"Who's Omar?"

No answer.

I grabbed both her hands. "Tell me. Who's Omar?"

She pulled her hands away and pressed them against her eyes. "I . . . don't know."

"You don't know?" I was practically screeching. "Was he wearing a name tag, for God's sake? You said Omar. You must've known him."

She started trembling. "I didn't. I . . . no, I . . . didn't say that."

"You did."

"I said . . . I said, oh, my . . . oh, my . . ."

She wouldn't look at me. I tried a different tack, forced myself to speak quietly. "You were in there for more than an hour. I've been parked on the street at least that long. Why'd you stay there if you . . . you found . . . if someone was . . . Why didn't you call 911?"

"I don't know, I don't know," she cried. "Somebody hit me or . . . no, I think . . . I guess I fainted. Whoever killed him must've . . . locked me in." She took off a glove and gingerly touched the back of her head. How she got to scalp through that tangled mess I'll never know, but her hand came away red. A dazed expression settled on her face. "I'm bleeding," she said.

I handed her a crumpled tissue. "Put pressure on it. It's not bleeding badly. I'll look at it when we get home." I began clutching at straws, desperately reaching for any kind of explanation that would make this nightmare go away. "Why do you think someone killed this guy? Maybe what you saw running down his face was the soup. Maybe it was tomato soup. Maybe he died of natural causes. Or maybe he just passed out."

"It wasn't just . . . blood, and there . . . was a . . . a bullet hole in his head."

Unbidden, the words of an old nursery rhyme sprang to mind.

There was a little man and he had a little gun.
And his bullets were made of lead, lead, lead:
He went to the brook and saw a sitting duck
And shot him through the head, head, head.

No wonder children were killing children. What the hell kind of nursery rhyme was that?

I didn't want to deal with this. I wasn't equipped to deal with this. This was Ted's province. Not mine. My job is healing. It's life-affirming. Calming. Ted's the one who has to deal with bullet holes and death. I needed to find a phone and call Ted.

Halfway up the block I noticed a cruising police car. Part of me knew I should flag him down. The other part wanted to get as far away from this place as I could. If Eve had it right and someone had been murdered, we were leaving the scene of a crime. But she was distraught and I didn't know what had happened to her other than that she'd found some dead person's head in a bowl of soup. And that would put us in the soup, and the cops would probably arrest her, or maybe both of us, on the spot. I also knew there was a helluva lot more to this story and, much as she irritated me, she was my father's wife and I couldn't just abandon her to the vicissitudes of the NYPD. As soon as we got home I'd page Ted, and then I'd call a lawyer. She had a right to talk to a lawyer before we went to the police. I owed her that much—at least, I owed my father. Convinced by my own pep talk, I went with my second impulse, threw the getaway car into drive, pulled out into traffic, and headed for the FDR. Eve had stopped crying. Shock was setting in, so I left her alone and concentrated on maneuvering on the slippery road surface.

Somewhere around a Hundred Sixteenth Street, I had to break the silence. "Where's your handbag?" I asked.

Her eyes wandered over to me. "What?"

"Your handbag. You had one, didn't you? Tell me it's not in the apartment."

"I don't know where it is." She reached up and touched her head. "I . . . I lost my hat too. It must've come off when I fell."

Under other circumstances that would've been a plus. But not today. Talk about dead. We were dead in the water. Not only had the browser in the bookstore seen Eve walking up and down the street, but he'd particularly noticed her hat, and that hat was unique. Probably the only one like it in existence, and it was still at the crime scene along with her purse, which undoubtedly had identification in it.

It flashed briefly through my overloaded brain that the body wouldn't have been discovered yet. We could go back and retrieve the incriminating objects. But there was no way I was going to climb up that fire escape, crawl in a window, and share space with a corpse. Not for a minute, not even for ten seconds, and not even to pull my foolish stepmother's fat out of the fire. Besides, the killer might still be in the vicinity, and we were implicated anyway. I'd been asking questions, giving Eve's description to every store owner in the neighborhood. The thing to do was go home, call Ted, and dump the mess in his lap.

An eternity later, tension by now having permanently welded my hands to the steering wheel, I turned the corner onto my street. All I needed to send my EDR (that's *electrodermal response*—biofeedback for fight-or-flight response) into orbit was seeing Rich's Mercedes parked in front of my house. Rich was back early with the kids. The weather must've put a crimp in their fun. Until now he'd only ranted and raved each time I'd stumbled on a murder victim. If I walked in the door toting a shell-shocked Eve, capable of blurting out God knows what, I could expect a knock-down drag-out. Being in no condition to fight, I decided to flee. I kept driving.

My office is in Piermont, as is my best friend, Meg Reilly. She owns and runs a café called Meg's Place, and it's where I go whenever I need solace or wonderful food. Right now what I needed was a hideout, a place where I could stash Eve till I figured out what to do. Meg has a storeroom and, more important, she has a good head. I was in desperate need of both. I turned the car around and headed for Piermont.

5

I LEFT EVE locked in the car with the motor running and the heat on while I dashed into the café. Fortunately, it was downtime between lunch and dinner and there were few customers. Meg was behind the counter talking to Betsy, her part-time waitress. She looked up when I—and the accompanying blast of frigid air—blew in.

"Well, what happened to you?" she called. "You look like someone threw you in the Hudson. You need one of my hot toddies."

"I need more than that. Can I talk to you privately for a minute?"

"And what is the crisis du jour?" she joked, taking note of my frazzled expression. "Shall I break out the chamomile?" When I didn't answer, her face grew serious. "Come on, we'll go in the kitchen."

I followed her through the swinging door and fell into a chair next to the chopping table. "You're not going to believe this . . ." I began.

"With you, I'll believe anything." She perched on a stool next to me. "Just don't tell me it's about another dead body."

"It's about another dead body."

She jumped off the stool. "Cut it out!"

"You've got to help me."

"Carrie, stop it now. If this is your idea of a joke, it isn't funny."

"D'you see me laughing? We're in trouble."

"*We're* in trouble? How did I—"

"Does that door lead to your storeroom?"

"Why do you want to know? You planning to hide the corpse in my cooler?"

"I've got Eve in my car," I whispered.

Her eyes opened wide. "God, Carrie, you don't mean—" She shook her head. "No, of course you don't. That's ridiculous. What was I thinking?" But she wiped perspiration off her forehead with her sleeve.

"She's not the one who's dead, but I've got to park her somewhere. Rich is at the house with the kids."

"You're not making sense. Why do you have to hide Eve from Rich?"

I gave her the *Reader's Digest* version. "I can't get anything else out of her," I finished. "But it's only a matter of time till the cops put two and two together."

"Jesus, Carrie, how do these things keep—"

"How the hell should I know? Somebody's put a curse on me!" I snapped. My tone changed to pleading. "Just help me, Meg. I need time to talk to her and work out what to do."

And, being the friend she is, she agreed. I left her dragging a chair into the storeroom while I went back to my car and drove around to the rear of the café. Between us, we lugged a nearly catatonic Eve inside and deposited her in the chair. Meg went into her efficiency mode and brought a cool washcloth, placed it on Eve's forehead, and began massaging her wrists. I went to work on the cut on her head, which didn't turn out to be very deep. *That hair's better insulation than the stuff in my walls,* I thought. Eve sat like a robot, passively allowing us to minister to her. When we saw color begin to return to her face, Meg went into the kitchen and appeared minutes later with three cups of chamomile tea on a tray, chamomile tea being her cure-all for any emergency. I've been the recipient of many a cup in my time. I'm not sure if it's the tea or Meg's compassion or the combination that works, but I'd swear by its calming effect.

"Drink, Eve," I commanded. She took a sip. "More," I said. "The whole cup."

Like a child, she did as she was told. When she'd finished, her breathing had slowed and her eyes had lost the glazed look. She focused on me, and a shudder convulsed her body. I took that to mean she was coming out of her fog, but it could've just been the effect I have on her. I plowed ahead despite it.

"Eve, this is my friend Meg," I said. "You met her at Allie's Bat Mitzvah, remember?"

She nodded.

"She's going to help us. But we need you to tell us exactly what happened in that apartment today. We need to know the whole story so we can plan how best to deal with this . . . crisis."

Silence.

"That man you saw, Omar—" She started to protest, but I overrode her. "Who was he? Was he the piper—I mean, the guy you were bringing the money to?"

The pause lengthened. Eve refused to meet my gaze. As I watched her, an expression I can only describe as crafty flashed over her face and was instantly gone. She reached into her coat pocket, pulled out a tissue, blew her nose, and looked at me. "I've been thinking about what you said in the car, Carrie, and you were probably right. You're so smart to have figured it out. I'm not sure that what I saw really was a bullet hole. Maybe it was a bruise from when he hit his head. Maybe the man did have a heart attack or something."

The minute she said it I knew I wasn't smart and that wasn't at all what had happened.

"What I'm saying is, maybe I was so upset when he fell over and I saw what I thought was blood that I fainted. Maybe it was tomato soup—"

"You said you saw more than blood, and you said there was a bullet hole! A bullet hole doesn't look like a bruise. And you said somebody hit you."

"I *thought* someone may have struck me. But maybe I fainted and fell and hit my head. When I came to and tried to leave, the door stuck and I assumed I was locked in."

I exploded. "That's crap, and you know it!"

She went on as though I hadn't spoken. "It was such a shock, you see, seeing someone dead like that. I'm afraid I got all muddled."

"Who was the guy?" I asked. "Just tell us that."

"I don't know. I never saw him before."

The transformation was mind-boggling. Before my eyes, in the space of five minutes, the woman had gone from zombie on the verge of collapse to the Eve I'd never been quite able to like: guard up, defenses well in place. I'd be damned if I was going to let her get away with it.

"What was so important that this guy was going to tell your friend? Surely you can tell us that now."

There was a pause while she invented what I was certain would be an interesting fantasy.

"When my friend was young she had an illegitimate child, who she gave up for adoption. Later she wanted to find the child, but the records had been destroyed. This man had worked for the adoption agency. Recently, he wrote her and said he had information as to her daughter's whereabouts, but he wanted money. She's never told her husband about the child. That's why she asked me to go in her place."

It was a pretty good story. Not implausible except for a couple of big holes. How had the man known Eve was looking for her child? Because this had to be about Eve. And why would somebody kill him? The only person with a motive in this scenario was Eve, and she wouldn't have killed him till after she'd obtained the information she wanted. Besides, she'd been too upset to be the murderer. Unless she was a wonderful actor, and if she was that good she'd been keeping a great talent from the theatrical world all these years. Hard to believe that the woman sitting here had ever been passionate enough to have an illicit affair. But it all was beginning to make sense. Her not wanting to tell my dad the truth. The book about lost children the piper had left for her. Her willingness to pay him off. With my dad's money, I'd bet. None of it made me like her any better.

"I assume the money's gone," I said.

"What money?"

"The payoff. Wasn't it in your handbag?"

"Oh, no," she said, patting her middle. "I have it."

"May I see it?"

Her brows drew together in a frown. "It's in a money belt under my blouse. Are you implying that I'm lying, Caroline?"

Nobody calls me Caroline. I wanted to choke her. "Your story has holes in it as big as the state of Texas. Why would somebody have killed the guy?"

"I told you. I think maybe he died of natural—"

"Oh, stop it. Do you realize the police are going to find your hat and your purse there?"

"I left my credit cards at your house. There's no reason anyone has to know I was there. I didn't have anything in my purse that had my name on it—" Her brow furrowed. "Unless I—"

"Are you kidding? There're pieces of you in that apartment you haven't a clue about. Your blood on whatever you hit when you fell, for one thing. Ever hear of DNA? Besides which, I described you and that hat to every—"

Meg stepped on my foot. "Let's you and I go make some more tea and let Eve rest for a few minutes."

Eve looked at Meg as though she were the Virgin Mary come to save her from the devil incarnate. "Thank you, Meg," she said. "I'm so exhausted. It's been such a terrible ordeal, and I really don't want to talk about it anymore."

Meg got up and half-dragged me after her into the kitchen.

"She's lying," I fumed. "She knew who the guy was. She called him Omar."

"Of course she's lying, but you gave her a way out. The perfect explanation."

"It won't fly with the police. I described that stupid hat to every store owner on the block. Besides, she probably left fingerprints all over the place—"

"Wasn't she wearing gloves?"

I recalled her removing her gloves in the car. "Yeah, she was. But there're probably hair fibers and blood from when she cracked her head—"

"And the very real possibility that she killed him."

I'd just convinced myself she couldn't have, and the suggestion undid whatever good the chamomile tea had done me. "I can't imagine—I mean, this is Eve we're talking about. This is a woman who swoons if I use the S-word. I really don't think she's capable of killing anyone. And she didn't get the information she needed."

"How do you know that?"

She was right. I didn't.

"You don't know what anyone's capable of if their back's to the wall," my street-smart friend continued. "Where's Ted?"

"He got called out on a homicide. He's not home yet."

"Are you going to tell him?"

"Of course."

"He'll inform Homicide in New York that you and Eve were there, you know. He'd have to."

Talk about dilemmas. "I . . . I can't lie to him. But I've got to get rid of Rich before I can even think about anything else. Can I leave Eve here till I do that?"

Meg nodded. "We'll give her time to mull things over, and then we'll have to make her understand the trouble she's in if it's discovered she was at the crime scene. Maybe then she'll tell us the real story."

I threw my arms around her. "Meg, thanks. I'll be back in less than an hour."

"What're you going to tell the kids?"

"I don't know. I'll think of something."

"I don't think it's a good idea to bring Eve to your house tonight."

"Well, I can't pack her up and send her home. Who knows what's going to go down tomorrow?"

Meg heaved a great sigh. "I must be crazy to get involved, but I'll take her home with me for tonight. Bring her stuff when you come back."

I felt tears stinging the back of my eyelids. How many people have a friend who'd go out on a limb for them like this? "Meg . . ." I choked. "You're really . . . the . . . the best. I don't know how I can ever—"

"Oh, shut up. Go home and get rid of that prick of an ex-husband of yours. Then make some excuse to the kids and get back here. Meanwhile, I'm going to get the truth out of that crazy lady in there if I have to pry it out of her with a can opener!"

6

MEG AND I GO back a long way. Not so much in time as in trouble. I thought about it on my way home. She got me through the worst of my divorce and all the Sturm und Drang that followed, and I got her through her brother-in-law's murder and the disappearance of her husband, Kevin. You form a powerful bond when you've been through the wars together. It's a bond forged by fire and built on trust, like the ones you're supposed to form in marriage but without the sexual component. Which is maybe why it lasts. Meg is the sister I never had, the mother I never knew, and the confidant I never had in my husband. She's beautiful inside and out. I love her.

Speaking of husbands—or ex-husbands, to be completely factual—I caught a glimpse of Rich pacing by the open front door as I pulled into the driveway. I jumped out of the car, opened the garage, got back in, pulled into the garage, slowly got back out of my car, and closed the garage door. Then I strolled up the walk.

"Hi," I said, feigning surprise at seeing him. "You're early. What happened?"

Part of the problem I have when I see Rich is that he still looks like the man I married, and there's always that tiny stab of longing for what used to be. At least until he opens his mouth. "Weather sucked," he groused. "Lousy drive home."

"Well, yesterday was nice," I ventured.

"Yeah, kids had a good time and we had seafood for lunch today before we left."

"Oh, good," I said struggling to keep up my end of the conversation. "Then we'll just have something light for dinner." I shifted uncomfortably. It's really weird how impossible it gets to have a normal conversation with the person to whom you used to bare your soul.

He has the same problem. "Well," he mumbled. "Wish I could stay but I gotta run. Just wanted to tell you I can't take the kids on my next weekend."

"Why? They'll be disappointed."

"Gonna be in Paris. But I'll make it up to them when I get back. Bye, kids," he called from halfway down the walk. "Be good," he threw my way.

"Yeah, you too," I called after him, doing my best to bind and gag the green monster inside me who wanted to do him violence at the mention of a Paris trip. I gave his retreating back the finger instead. The littlest finger. For those who don't deserve the very best.

Allie and Matt were curled up on the couch in our kitchen–family room when I walked in, shedding my coat. Horty was snuggled between them, head on Allie's lap. He perked up and wagged his tail as I dropped kisses on two silky dark heads. I scratched behind his ear and he slobbered on my hand. His expression of undying affection.

"I hear you had a big lunch so I'm off the hook for dinner," I said to the kids.

"Not me. I'll be starvin' in a coupla hours," Matt responded.

"Glutton," his sister said. "How can you even think about food?"

"Listen," I chattered, trying not to reveal my nervousness. "Ted's out on a call and I'm not sure when he'll be home. I'm just going to slice some cucumbers and heat up last night's spaghetti, and everyone can help themselves when they get hungry. Okay?"

"Fine with me," Matt said.

"What's wrong?" asked Allie, who knows I'm a stickler for the family sitting down to dinner together.

"I just promised Meg I'd help her with something, and so long as you've had a big lunch, I won't have to cook and I can run back to the café."

She looked at me suspiciously. "You sure nothing's the matter?"

"What could be the matter?" I asked as I transferred the spaghetti from the refrigerator dish to a pot. "I'll leave this on warm. Just stir it every so often, Allie, and it should be fine." I picked up my coat. "Do your homework. Feed the cats, and let Horty out back if he needs to go. If I'm not home by dark, which I probably will be, put on the alarm."

I was halfway out the door when I realized I hadn't taken Eve's suitcase. Obviously, Allie hadn't been up to her room or she would have asked me who'd been sleeping in her bed.

"Forgot something," I yelled, dashing upstairs.

José was asleep in Eve's suitcase, which I'd forgotten to close. He meowed in friendly greeting till I unceremoniously dumped him on the floor. Then he spit at me.

"Watch it, buster," I muttered. "Don't spit at the hand that feeds you." He rubbed up against my leg. José's feisty, but he's not stupid.

I didn't want to walk out carrying a suitcase, so I tossed Eve's belongings into her shopping bag, ran into the kids' bathroom, grabbed her toothbrush and toothpaste, and hid her suitcase and the gifts she'd brought the kids under my bed.

Paper bag in hand, I flew back down the stairs. "If Ted calls, tell him he can reach me at Meg's. I'll bring you guys back one of her yummy desserts."

"Death by chocolate," Mattie yelled after me.

I wish he hadn't said that.

Meg was behind the counter on the phone with Ted when I got back to the café. The restaurant was beginning to fill up.

"You tell him anything?" I whispered.

"Not me. I'm only the baby-sitter."

I threw her a desperate look and reluctantly took the phone. "Hi."

"How come you're at Meg's?"

"I brought Eve here. She's upset and I didn't want the kids to see her like this. When're you coming home?"

"That's why I'm calling. I don't know how long I'll be stuck here. What happened to Eve?"

I glanced around at the crush of people gathering at the entrance. "Hard to talk here. Tell you when I see you. You're not going to be there all night, are you?"

"Hope not. You didn't do anything crazy, did you?"

I cannot tell a lie. I chopped down the cherry tree.

"I just picked her up in the city. She took the bus before we got up."

"Damn. Where'd she go?"

"Tell you later."

"You don't want to tell me now?"

"Can't. Long story."

Pregnant pause, followed by a sigh. "Okay. See you at home."

"All you did was postpone the agony," Meg whispered as she passed by me on her way to greet a couple at the door. "She's having a bite to eat in the kitchen."

Glad she *can eat,* I thought grumpily, and gave the swinging door a vicious push. It got even, swinging back at me and grazing my head, so it was a minute before I noticed Eve wasn't in the kitchen. On the chopping table were the remains of a sandwich and a cup of tea, but the chair by the table was empty.

"Eve?" I called out. "I brought your stuff. You're going to be staying at Meg's tonight." No answer. I crossed to the storage room, thinking she'd opted for more privacy than the busy kitchen allowed. When I pushed open the door, it was like stepping into Meg's cooler. The cold blast of air was coming from the open door leading to the alley in the back of the café. I ran outside and stared at the empty space where not five minutes earlier I'd parked my beautiful new black Honda.

A guilt-ridden Meg took me home. "I'm so sorry. I feel terrible."

"It wasn't your fault. You have a restaurant to run. You couldn't watch her every second. Besides, she must've been looking out for me—waiting for me to get to the café."

"But where could she have gone?"

"Damned if I know." I stared out the window at the icicles forming on the trees and tried to ignore the fear that was tying all the muscles in my chest into one huge knot. "I swear I could kill her with my bare hands. She's always rubbed me the wrong way, and now I know why."

"Give her a break. She's obviously in some sort of trouble."

"Maybe she did kill that guy," I grumbled. "Why else would she be running away?"

"People do crazy things when they're afraid."

"You know the irony of all this? Almost from the day I knew her, she's been acting like my dad needed protecting from *me*."

"Well, even you have to admit your life the past couple of years hasn't exactly been a sitcom."

Actually more of a daytime soap.

"She have any friends in the area?"

"Far as I know she doesn't know anyone around here except the lawyer who handled her husband's estate."

"You have his name?"

"No, but I'm sure my dad does. Not that I'm about to call and ask him."

"You may have to."

"I'll sic the cops on her first. I'll have Ted put out an alarm on my car as a stolen vehicle."

She patted my leg. "You won't. You're just saying that because you're upset and worried about her."

"Of course I'm worried about her. She's important to my dad and she was staying with me. I'm responsible for her. Doesn't mean I have to like her."

I didn't want to think about the impending conversation with my dad. I didn't want to think about the one with Ted either. "I should've reported the crime. I could've done it anonymously. Ted's going to freak."

"You could still do it."

"Oh, sure. How's this? Hello, Police? I'd like to report a dead body I happened to run into recently. Well, actually it was this afternoon, but I didn't want to bother you. No, I didn't run into it personally, but I have it on good authority, there's a hole in its head." We pulled into the driveway and I opened the car door. "You'd better get back. I'll let you know if she shows up."

"I'll call you after we close and come over if you need me." I gave her a quick hug. "Thanks for everything."

"You bet," she said, reaching into the backseat and handing me the shopping bag with Eve's things. "Count on me. I'll lose your stepmother for you anytime."

Despite everything, I smiled. "Under normal circumstances, that'd definitely be a plus."

Quietly I let myself in the front door, hoping not to have to field any questions from the kids until I'd had a chance to put something in my stomach. I hadn't eaten since early this morning, and I was beginning to feel woozy. I stood at the foot of the stairs listening to the robotic voice emanating from Matt's computer and to Allie's clear soprano as she ran scales. Satisfied that I'd have a few minutes to myself, I slipped out of my shoes and padded softly into the kitchen–family room. Dropping Eve's shopping bag beside the table, I tossed my coat over the back of a chair and reached simultaneously for the kettle and the Advil. I swallowed two pills and lit the burner under the kettle. Horty's tail beat a rhythmic greeting on the floor before he heaved himself to his feet and lumbered over to me. He licked my hand and rolled over. I leaned down and stroked his belly, our ritual greeting. Not to be ignored, Luciano came over and rubbed Siamese cat fur against my pants leg. As I sank down onto the couch, he crawled onto my lap and inched his way up to my shoulder. I leaned back and rested my pounding head against his soft body. The low rumble of his purring soothed and relaxed me. *Maybe I should bring him to the office*, I thought. *A new biofeedback technique guaranteed to ease the troubled soul.*

"Where do you suppose she's gone, Lucie?" I whispered into his fur. I have this habit of talking to any creature that will listen to me.

"Murrrr," he responded.

"What am I going to tell Dad? I can't tell him about what happened this morning, but I'll have to tell him I don't know where she went. He'll go bananas when he hears she's disappeared."

A flicking tail tickled the back of my neck.

"Unless he knows more about why she's here than he's letting on." Which was something I hadn't considered. I thought back to my conversation with him this morning. What had he said just before we hung up? *Tell her I said to be good and keep out of trouble.* Did that mean anything? Just a manner of speaking, probably. Or maybe not. Maybe he suspected something. "Who do you suppose the dead guy was, Lucie?"

Lucie rose, stretched, and moved to the other side of the couch. The problem was out of his area of expertise.

Seconds later the piano stopped and Allie appeared in the doorway.

"Who brought you home?"

What is she, psychic?

"How'd you know I don't have my car?" I asked, while I picked cat fur off my sweater and dog fur off my pants.

"The garage door didn't go up, and besides—"

"You were vocalizing. You must have pretty good ears."

"I was taking a break. Besides, Aunt Eve stopped by looking for her suitcase. She went ballistic when she couldn't find it. Whatsa matter with—why're you looking like that?"

I was staring at her, mouth agape. I snapped my mouth shut and jumped to my feet. If I'd been standing I would have sat. I had to move or I was going to scream. "How long ago?" I asked when I could speak in a normal tone of voice.

"How long ago what?"

"Was she here. Did she leave."

"About fifteen minutes ago. She said you'd lent her your car. How come Grandpa didn't come down with her?"

Despite my best efforts my voice rose. "She said I lent her my car? Did she say where she was going?"

"No. Mom, what's the matter?"

I did the good-mother thing and managed to bring myself under control. "It's okay, honey. Just, Aunt Eve took my car without asking me, and . . . uh . . . she sort of isn't herself. She has a kind of problem and I'm worried about her."

"What kind of problem?"

Motherhood isn't easy. Schools don't give courses in parenting. At least they didn't in my day. Allie's thirteen, and in many ways she's pretty mature. But I'm forty-one, and I'm not doing well with this. To tell the truth, the last couple of years have been an emotional seesaw for me, and my children weren't left unscathed either. I didn't want more tumult in their lives, and I wasn't sure how much I should tell her. I opted for part of the truth.

"Aunt Eve is very upset over some kind of crisis that she told me a good friend of hers is having. This morning she went into the city to try and help her—the friend—and she got in sort of over her head. Now she's taken my car and I don't know where she's gone."

"When you say her friend you mean her, don't you? She's having the crisis?"

This kid is either more astute than I've given her credit for, or I'm as transparent as Ted tells me I am.

"I only know what she told me."

"What happened to her this morning?"

"It's complicated, and I need to call Grandpa and see if he has any idea what's going on. So if you don't mind, honey, I'd just like to eat something and relax before I do that. When I know more, I'll tell you. Okay?"

I walked over to the stove and lifted the lid on the spaghetti pan. "Bless you, you saved me some food."

Suddenly she was the mother and I was the child.

"You just sit. I'll heat up the spaghetti. What d'you want to drink?"

A double martini.

"Club soda'll be fine."

"How about a glass of wine?"

"Good thinking. Now tell me about your weekend."

And I tried to shut everything out as she described their visit to the aquarium. The whales and the sharks were kept in tanks too small for them, and Allie planned to write a letter to the Connecticut chamber of commerce about that, but the penguins were adorable, and the dolphin show was great and we should never ever eat canned tuna unless the company promises they don't use nets to catch the tuna, because the dolphins become ensnared and die.

I'd managed to polish off all my wine and a good half of the spaghetti on my plate when I heard a key in the front door. I scrambled to my feet, thinking it might be Eve using my key, but seconds later Ted walked in.

"Hi, you two beautiful ladies," he said. "Smells wonderful. You save any of that for me?"

"It's last night's leftovers, but there's plenty." I brushed his scratchy five-o'clock-shadowed cheek with my lips and hurriedly moved to the stove. "You got out of there much earlier than you expected to, didn't you?"

"Yeah, the Evidence Tech had finished up, so I figured I could—"

"I didn't cook tonight because the kids had big lunches and nobody was very hungry, so we're having the spaghetti again. . . ."

I was babbling, dreading what was coming, and he shot me a quizzical look.

"I love your spaghetti," he said. "You can make it five nights a week and I won't complain."

I turned to Allie. "Honey, will you run up and see if Mattie's finished his homework? I need to talk to Ted."

"Doesn't he know about—"

Ted stopped scratching Horty's ears. "What don't I know about? What happened this morning with Eve? No, I don't. Where is Eve, by the way?"

"Go, Allie."

She glanced from one of us to the other. "Uh-oh. Sorry. I'm going."

He waited till we heard her footsteps on the stairs. Then he came up behind me and wrapped his arms around me. "Uh-oh?" he murmured into my hair. "I don't like that word. It gives me heart palpitations."

Normally, his wrapping his arms around me gives me heart palpitations. The nice kind. But not tonight. I pulled away. "I'll fix you a drink."

He groaned and walked back to the table. "I need a drink for this?"

"Well . . ."

"Just feed me. And talk."

So I did. I told him everything, sure Eve would never forgive me, but hell, what did she expect? When I'd finished, there was silence except for the drumming of his fingers on the table. I focused on my place mat and began fidgeting with the fringe. Finally he said, "I'll take that drink now."

"Scotch?"

"Make it a double."

After the first swallow he put the glass down and looked at me with an expression that definitely could not be categorized as loving. "You haven't reported this, I take it."

"I . . . she was . . . they would've—"

"You didn't."

"No."

He got up and went to the phone. I poured myself another glass of wine and listened to him as he gave someone at the NYPD the address of the brownstone. There was a pause punctuated by a couple of grunts, and then he gave them my name and address and Eve's name. So much for anonymity.

"What's your license-plate number?" he asked.

"I don't want her picked up, Ted. She didn't really steal my car—"

"She won't be arrested. Yet. I just want her located before something else happens." I heard him give my license number, then he walked out to the foyer and talked another couple of minutes. When he came back to the table and sat, he looked tired, and the lines around his eyes seemed more deeply etched into his face. I didn't like feeling responsible for that.

"I wonder if you realize you're not the easiest person to be involved with," he said, reaching for the tumbler.

"I know I probably should've called the police right away, but—"

"*Probably?* Jesus Christ, Carrie, you have to be the only person I can think of who wouldn't have under those circumstances!"

I was quiet. I was filled with mixed emotions, not the least of which was anger at Eve for having put me smack in the middle of her mess. "What's going to happen?" I asked finally.

"We'll get a visit from some friends of mine from New York later tonight. They're going to want to know everything you know."

"Which isn't much," I muttered. "What'd they say about my not reporting it right away?"

He polished off the Scotch and put the glass down. "God help me, I lied for you. I said Eve hadn't told you what happened till you got to Meg's. That she was almost hysterical and you couldn't make much sense of what she did say."

"Thank you." I got up, went over to him and sat down on his lap, wrapped my arms tightly around his neck, and kissed him. "You won't go to hell," I whispered. "It's only a tiny white lie."

"Yeah, yeah. Tell that to Congress."

But he smiled and kissed me back. A minute later the ringing of the phone made us both jump. I grabbed it.

"Hi, sweetheart."

"Hi, Dad," I breathed.

7

TED'S EXPRESSION was incredulous as I hung up the phone. "Why didn't you say anything about the murder? Maybe he knows something."

"I couldn't. He's upset enough as it is," I snapped, resenting his tone. "I couldn't dump that on him."

"Carrie, he's a big boy."

"A big boy with a weak heart."

"What a role reversal. You know who you're behaving like, don't you?"

That brought me up short. "Maybe now I understand how she's felt the last couple of years."

"You're being silly. How long do you think you can keep him in the dark?"

"Till he gets here anyway." I walked over to the table and slumped wearily into a chair. "He's driving down in the morning." I put my head down and rested it on my arms. The conversation with my dad had been nerve-racking, a balancing act, trying to extract information from him while attempting to make light of Eve's disappearance and what had caused it. "Maybe she'll be back by then."

He tossed down another Scotch, then joined me at the table. "Tell me what he said."

"Just that she was rattled by a letter she got from her lawyer and all of a sudden she was packing to come here."

"Didn't he ask her what it was about?"

"If he did, I guess she didn't tell him."

"Nice relationship."

"You don't tell me everything."

"Who says?"

"You said."

"You're talking about my work. That's a different issue."

"So you keep insisting. Anyway, all he said was that she's been in touch with this lawyer a few times to straighten out some estate problems." I raised my head. "You think the lawyer's involved in what happened? Maybe there *was* an adoption. Maybe it was an illegal adoption and this was the lawyer who arranged it."

"There's always that possibility, if any of what Eve told you is true. If someone found out about your dad winning the lottery and saw a way to get his hands on a nice bit of change, it could've been tempting."

"The lawyer obviously knew her when she was married to her previous husband. That's longer than any of us have known her."

"Did your dad know his name?"

"I forgot to ask him. We'll find out tomorrow. None of it explains why that guy was killed, though."

"Saints do not cook up extortion plots. You get a bunch of pond scum together and they'd off each other for ten bucks, much less thousands."

I got up from the table and started clearing the dishes. I'm one of those people who has to keep busy when I'm nervous. "It's so hard to accept that Eve had a baby and gave it away."

"Your very staid and proper stepmother may have had a far more intriguing past than you've given her credit for." He grinned. "Want me to run a check on her?"

"You probably should."

"Good you said that, because I plan to."

"If she does find this person, what will she say? How do you make up to a child for abandoning it?"

"I guess you explain that you were young and made a terrible mistake. A lot will depend on what kind of life the kid's had."

I shook my head. "Imagine keeping a secret like that all these years."

"Remember, we don't know the whole story. We don't even know if she's telling the truth now. You're sure she called that guy Omar?"

"Uh-huh. She denied it later, but I'm sure. Isn't that a Turkish name?"

"Could be any of the Middle Eastern countries."

"So he was a foreigner. That narrows it."

"Nope. We had a general, Omar Bradley, remember?"

"I don't know why she had to drag me into this. It isn't my problem."

"A man's been murdered, and your dad's wife is involved in it up to her eyeballs. Which, I hate to say, kind of makes it your problem."

There was clattering on the stairs and Matt, barefoot and wearing only shorts and a T-shirt, came charging into the room.

"Mattie," I scolded. "It's February. Why're you wearing shorts? You'll catch pneumonia."

"I'm fine. It's hot upstairs. Where's the death?"

My heart leapt into my throat. "*What?*" I croaked.

"You promised to bring some death by chocolate from Meg's. You forget?"

My heart dropped back to where it belonged. "Oh, sweetheart, I'm sorry. I'll call Meg and tell her to save some, and I'll get it tomorrow."

He scowled. "Shit," he mumbled.

My hair stood on end. "WHAT? WHAT DID YOU SAY?"

"Shoot. I said shoot." He got a running start and slid across the floor to the foot of the stairs, then took them two at a time.

"Matthew Burnham, if I ever hear that word out of your mouth again, it's no TV and no computer for a month! You hear me?"

"I hear you. The whole world can hear you."

"Don't be fresh. I'm not kidding. Now, go put something on before you catch *your* death."

"I'm okay. Don't you know heat rises?"

"Just do what I said!" I turned to Ted, who was doing his best to look serious. "Did you hear that? You think that's funny?"

"It's the world we live in. And his age."

"It's the TV. It's the Internet. It's his father's foul mouth."

He broke out laughing. "I can't believe the hypocrisy. Correct me if I'm wrong, but I do believe I've occasionally heard that horrific word pass his mother's pretty lips."

"Never in front of the children!"

"He's seeing how far he can push you."

"Well, it's this far. If I ever—"

The sound of cars pulling into the driveway stopped me and brought Horty to his feet. I ran to the window and pulled back the drape. Blinded by flashing lights, I let it drop back. "Oh, God, they're here. It didn't take them long."

"You'll be okay," Ted said, getting up. "You haven't done anything. At least nothing they know about."

"It brings back memories. Cops make me nervous. Some-times I wonder how I ever ended up with a cop."

"I'm irresistible."

"You were pretty resistible at the time."

"Come on. I wasn't that bad."

"You don't know what it's like being on the other end."

"Let's keep it that way. Don't put me in a position of hav-ing to lie for you again."

The doorbell rang, three short, sharp bursts. Horty started howling and José rose from his perch on the arm of the sofa, fur bristling, back arching like a Halloween cutout.

"I'll get it," Ted said. "See if you can keep Man-eater here under control. We don't want any accidental shootings."

I grabbed hold of Horty's collar and dragged him to the couch. "They've got more to fear from José," I grunted. "Sit, Horty, you loudmouth. You want to get shot?"

A few seconds later I heard raised voices in the foyer. Then Ted, his face somber, reappeared, followed by two plainclothes detectives, two uniforms—and a disheveled, clearly terrified Eve, her face streaked with tears. Her hands were behind her back, and one of the detectives was hold-ing her firmly by the arm.

Stunned, I scrambled to my feet, my fingers going limp on Horty's collar. Ted grabbed him as he made for the strangers, intent on licking them to death, but how would they know that? One of the uniform's hand slid down to his hip and remained there.

"What's going on?" I gasped. "Eve, where've you been? Are you okay?" I started to go to her, but the look she shot me was so filled with malevolence, it stopped me cold. *She* was angry with *me?* It was then I realized why her hands were behind her back. Horrified, I glanced at Ted. "Are those . . . Is she in *handcuffs?*"

One of the detectives fixed his icy gaze on me. "This

lady was caught breaking into the apartment where the murder was committed," he said. "She says she's your step-mother, and because the lieutenant here had already no-tified us about the crime, we gave him the courtesy of bringing her here before booking her. We thought you might be able to convince her, for her own good, to fill us in. She admits she was in the apartment earlier today, which we knew from the lieutenant and from the descrip-tion of her from witnesses, but she refuses to tell us why she went there or why she went back."

I knew why she'd gone there, and I was pretty sure I knew why she'd gone back. She'd remembered there was something in that handbag that would lead the cops to her. But she'd arrived too late. Now that the cops had her, why didn't she tell them what she'd told Meg and me? Maybe because the whole thing had been a crock.

"I think she went back for her hat and her handbag," I said. "She was so upset when she saw this person dead, she ran away and left them there."

"You telling me this woman went back to a murder scene because she didn't want to lose her handbag?" the second detective sneered. "Must've been somethin' pretty valuable in it." He fixed his gaze on Eve. "Wanna tell us what that was?"

"That's not why she went back," said the first detective.

We all looked at him.

"There was no hat found at the crime scene," he said. "And no handbag."

Our gaze shifted to Eve.

"I want a lawyer," she whispered.

8

"WHERE DID I file those names?" I was talking to myself as I frenetically flipped through my Rolodex. Ted had gone with Eve and the detectives back to the precinct in Manhattan in an undoubtedly futile attempt to get Eve released into his custody. She'd remained adamantly silent, but I was pretty certain we could get the real story out of her if we could just get her alone. Neither of us had mentioned the book, the illegitimate child, or the conversation with my dad. Silently, I thanked Ted because I knew holding back any information he deemed relevant to a murder case was going against every fiber of his cop being. That made twice in one day he'd gone out on a limb for me. I also knew the reprieve would be short-lived.

"I don't hold out much hope," he'd said in an undertone on the way out. "They can hold her for forty-eight hours without charging her, and if I were in their shoes, that's exactly what I'd do."

"You can't let her spend a night behind bars," I'd pleaded. "She'll go out of her mind."

"One night may be the least of what she's facing, the damned fool woman," he'd muttered, tight-lipped. "What the hell's wrong with her? For starters they've got her on breaking and entering, which could—" Catching the expression on my face, he'd stopped. "I'll do what I can."

I'd watched through the window as the detectives helped Eve into the patrol car, my stomach plummeting into my shoes as I saw one of them push her head down the way I've seen them do to criminals on TV. Why do they do that, for God's sake? Are they afraid the perp might bump his head and accuse them of police brutality? I'd have to ask Ted at a more propitious time. The only silver lining to this storm cloud was that my father wasn't here to observe it. A circumstance that, unhappily, would no longer exist by tomorrow afternoon.

"Why wouldn't I have put lawyers under *L*?" I muttered in frustration.

Allie appeared at my side, reached out a hand, and flipped back to the *A*'s. "Maybe you put 'em under *A* for *Attorneys*."

Which was exactly what I had done. "Here it is." I pulled out a card, grabbed the phone, and dialed.

"Mom, it's Sunday. Nobody's gonna be there," said Allie, the voice of reason.

I slammed the receiver back into its cradle and dropped my head into my hands.

"Who was it got killed?" Matt asked, bumping noisily down the stairs. "A friend of Aunt Eve's?"

"I don't know, honey," I replied, lifting my head. "When they let her come home, I'm sure she'll tell us what this is all about."

"I don't like this," Allie said. "Everybody in school'll be asking us questions again. Why can't we have a normal life like other people?"

Because I've been cursed. I must've done something terrible in a past life. "Unpleasant things happen in everyone's life, Allie. They just don't talk about them."

"They don't keep falling over dead bodies, or they *would* talk about it. They talk about us. I wish Daddy was here."

I wish Daddy was anywhere but here.

"Ted's a cop," Matt said. "He'll know what to do."

I wanted to hug him.

"He's not Daddy," Allie murmured, avoiding my eyes.

I got up and put my arm around her, grabbed Matt's hand, and propelled them both back toward the stairs. "Everything's going to be okay. I know you're freaked, and I am too, but this'll all be straightened out in the next few days. Ted's going to take care of things with the New York police, and Grandpa's coming tomorrow. I'm sure Eve'll be released by the time he gets here."

"I feel all jumpy," Allie said. "I don't think I'll be able to sleep."

"Me either," chimed in Matt. "Can't we wait up for Ted?"

"No. It could be hours till he gets back, and you have school tomorrow. Try reading yourselves to sleep, okay?"

"What're you going to do?" Allie asked.

"The same, just as soon as I load the dishwasher," I lied. "I'll be up to kiss you good night when I finish."

Reluctantly, they trudged upstairs. Feeling jumpy myself, I punched in the code that set the burglar alarm Ted had insisted I install last year. Then I went into the kitchen and let water run over the sticky plates I'd piled in the sink.

Maybe Omar was the lawyer who'd arranged the adoption, I thought. If there had been an adoption. Like Ted had hypothesized, maybe he'd found out about the lottery win and decided to cash in. But who would've killed him, and why? And why wouldn't Eve tell the police who he was if that was the case? The extortion plot was bound to come out. Eve had the money belt on her, and the cops would certainly frisk her and find it. God, they'd probably strip-search her. The thought made me cringe.

"Mom?" Matt called from the head of the stairs.

"What, Matt?"

"There's a guy standing out front looking at the house."

Damn, I'll bet it's the press was my first thought. Could they have found out about this so soon? I dashed into the living room, flipped off the light, and peered out the window. Nobody. I crept into the kitchen, being careful to stay close to the wall, and peeked out through the glass pane on the back door, where I had a clear view of the garage and the yard. No one lurking anywhere that I could see. Of course, he could have gone behind the garage, but why would anyone from the media do that?

"I don't see anybody, honey. You sure it wasn't just a shadow from a tree?"

"I know a person from a tree."

"Well, whoever it was, he's gone now. Probably somebody just looking for a particular address," I added, keeping my tone light. "I've got the alarm on. Go back to bed and I'll be up in a minute."

I went back to the sink, reached under the cabinet for the dishwasher detergent, and poured it into the depression in the door, managing to spill it all over the floor in the process. My nerves were totally shot. Was Matt right? Was someone watching the house? Where the hell was Ted anyway? He should've been back by now.

The doorbell rang just as I turned on the machine. I must've jumped four feet in the air. Horty started barking, and I shushed him as I hurried to the door. "Quiet, Horty. Who is it?" I called.

"Me. Meg."

Relieved, I turned off the alarm and opened the door.

"What's up?" she inquired, as she shed her coat.

"You see anybody out there when you drove up?" I asked, taking a furtive glance around before I shut the door and re-set the alarm.

"No. Who're you expecting?"

"Nobody. Mattie said he thought somebody was watch-ing the house. I think we're all getting paranoid."

"Well, there isn't anybody there now. Any news about Eve?"

"You're not going to believe it."

"Oh, yes, I will," Meg said, following me into the living room. "At this point I would believe you if you told me she was in jail."

"She is."

Meg stopped dead. "Come on."

"Sit. I've got a lot to tell you."

"Wait. Before you do, I've got something to show you." From her tote bag she pulled out a black nylon belt about three inches wide in the front, with a buckle on the narrow end and a zipper dissecting the middle.

"Is that what I think it is?" I breathed.

She nodded.

"Where'd you find it?"

"In my cooler. Believe me, the way things are going around here, I was glad this was all I found."

"So that's where she stashed it. Well, at least they didn't find it in the strip search."

"They strip-searched her?" Meg asked, horrified.

"I don't know. Don't they do that after they book you?"

"How should I know? Kev never gave me the details."

"Sorry. Didn't mean to reopen old wounds." Meg's

husband spent some time in jail for something his brother had done. It's a whole period in their lives Meg would like to forget.

"How'd she get arrested?" Meg asked.

I gave her the lurid details while I unzipped the money belt and pulled out the wad of cash. "My God, how much is in here?"

"Twenty-five thou. But that's not all that was in there."

"What do you mean?"

From her tote bag she drew out an envelope and carefully extracted two snapshots. "These were on top of the money."

One of the pictures was of an adorable, sandy-haired, freckled-faced little boy about nine or ten years of age, wearing bathing trunks. He was holding up a fish half as big as he was, a gap-toothed grin lighting up his whole face. The other was of the same boy, standing unsmiling between two men—one a dark-haired young man in his twenties, wearing cutoffs and a T-shirt, who had his arm around the boy; the other a fortyish man, who would have been good-looking if he hadn't been scowling at the camera. I took the pictures from Meg and flipped them over. On the back of the first was written the name *Jamie*. The second, scrawled in a different handwriting, had the names *Omar*, *Jamie*, and *Frank*.

"Omar," I whispered. "Which one?"

"I think the younger guy," Meg replied. "At least, if the names on the back correspond to the pictures."

Matt's head poked over the railing. "Hi, Meg."

"Hi, Mattie. How're you doing?"

" 'Kay."

"Your mom tells me you've had a little excitement around here tonight."

"Never dull in this family, that's for sure." He paused. "Mom?"

"Yes, Matt?"

"You said you were comin' up." I could hear the anxiety in his voice.

"The kids're upset," I whispered to Meg. "I'm just going to run up and kiss them good night."

She nodded.

"Meg?" I said as I started up the stairs.

"Yeah?"

"The paperback book in Eve's shopping bag . . ."

"What about it?"

"It said, *For Jamie* on the flyleaf."

"The cast of characters from Eve's mysterious past. That's two out of three. Now, who's Frank?"

"Eve's going to have a helluva lot of explaining to do when she gets here," I muttered grimly as I started up the stairs. "That's all I can say."

"Like Mattie said," Meg replied. "Never dull in this family."

Ted didn't make it home till after midnight. I heard the car as he pulled into the driveway and met him at the foot of the stairs. He was alone.

"Sorry, Carrie. Couldn't swing it. Christ, I'm beat." His jacket and shirt were off before he made it up to the bedroom. I massaged his neck as he sat on the edge of the bed removing his shoes and socks.

"How was she—I mean, what was she like when you left?"

"Relatively stoic. Probably in shock."

"Did they . . . is she in a cell?"

"She'll survive. I told her we'd probably have her out by tomorrow. Unless they charge her, in which case bail will take a little longer."

Bail. It struck me then that this was going to be an expensive proposition. It looked like my poor father was going to lose his lottery money one way or another.

"Probably?"

"I told you, they can hold her for forty-eight hours if they want. If she comes clean and they don't think she did it, they'll probably let her go. I called in a couple of favors and got the guys to say they'll lay off interrogating her till after your dad gets here. Can't guarantee anything, of course. But I figure he can talk some sense into her if we can't. What time do you think that'll be?"

"I guess by late afternoon. I have patients till four. I told him to come directly to the office, but maybe he should go right into the city."

"Page me when he gets to you. I'll drive him to the precinct." He got to his feet and staggered to the bathroom. I waited till the water had stopped running.

"I've still got the names of the criminal lawyers Meg gave me," I called out. "I thought I'd try—"

"Taken care of," he called from the bathroom. "I've arranged for someone to be there first thing in the A.M. Lady I've run into a few times. She's good."

He'd gotten a woman lawyer for Eve. Full of surprises, this man. "How'd you get home?" I asked when he emerged, drying his hair with a towel. "You went in the patrol car with Eve."

He tossed the towel on a chair and flipped off the overhead light. "Your car. Let me have it after they did a search."

"You must've called in a couple more favors for them not to have impounded it," I murmured.

"For you. Knew you'd need it." He started to switch off the lamp on the bed table.

"Leave it on for a minute." I waited till he'd crawled into bed beside me to show him the money belt and the snapshots. I pointed to the dark-haired young man. "Meet Omar," I said.

9

"FUCK YOU, Carlin, and fuck Ruth-Ann, and fuck that pansy Dr. Golden, and fuck the world! I ain't doin' this stupid shit no more!"

I looked up from the chart I was reading and gazed into the belligerent watery blue eyes of my ten-o'clock, who, hands on massive hips, was straddling the threshold of my office doorway.

I suppressed a sigh. The day had not started out well. I hadn't slept much the previous night—couldn't get the image of Eve sitting up all night on the edge of an unmade cot in a jail cell out of my head. Was she in a cell alone, or had they thrown her in with prostitutes and thieves? Ted hadn't answered me directly when I'd asked. And the look Eve had darted my way as she stood, hands cuffed behind her back, in my living room had made it abundantly clear whom she blamed for her present situation. Having ratted to Ted, who'd sicced the NYPD on her, I was guilty as charged, and sleep had eluded me until nearly three-thirty.

At six-thirty I'd dragged myself down to the kitchen, leaving Ted to shower first. The kids had ignored their alarms and my wake-up calls, quarreled over who got to use the bathroom first, and almost missed their car pool. Matt had been especially cranky. He'd dawdled over his breakfast, complaining about a headache but jerking away from me when I reached out to check his forehead. Finally, pressing a half-eaten bagel into his hand, I'd yelled at him to get a move on and practically pushed him out the door. Somehow I'd managed to bathe and dress, feed the animals, make our bed, and get to my office by nine-thirty. I try to get in at least a half hour before my first patient so I can set up the computer and review my charts quietly. This morning it was a struggle to concentrate, and I'd really been hoping Doris wouldn't show up.

"I know you don't like doing this, Doris," I said as sweetly as I could manage. "But since you're already here, why don't you ask Elaine to come out?"

"She don't want to see you today. She's busy plannin' to spend my hard-earned cash on redoin' the bedroom. Hopin' for company, I guess." She gave a raucous laugh. "Never happen."

"Well, then, get me Patty."

Elaine/Doris/Patty/Gloria Wiszneskie is my first, only, and last Dissociative Identity Disorder (more commonly known as Multiple Personality) patient. I treat her as a special favor to Joe Golden, who happens to be one of the few psychiatrists who sends me patients, but DID isn't my thing. I'm not really trained to deal with it. Joe insists that, as an adjunct to psychiatric therapy, the biofeedback relaxation techniques are beneficial, especially to Elaine and Patty, who are more than willing to work on stress reduction. I always give her (or them) my first appointment to protect my other clients' ears and sensibilities from the trauma of Doris's colorful language, should she be the one who's out.

Elaine/Doris/Patty/Gloria is a big woman in her late forties, almost five feet ten inches tall, broad-shouldered with strong, heavy legs, feet that require men's size-eleven shoes, and stringy brown-gray hair that's begun thinning on top. Physically, she makes me think of a peasant who, in the old country, squatted in the field to have her babies and picked up the hoe minutes later. Despite all her shouting and cursing when she's Doris, I'm not afraid of her, because three of her four personalities are rather likable and, if I work at it, I can usually coax one of them out.

Each personality is different; in this case each one sees itself as separate and distinct both physically and age-wise. Elaine is the host personality, the one she was born as and the most intelligent. Elaine sees herself as a born nurturer and homemaker, accepts her body and the fact that she doesn't conform to *Vogue*'s standard of beauty. She's artistic and does beautiful crochet work and embroidery, loves animals, and has two dogs and four cats whom she adores. She rarely raises her voice. Not so Doris. Doris doesn't like the animals to be kept in the house. Elaine is always shocked to find the animals wandering around in the yard after Doris has been out. Especially interesting to me is that Elaine is only vaguely aware of the other personalities and never cognizant of what has happened when one of the others has emerged. Doris knows them all and dislikes them all. Patty, who is twenty-eight, sees herself as petite and blond, speaks in a wispy voice, and is frightened of everything and everyone. Doris has only contempt for her. Gloria is seventeen, an overt flirt who exploits her sexuality every chance she gets. She envisions herself with long hair and a tall, willowy, sensuous body, and she laughs a lot. Doris thinks she's an idiot. Doris herself is the same age as Elaine, forty-seven, but she's coarse, vulgar, and mad as hell at the world. Recently, she's taken up boxing. One of the more fascinating phenomenon I've discovered in working with the woman is that each personality's handwriting is different from the others. Even more interesting is that the brain waves are different. Elaine is very high in the theta and delta areas, these being the dreamy, sleepy brain waves, whereas Doris and Gloria register high in the high beta, which indicates an excessive degree of anger and/or tension. Patty registers high in both areas. Joe has me record the brain waves twice a month for his research. I don't mind telling you the whole experience has been quite an education for me. I've done some reading on the subject just to convince myself that this disorder is real and not some bizarre joke being played on the psychiatric community by a few psychotics. From everything I've learned, it's real.

Doris sauntered into the room and plopped herself down hard in my reclining chair, causing it to rock and groan in protest. "Patty's a prissy wimp. She's all stressed out today."

She and I both.

"That's why it would be good for me to see her. Maybe I can help. Do you know why she's stressed out?"

Doris grinned. "Yeah, when we was in the city last night, some guy in the subway station grabbed her tits."

I found myself wondering what feeble-minded twit would even think about making a pass at a woman who looked like Elaine/Doris/Patty/Gloria Wiszneskie. "That's terrible. What did she do?"

"She's such a wuss, all she could do was stand there and yowl like one of Elaine's tomcats. Lucky for her, I came out and kicked him in the balls. You shoulda seen him fold up, the pervert. Anyway, she's been shakin' and cryin' ever since."

Someone making a sexual advance to Patty could be very

destabilizing to all of the personalities. Elaine *et al.* comes
from Appalachia. She/they suffered from incest and malnu-
trition and was alternately abused and neglected as a child
by alcoholic parents. The child survived physically because
of her God-given genetic strength. Emotionally, she paid
a heavy price. The personalities evolved, Joe tells me, for
self-protection. There used to be five of them, the fifth
being a man—a pimp—a character I assume Elaine had met
knocking around in her young adult life. I used to get a little
shook up when he was out, not sure I could handle his out-
bursts, but he seems to have died prematurely, probably
knocked off by an irate john. So I guess you could say we're
seeing a very small light at the end of the tunnel. Doris has
appeared less and less over the past few months. Mostly she
shows up, as happened last night and today, when one of
the others feels threatened. She/they is finally able to hold
a job cleaning office buildings at night, my building being
one of them, and that, too, is progress. Joe is paid by insurance, and he pays me out of his pocket.

"You don't look so hot yourself today," Doris leered. "You
got circles under your eyes. Boyfriend been poundin' you
into the sheets?"

Man, I wasn't in the mood for this.

"Doris," I said firmly. "We're here to work on you, not to
discuss my personal life. Now, you can stay if you have
something you want to talk to me about. If not, I really
want to talk to Patty."

And suddenly Doris was gone, the face freezing into an
eerie blank stare, then melting like a wax candle and becoming Patty. She shrank into the chair, curling up into a
ball—quite a feat when you're five foot ten—and tears
started rolling down her cheeks. Every time I see the transformation, I'm startled anew.

"Hi, Patty," I said, reaching for the leads.

"Hello, Ms. Carlin," she whispered in a high, thin voice. "I'm so scared. Something really awful happened to me last night."

"I know," I replied sympathetically. "I hear you had a real bad experience."

Guess what? Me too.

The rest of the day continued on a downward trend. Ted called at eleven-thirty to tell me the lawyer he'd hired for Eve had met with her this morning. Eve had admitted to her that the friend was an invention and that the man, Omar, was someone from her past who had contacted her after he'd seen us all on television in Boston. She'd refused to say why she'd gone to meet him, only that he had some important information for her. She didn't mention the illegitimate child either, which worried me. She didn't admit to having brought any money and, of course, when she was searched, no money was found on her. She hadn't killed him; he was dead when she got there. The lawyer, a woman by the name of Vivian Holbrook, didn't press her for more details just then, but she made it clear to Ted that she would represent Eve—assuming charges were brought against her—only if Eve came clean with her. The murder weapon had not been found.

Everything now depended on my father, but by four o'clock he still hadn't come and I began to worry. To top things off, my one-o'clock canceled, which left me sixty-five dollars short for the day, and I got bawled out by eight-year-old Jerry Trainor's mother because his grades haven't improved. Jerry is ADHD (Attention Deficit Hyperactive Disorder), and I've had him for only seven sessions. It took me six of them to get him to sit in my chair and stop cracking his knuckles long enough for me to attach the

sensors to his fingers. I'd been hoping to turn him over
to Ruth-Ann, my assistant, but she called in sick. I didn't
question it. If Ruth-Ann says she has the flu, she has the flu.
She's an Orthodox Jew and an ex-patient who's become a
dear friend. So I ran my overeaters' group, of which she is
a proud graduate, without her, keeping an ear out for the
door buzzer, hoping my dad would arrive before the end
of the day. Jerry was my last patient, and when I checked
my answering machine after finishing with him, there was
a message from the school nurse. Matt had thrown up his
lunch and was running a hundred-and-one fever. More
guilt. The symptoms had been hitting me in the face at
breakfast, but I'd chosen to ignore them. The nurse felt he
shouldn't go home in the car pool and expose the other
children, so would I please come and collect him?

Mrs. Trainor chewed my ear while I set the alarm and
tacked a note to the door telling Dad to meet me at the
house. She followed me to my car, and I tried to maintain
my sanity while I explained that it'd probably take thirty or
forty sessions of brain-wave training for Jerry to show any
significant improvement.

By four-thirty I had a peaked-looking Matt in the car and
was headed home.

"When you didn't pick up your phone, the nurse called
Dad's office, but he said I should wait for you; he couldn't
come get me," Matt complained. "Why didn't you answer
your phone?"

I was on guilt overload. "I'm sorry, Mattie. I can't really
check my messages during a session. And you know how
busy Dad gets. Does the ear hurt?"

"Nah, I just feel queasy. And it isn't 'cause I was wearing
shorts yesterday," he added defensively.

"I didn't say it was. I'm sure it's the flu. Ruth-Ann has it too. We'll get some Tylenol into you and get you to bed and you'll feel better."

"I didn't tell Dad about Aunt Eve."

I couldn't afford to get the flu, but I pulled him to me and gave him the hug I'd wanted to give him yesterday.

As I drove I was mentally arranging sleeping quarters. I'd intended to put my dad in with Matt, and Eve in with Allie—depending on whether or not she was released, of course. The kids both have twin beds in their rooms, but that clearly wasn't going to work out now. Ted was probably going to have to stay in his apartment for a few days.

"I'll bet I barf the Tylenol," Matt sniffed.

"Maybe not. We'll see if you can hold down toast and tea first. Here we are," I said cheerily, refusing to bow to the stubborn dark cloud hovering over my head.

I made a sharp left into my street and swung into the driveway directly behind a shiny new green Buick.

"Grandpa's here!" I exclaimed. "He must've come directly. Stay in the car where it's warm till I open the door and let you both in the house." And I was out of the car and hugging the lean, white-haired, comforting Rock of Gibraltar who is my father.

Twenty minutes later Matt was tucked in bed, nibbling at his toast and tea and watching TV. I'd told Dad we'd found Eve, she was all right (a slight exaggeration), and I'd give him the details as soon as I'd gotten Matt set. When I came back down he was standing at the foot of the stairs, arms folded across his chest, frowning, brows knitted into a straight line across his forehead. He looked drawn and thinner than he had since the last time I'd seen him, and I felt a sudden pang of fear.

"Are you okay, Dad?" I asked. "You look tired."

"I'm all right." He walked over to the couch and sank heavily into it. "It was a long drive to make by myself. I guess I'm not used to doing things alone anymore."

He couldn't have made it clearer. Whatever Eve was or had been involved in, whatever I might think of her, he needed this woman in his life. Probably, much as I hated to admit it, more than he needed me. "You must be hungry," I gulped after I'd choked down that bit of reality. "Can I fix you a sandwich?"

He shook his head impatiently. "Just tell me what's going on. Where's Eve?"

I followed him to the couch and collapsed beside him. The day was beginning to take its toll on me. This was the pits, the absolute river bottom, my having to sit here and tell my father that the woman who had become so important to him was in jail. Even harder was telling him how she got there. I decided to omit the part about the child. That would be up to Eve to tell him. I put a glass of brandy in front of him, and he'd drained it by the time I'd finished.

"She hasn't told her lawyer yet, but she was going to give this guy twenty-five thousand dollars. Meg found it in the money belt. Either he knew something about her that she wanted to keep quiet and she was paying him off, or he knew something she desperately wants to know and she was buying information. Either way she could become a suspect in his murder if she doesn't tell what she knows. I don't think she understands how serious her situation is. You're probably the only one who can get through to her."

He nodded and rose to his feet, his tall frame suddenly stooped as though bending under the burden I'd forced him to shoulder. I wanted to tell him that now it was his turn to lean on me, that I would be his safe haven now as he had been mine all my life, but before I could think of a way to say it, the moment passed.

"Let's get going, then," he said.

"I'll call Ted. He said he'll go with you. I've got to stay here with Matt, at least till I'm sure he's feeling better and Allie gets home from her singing lesson."

Ted wasn't at the precinct. While I waited for him to call back, I insisted Dad eat a tuna sandwich, which helped to fill the awkward silence that had fallen between us.

"No mayonnaise," he warned as I reached for the jar. "Haven't had any of that poison since Eve and I tied the knot. She makes up some kind of concoction that tastes pretty damned good and doesn't have any cholesterol."

"Oh," I said, feeling inadequate. "Well, I have some light dressing. Should I—"

"No, no, I'll have it without anything."

I brought the sandwich and a glass of juice to the table and sat opposite him.

"She's a wonderful woman, you know," he said after he'd polished off the first half. "You never really got to know her."

"I guess that's true," I replied, eager to take advantage of the opening he'd given me. "I don't know a thing about her, really, about her past, about her family, anything."

I waited, hoping he'd fill in the blanks. When he just kept eating, I rattled on. "It's weird, you know? I mean, you married a woman who had a whole life before she met you. And really, how much do you or any of us know about what that life was like. . . ." I left it hanging.

"She was married for twenty years. I suppose her life was fairly uneventful till her husband got sick. She'd been a widow for a couple of years when I met her."

The black widow?

"What'd her husband do? What'd he die of? Where did
they—"

"He was a dentist. He died of pancreatic cancer, and they
lived in Framingham." He gave me an appraising look.
"What were you thinking? That she killed him?"

"No, no, don't be silly," I protested. "It's just, well, you
have to realize we have a situation going on now and
Eve's not talking. I just wondered if she ever discussed her
family."

"As far as I know there isn't much family. I believe she
was an only child."

"And she and her husband never had children?"

"No."

"You sure?"

"Certainly I'm sure. You don't hide children away like some
out-of-date photograph. What're you getting at, Carrie?"

There was no way to do this delicately. "Well, speaking
of photographs, she had a couple in her money belt. I don't
know if they were hers or if she took them from this guy."

"Go on."

"The pictures weren't recent. They were pretty old, as
a matter of fact. One snap had this cute little boy about
Matt's age, maybe a year or two younger, and the other was
of him with two men. We don't know who the older guy
was—could've been the child's father. Age was about right.
The other was the victim."

"Where are the pictures?"

"Ted has them. I presume by now the detectives who're
investigating the case have them."

There was a long pause. I watched the expressions pass
over his face and thought I knew something of what he was
feeling. In the days and months after Rich left, I agonized
over the fact that there was so much about my husband, his
activities, his thought processes, that I never knew. And it

was a devastating realization because it told me things I didn't want to face about myself as well as about him.

After a minute he pushed his chair away from the table, got up, and walked to the window, keeping his back to me. He stared out at the deepening shadows, lit up now and again by a passing car. "I'd know if she had children," he said forcefully.

"People hide things from people they live with all the time."

Like affairs.

"I know that was your experience with Rich," he said, reading my mind. "But Eve would never lie about something like that."

Never say never.

"When I talk to her we'll clear it up."

"I hope so for all our sakes." And then I had to ask. "Was the money she had with her your lottery money?"

He turned and looked me in the eye. I could see the anger in his. "She's my wife, Caroline. As it happens, she has some money of her own, but the lottery money is *ours*. We were together when I bought the ticket."

Caroline from my *dad*? He hadn't called me that since I was a teenager and got caught fooling around in our laundry room with a boy Dad thought undeserving of me.

"I'm always here for you if you or the children ever need anything, you know that," he went on. "Eve and I had a prenup drawn that assures everything I had before we were married goes to you and them. And of course, the trusts for the children's educations can't be touched. But I want you to understand that whatever's left of the lottery money when I die is hers."

I guess I'd really underestimated the depth of his feeling and commitment to this woman. "I don't care about the money for me," I protested. "I want you to do all the things you never got to do while you were raising me. I'm glad you and Eve are planning to travel. I just don't want you to lose it before you've—"

Just then the phone rang. I grabbed it. It was Ted.

"Your dad get there yet?"

"Yes. You coming to pick him up?"

"Be there in twenty. Hope he brought his checkbook."

10

HE MADE IT in fifteen. I stood in the doorway watching the lights from Ted's car disappear as it rounded the corner, then, because it was already dark, I punched in the alarm code, picked up my dad's suitcase, and went upstairs. I dropped it outside my room while I went to look in on Matt. He'd fallen asleep with the TV on. I crossed to the head of the bed and touched his forehead, which was cool, then pushed the damp hair back off it. The fever had broken. I figured it was one of those twenty-four-hour bugs. He'd wake up famished and raring to go.

Taking advantage of what I hoped would be a little quiet time before I had to start dinner, I turned off the television, picked up the empty tray, and tiptoed out of the room. I set the tray down on Dad's suitcase in the hallway, went into my bathroom, and ran a steaming bath. With Dad and Eve here for I didn't know how long, this would probably be my last chance to luxuriate in my own bathtub. Besides, I figured I was entitled to fifteen minutes of returning to the womb. I dumped in half a cup of stress-reducing herbal

bubble bath, shed my clothes, and lowered my stressed-out
body into the silky foam. From events in my past I've developed an aversion to water. I avoid swimming pools, lakes,
and oceans, but fortunately for all who spend time with me,
the phobia hasn't extended to bathtubs. Hot baths com-
bined with the simple biofeedback exercise of putting myself in my "safe place" work for me the way tranquilizers do
for the general population. And it's a lot cheaper. I closed
my eyes and allowed the water to wash over me, the heat to
penetrate through my skin to my soul. Letting my imagination take over, I gave my senses free rein, putting myself
back in time to the tree house my father had built for me
when I was a child.

*But Eve is there, wearing her red hat and her tight spangled sweater,
sitting on the edge of the wooden platform with her pudgy legs dangling
in space. She has a basket filled with money on her lap, and she is scat-
tering handfuls of the bills into the wind. I am on the ladder trying to
climb up, and every time I get to the top, she kicks me away. Finally I
grab her legs and pull her with me and we fall to the ground together, and
then we are outside the bookstore and she is screaming, "His head's in the
soup. His head's in the soup."*

I came back with a jerk, splashing water all over my hair
and Lucie, who'd pushed open the bathroom door and had
been keeping me company while performing his own ablu-
tions. He gave a yowl of indignation, got up, and stalked
out. Lucie's aversion to water does extend to the bathtub.

Damn Eve, I thought angrily. *She's even managed to screw up my
safe place.*

Sweat had broken out on my forehead, whether from
the dream or the steam I couldn't say, but womb time was
clearly over. I rose from the water, dripping with foam like
some poor man's Venus, and kicked the door shut in case
Matt happened to wake up and come looking for me.

I wrapped myself in my terry-cloth robe and was sitting

at my dressing table blow-drying my hair when I heard Matt's voice.

"Mom?"

"Coming," I called. Unplugging the dryer, I crossed the hall to his room. He was out of bed and standing by the window that looked out onto the east side of the house.

"How're you feeling? You shouldn't be out of bed."

"I wanted to get somethin' to read. That guy's here again."

My heart started whamming against my ribs as I joined him at the window and peered out. "Where?"

"He was on the deck a minute ago."

"He was on our deck?"

"Yeah, standing over by the grill."

"I can't see anything. Turn off the light."

The room went dark, and my eyes traveled from the corner of the garage across the deck to the row of pine trees that wrapped the walk. Nothing stirred. Not even a squirrel. Not even a mouse. Except for the pines, the trees were bare, leaving little place for anyone to conceal himself. Could Matt be imagining this? I wondered. Was it possible that the events of the past couple of days had so thrown him that he was seeing danger behind every bush?

"I don't see anyone, honey," I whispered. "Could it have been a shadow from a tree branch? Sometimes the wind causes—"

"It's the same guy who was out there last night. He's wearin' a dark jacket with a hood. I'm not wacko. I can tell the difference between a tree branch and a guy."

"Well, he seems to be gone now."

He glanced up at me hopefully. "Maybe he was house-huntin' and now he went home."

"People don't come around to look at houses in the dark, and our house isn't for sale." Just then my eye caught a slight movement behind the big pine at the foot of the driveway, and I saw him. He stepped out from behind the tree as though he didn't care if he was seen or not, and for a brief moment he stood there in full view, looking up at the house. Then he trotted across the lawn and disappeared behind the garage.

"What do you s'pose he wants?" Matt asked.

"I don't know," I replied brusquely, drawing back from the window. "But I'm darned well going to find out." Ugly scenarios about what he probably wanted were skittering around in my head. I'd had a run-in with a stalker last year, and it wasn't an experience I'd want to repeat. Had I upset an unstable patient recently? Doris was always mad at me, but this wasn't Doris. It wasn't even Tony the pimp, who used to be one of her personalities, because Elaine/Doris/etc. was chunkier than this guy. Maybe this was someone Ted had arrested who was out of prison and bent on revenge. I'd certainly heard of situations like that, and it had been one of the reasons I'd hesitated about having Ted move in. Whoever he was, I wasn't going to sit around waiting for him to reveal the nefarious reasons behind his visit.

Matt trailed after me as I went into my room. "What're you gonna do?"

"I'm going to set off the alarm and let the police handle it."

"Then he'll run away and they won't catch him. And then he might come back later."

Out of the mouths of babes. My hand stopped just short of hitting the panic button. "You're right. I'll call the police and tell them not to use their sirens."

Keeping my back to Matt so he couldn't see how unsteady my hands were, I pressed 911 and gave them my name and address. I told them there was a suspicious person lurking outside my house; would they please come and check it out? While I talked I reached for my handbag, fished around for my pepper spray, then remembered that Eve had taken it. Damn the woman again. It was in the handbag that had disappeared.

"Maybe he's casing the place, plannin' to rob us," Matt piped up.

"He must be a pretty stupid burglar to stand right out in the open where we can see him," I replied with forced bravado. "Anyway, if it's money he's after, there're a lot better targets in this town than us." Clutching my robe tightly around me, I grabbed Matt with my free hand, and the two of us tiptoed into Allie's bedroom, which faced the street. From her window we could see down to the corner.

It seemed like hours to me, but probably less than five minutes had passed before two patrol cars pulled up and parked directly across the road, blocking access and egress. Four cops emerged, guns drawn. Approaching the house, they moved stealthily, intermittently cutting the blackness with beams from their flashlights. I watched as they split up, two circling to the right of the house and two to the left.

"Let's go downstairs," Matt said, wriggling out of my grasp. "I wanna see them catch him."

"It's dangerous," I hissed, running after him, fearful the next sound we would hear would be gunshots. "Stay away from the windows."

Horty lazily lifted his head from his mat in the corner of the living room where he'd been sleeping. He looked at me as if to say, "Oh, is something going on? Should I be barking?" Then, inspired by canine guilt or some noise belatedly picked up from outside, he started making enough racket to bring out the entire tristate police force.

I muzzled his jaw with my hand. "My hero," I muttered. "*Now* you open your big mouth."

More time passed, then one of the cops reappeared, speaking into his walkie-talkie as he made for the patrol cars. A few seconds later two of the others emerged, the man in the dark jacket wedged between them. They stopped at the foot of the front walk, waiting for the patrol car to be brought around. I could see that the man was shackled, but from this distance it was impossible to see much else. I couldn't tell if he was white, black, or green. I could only see that he was of average build and fairly tall, definitely not Tony. Seconds later the doorbell rang. "Matt, hold Horty," I said, moving quickly to answer it.

"We got him, ma'am," the young cop standing on my porch said. "Good you called us when you did."

"Thank you. Thank you very much," I replied, but my relief was edged with apprehension. "What was he doing? Do you know who he is?"

"He was casin' the joint, right?" Matt chimed in. "Was he gonna rob us?"

The cop smiled. "He says he was only looking for the number on the house."

"The number's clearly marked on that white rock at the top of the driveway. Besides, my son saw him out there yesterday."

"Well, we're gonna take him in and run a check."

I stood shivering in the doorway and watched as the patrol car pulled up. No one made a move to get in, and the man suddenly raised his head and looked over at me. I shrank back, thrusting Matt further behind me. "Well," I said. "I'm awfully glad you caught him. You guys do a great job."

"That's what they pay us for."

I caught a glimpse of my neighbor, Mr. Dressler, across the street as he opened his front door to see what was going

on. I started to close my door in response. I didn't want to
be the talk of the neighborhood again. "Well, thanks again."

"Uh . . . ma'am?"

"Is there something else? You don't need me to come
down and press charges, do you?"

He shook his head. "It's . . . he says he wants to talk to
the lady of the house."

"Who? The burglar?"

"Well, he hasn't actually stolen anything."

"I don't care. What could he possibly have to say to me?"

"You don't have to do it. It's just . . . there's something
about him. He's not what we usually run into, and we'd kind
of like to hear what he has on his mind."

"Is he high on something?"

"Don't seem to be."

I hesitated. I was torn between curiosity and repugnance
at the thought of being in the same room with some preda-
tor. "Isn't this . . . unusual?"

"Very irregular. Normally we'd ignore the request, but
there's something going on here we probably should know
about. For your benefit as well as ours. It'd only take a minute, but if you're afraid . . ."

The only thing we have to fear is fear itself. Sometimes I really
wish my father and his famous quotes would get out of
my head.

"He's cuffed. He can't hurt you. And we'd be right here."

"You mean you want to bring him inside?"

"If it's okay with you. It's pretty cold out."

Curiosity and the fact that I was freezing and Matt
would catch pneumonia if we stood here much longer won
out. Besides, if this was one of my more stressed-out patients gone loony, I'd better know it. "Okay," I said. "You
can bring him in, but only for a minute. Mattie, go upstairs."

"Aw, Mom—"

"No arguments." And to the cop I said, "Give me a minute to change."

They were huddled on the porch when I opened the door three minutes later—two of the cops and the would-be burglar/peeping Tom/child molester. The other patrol car had taken off. I'd thrown on jeans and a sweater, and I had my hand firmly gripping Horty's collar as they trooped into the foyer. Each one, including the burglar, carefully wiped his feet on the mat by the door just as though I'd invited them in for cocktails. Nothing like a well-brought-up burglar, I thought.

A low growl rumbled in Horty's throat as I closed the door and forced myself to face the shackled young man standing before me.

He wasn't at all what I expected. He didn't look like a drugged-out punk or a street-gang tough or some sleazy rapist–pedophile. I guessed him to be in his early to mid-thirties. He was wearing jeans and a knit shirt over which was a navy blue parka with a hood. The parka was open and the hood thrown back. There were mud stains on the knees of his pants and some on his sleeves and face, but otherwise he looked like the boy next door. More than that. He looked like the boy next door every girl dreams about. An Adonis. He was about five foot eleven, clean-shaven and even-featured, with blue-green eyes and wavy brown hair. With his coat open I could see that he was well-built, like a runner with long legs and long arms, and he moved with the easy grace of a young Henry Fonda or Clint Eastwood. In his chosen profession, I thought wryly, that should stand him in good stead. I'd've bet his smile was dazzling, but he wasn't smiling. He looked straight at me, unafraid to make eye contact. Suddenly I wasn't frightened anymore. I was mad. I didn't wait for him to get in the first word.

"What do you want?" I was shaking with fury. "Who are you? How dare you skulk around my home frightening me and my children?"

"I didn't mean to scare you," he replied in a low voice. "I wasn't sure I had the right place. My name's Garrett. I came here looking for my mother."

"I'm the only mother living in this house and my name's not Garrett," I snapped. "And you're not my son."

He smiled then—an engaging smile, the teeth even and white just as I'd imagined. "No, that wouldn't be possible. We're obviously too close in age. My mother's name is Eve. Eve Carlin. If this is the Carlin residence, and you're Caroline Carlin, I guess that would make you my stepsister."

FROM NOW ON when my kids tell me something's blown their minds, I'll tell them they haven't a clue what the expression means. I've probably had more than my share of shocks in my life; that's kind of the way the past couple of years have gone for me. But this caught me off guard. This completely blew my mind. I was still staring at the guy, speechless, when through the buzzing in my head, I heard a car pull into the driveway. Minutes later the scrape of a key turning in the lock brought me back to reality, and Ted was there with my dad and Eve on his heels.

"What's going on here?" he demanded of the cop nearest the door. His eyes took in the shackled prisoner. "Who's this guy?"

I started to answer, but before I could get the words out, the cop took over, his intent to calm the frightened "husband."

"It's okay, Mr. Carlin. Everything's under control."

Ted whipped out his badge. "Brodsky, Violent Crimes. What the hell happened here?"

Big change in attitude, like when a doctor realizes he's talking to another doctor.

"This lady called us about a possible break-in. Said her boy saw the perp on the grounds two nights in a row. We apprehended him at the rear of the house by the garage."

"I wasn't trying to break in," the perp said.

Ted's angry eyes raked the young man. "What the fuck were you doing, then? Who are you?"

"Says his name's Garrett," the other cop replied. "Says he came to see his mother and that this lady is—"

There was a strangled sound from Eve, half gasp, half moan, so unnerving it caused the officer to pause mid-sentence. Her face had drained of all color and I took a step toward her, fearful she'd fall. My father reached out a hand to steady her, but she pushed him away.

"No," she whispered. "Don't. I need to . . . I have to . . . see—"

"What in . . ." Ted began, but I grabbed his wrist, my nails digging into his flesh, and his voice trailed off.

It was like watching a tennis game at match point. All eyes shifted from the stranger to Eve and back again. But the featured players in this drama stood unmoving, eyes locked. When he spoke, it was to score the ace.

"It's been a long time, Mother," he said.

The room went deathly quiet, the only sound breaking the silence a soft whine from Horty as he pressed against my leg. Eve stood rigid, a panoply of expressions playing across her face as she struggled for control. Her eyes never left his face as she searched for—what? The little boy in the picture? Were they one and the same? The air in the room seemed stifling, as though the breath had been sucked out of all of us, and for a brief time it seemed no one dared take a breath at all. Finally, almost in slow motion, Eve propelled herself forward. She stopped in front of him, reached up as if to touch his face, then hesitated, fearful perhaps that he'd pull away, and drew back.

He grasped her hand. "Please don't be afraid. I'm here. I've found you."

I could feel my cheeks getting wet. My father's hand found mine. One of the cops coughed and blew his nose. Ted cleared his throat. Horty whimpered.

There was a long pause, then Eve's voice, choked, almost inaudible, broke the silence. "Jamie?" she whispered. "Jamie?"

All hell broke loose after that. Everyone talked at once. I said I would drop charges, and the cops uncuffed their prisoner after Ted promised he'd bring him and Eve to the station in the morning to make out a report. While they worked out the details, Eve—mute with shock, tears raining down her mascara-streaked cheeks—and this man who claimed to be her son sank down onto the couch, so deeply engrossed in each other the rest of us could only have been background noise to them. While he talked, her eyes never left his face. From time to time she reached up and ran her fingers over his features, as though through touch she would discover the little boy from the photograph who she so desperately needed to find in the man. I realized she was still wearing her clothes from yesterday: the brown skirt, rumpled and creased now from having been slept in, the dark panty hose, and the tight cherry-red sweater with the sequins. The panty hose had acquired a run, and the sequins on the sweater had gone dull, having somehow lost their glitter in that jail cell, the way stars dim under threat of a storm. And the tears were doing a bang-up job on what was left of her two-day-old makeup. On her best days (except for that size D bra cup) Eve was no Sophia Loren, but it wasn't fair that on such a momentous occasion she should be caught at her worst. I wanted to freeze-frame the scene, take her upstairs, run a bubble bath, help her don clean clothes, and do something with that rat's nest of a hairdo. Then I'd deposit her back on the couch and unfreeze the frame so she could meet her son looking crisp and clean and decently coiffed. But I did the best I could under the circumstances, reached into my desk drawer, pulled out a box of tissues, and as unobtrusively as possible slid the box onto the coffee table. She caught my hand as I was about to sneak back to my chair.

"Carrie, Carrie, don't run away. Wait. I want you to—" She grabbed a handful of tissues, blew her nose, and wiped her eyes, leaving two black splotches under each eye. "Isn't this . . . can you believe what's happened? Can you believe I've found my son? My little boy, Jamie. I want you to meet . . . this is Jamie—my son." She tugged at his sleeve. "This is Carrie—my David's daughter. She's a bio-feedback . . . she does . . . uh . . . this is her house, you know. She . . . I've been staying here—"

"Yes, I know." He smiled. "We've met."

Before I could think of a suitable reply, she beckoned to my father, who, after the initial excitement had abated, had moved to the other side of the room and was sitting in the rocker, quietly watching the drama unfold. At her summons he got up and joined us.

"And this is David, my husband," she said. "He's such a wonderful, wonderful man. You're going to love him."

She didn't say he was going to love me, but considering I'd ratted her out to the cops, how could I take offense?

Was this truly Eve's illegitimate son? I wondered as I shifted uneasily from one foot to the other. How could she know that if she hadn't seen him since he was a child? Or, even more incomprehensible, since he was an infant? She'd talked about her "friend" having a girl baby. Were there two missing children, or had she said that to throw me off?

"David, sit down," Eve blubbered. "Just look at him. Isn't he beautiful? Oh, my God, my God, I can't . . . how did this . . . it's . . ." And again she dissolved, a dam unleashed that gave no sign of slacking. "I'm sorry, I'm sorry. Just give me a minute. . . ."

Dad looked about as uncomfortable as I felt. If I was freaked out I could imagine his state of mind. But, gentleman that he is, he squeezed in next to his wife and extended his hand. "I . . . uh . . . I'm glad to meet you, young man. I don't really understand how all this has come about, and I hope you'll enlighten me, but, well . . . you're welcome here."

It came out stiffer than he'd probably intended, but Jamie took his awkwardness in stride. He reached over Eve and took Dad's hand. "Thank you, sir," he replied. "I appreciate that. It's been a long time since I had a family to welcome me."

I could tell Dad was touched and a little taken aback by his response, but he struggled on valiantly. "Well, whatever makes your . . . uh . . . mother happy, makes me happy," he said.

"I looked for you . . . for so long . . . it was like you went up in smoke," Eve choked. "How did you . . . after all these years, how did you find me?"

Jamie flashed a smile and pulled his wallet out of his pocket. He opened it and extracted a photograph. "I've always kept this," he said. A younger, somewhat slimmer Eve, no older than Jamie was now, looked back at us. But for a few more wrinkles and a few more pounds, Eve really hadn't changed that much.

"I live in Boston now. I saw you on TV. I saw all of you."

Before I could react to that, one of the cops standing in the foyer entranceway motioned to me. He and his partner were getting ready to leave. "Be right back," I mumbled, and scurried over to them.

The younger cop grinned. "Well, that turned out better than we expected, didn't it? I like happy endings. Reminds me of that TV show where they hook up people who've been separated for years."

"How long since they've seen each other, Ms. Carlin?" asked his partner.

The image of the little boy from the snapshot, grinning from ear to ear as he proudly displayed his trophy, sprang to mind. I went with it. "A very long time," I said. "Probably not since he was nine or ten years old."

"What happened?"

"I'm not sure. I guess we'll hear about it later. But it would've never turned out this way if you hadn't convinced me to see him."

"Take my word for it," said the first cop. "Most of our calls *don't* turn out this way."

Ted came up behind me, rested his hands on my shoulders, and whispered in my ear. "I'm going out to the patrol car—give these guys a rundown on what's gone on. Back in a few minutes."

I nodded, moved to behind my desk, and sat in the chair, trying to make sense of the bombshell this young man had exploded in our midst. I found myself sneaking looks at him, searching for the boy in the photograph. The coloring was the same, the light eyes and fair skin. If Eve had given up Jamie at birth, how had she come into possession of those photographs? Had she ferreted out his adoptive parents and gone to see him when he was growing up? Or maybe Omar had the photos and had taunted her with them. But then Omar would have had to be alive when she arrived at the apartment, and I didn't want to consider that possibility. Omar himself had been in one of the pictures, his arm draped around the boy's shoulder as if they were great buddies. I wondered how Jamie had known Eve was here. Only my father had known she was staying with me. So many questions I wanted to ask, but I had to contain my curiosity for the moment.

Eve was talking now, alternately laughing and crying between bursts of hysterical chatter. Soggy tissues were fast carpeting the floor. I decided wine might stem the tide, then concluded it would probably make it worse. Chamomile tea, Meg's panacea, that was the solution. I got up and headed for the kitchen. "I'm going to put the kettle on," I mumbled in passing.

"Mom? Can I come down now?"

I'd totally forgotten about Matt. "Sweetheart, yes, I'm sorry. Come on down."

"I heard the whole thing." Matt racketed down the stairs and skidded to a stop in front of Jamie. "Hi," he said. "I'm Matt."

"Hi," Jamie responded solemnly. "I'm Jamie."

"I know. You don't look like Aunt Eve."

"I've got her coloring, though."

"Yeah," Matt said. "That's how it works sometimes. I look like my mom, but my hair's the same color as my dad's. D'you look like your dad?"

I could feel my face burning. I wanted to say something that would save Eve embarrassment, but I couldn't think what. *I should've made Matt stay upstairs till the explanations are over*, I thought unhappily.

"Actually," Jamie said easily, "I don't really look a whole lot like him either." He stretched out his hands. "I've got big hands and feet like his, though. Funny the things we inherit."

How would he know that?

Eve looked over at my flushed face, clutched at my shirt. "Carrie . . . it isn't what you think . . . David . . ." She turned to Dad. "I'm . . . sorry I never told you about Jamie."

She looked so tormented, so guilt-ridden, he took her hand and said, "It's all right. It's all right. You don't owe me an explanation."

But it wasn't all right, and she did, and she knew it.

"No, you don't understand. It . . . I do . . . I haven't been . . . honest with you. You see, I . . . I never told you . . . I was married to Jamie's father."

The stunned silence that followed was broken seconds later by the sound of the front door opening and closing.

Ted walked in the room and halted as he took in our expressions. "Did I miss something?"

Only bombshell number two.

"Eve was telling us," I murmured, "that she'd neglected to mention to anyone that she and Jamie's father were married. . . ."

I wondered if there were any more husbands she'd forgotten to tell us about. And if they were all dead.

Jamie got to his feet. "Listen," he said, his focus on my father. "I had no idea you didn't know. I seem to have put my mother in a very awkward position. I'm sorry. Maybe I should come back tomorrow, after you've had time to—"

"No," Eve cried, distraught, hanging on to his arm. "No, no, no! You can't go. Don't let him go," she implored my father. "Please, let me explain. David, I thought . . . I thought I'd never see Jamie again. I was trying to forget . . . to get on with my life. That's why—"

"Forget what?" I asked, all my old feelings about Eve returning in force. "That you had a son?"

"No," she moaned. "That I'd lost my son. His father stole him. He came with hired thugs to where we were hiding

out and he—he—he tore him screaming out of my arms."
Her hands moved to cover her ears, as if by the action she
could block out his cries. "I still hear him—even now at
night I hear him—calling to me, *'Mommy, don't let him take me.
Help me.'* And I couldn't. I couldn't. They knocked me down
and took him, and they disappeared, and I never saw him
again. Till now." Her voice broke. "Till now."

Her story shattered me. I felt almost physically ill. I
couldn't imagine what I'd do if Rich stole the children. For
some perverse reason, which I can never explain to my
friends, when he betrayed me with Erica, I wanted to kill
her, not him. But there's something so visceral about the
mother–child bond, the animal instinct to protect your
young that overwhelms you the minute that tiny helpless
thing is placed in your arms. If he'd taken my children,
there's no question in my mind, a tigress would have nothing
on me. I would not have been accountable for my actions.

Tears were again streaming down Eve's face. Jamie was
sitting quietly, his eyes never leaving her. I had to get out of
the room, so I offered to make tea for everyone. Five minutes alone of diaphragmatic breathing in the kitchen gave
me time to collect myself, and after several cups of chamomile tea, both Eve and I had calmed down sufficiently for
her to go on.

She'd married, she told us, when she was relatively young
to a man by the name of Frank Garrett. The brutality had
started on their honeymoon and had gotten progressively
worse, to the point where she'd realized her son's life as well
as her own were in danger.

"Jamie . . . he wasn't even as old as your Matt is now
when we ran away from Frank," she said. "That night—"
Her hand tightened on Jamie's. "That night he'd beaten
Jamie with a belt for forgetting to turn out a light. I . . . I'd
tried to . . . I threw myself on top of Jamie, but he yanked

me off. He was . . . big . . . so much stronger . . . I couldn't . . . I couldn't stop him. I knew if we didn't get away, he'd kill us one day."

Involuntarily, my hands tightened on Matt's shoulders. I wished he hadn't heard this, and I was filled with remorse at the unkind thoughts about black widows and dead husbands that had gone through my mind.

"I didn't . . . I didn't even have a plan. There were no shelters for battered women and children then—at least none I knew about. I didn't have any money. I thought if we could just get somewhere safe, I'd . . . I'd think what to do, so I ran to my friend Louise's. Her brother was there—he must've called Frank and told him where we were—and . . . and Frank came with those horrible men. . . ." She took a deep shuddering breath and her eyes found Jamie's. "I looked for you for eight long years. The police wouldn't listen—in those days they wouldn't get involved in a kidnapping case if a parent was the kidnapper—so I hired private detectives. Nothing. It was as though you'd been snatched by space aliens. But there was never a night in the next God-knows-how-many years that I didn't . . . that I didn't go to bed with a stone on my heart, wondering where you were sleeping, if you were sleeping on the cold ground somewhere, or . . . or if you were buried somewhere *in* the ground. . . ." Her voice trailed off.

There was silence for a long, long moment, and then Jamie got slowly to his feet. "It wasn't Louise? It was Omar who called him?"

Oops. Bombshell number three.

Ted didn't miss that cue. "Omar?" he asked, his eyes drilling Eve. "As in the Omar who is now residing in the city morgue? That Omar?"

Aghast, Jamie stared at Ted. "What're you saying? He's dead?"

"I didn't kill him," Eve moaned. "I swear it wasn't me. You have to believe me."

Up till now I had believed her. But up till now I hadn't known how strong a motive she'd had.

There was the sound of a key turning in the lock and Allie opened the door, bringing with her a rush of cold air that worked like a slap in the face to break the tension.

"Hi." Allie paused in the doorway, eyes flicking from me to her grandfather, to Eve, and coming to rest finally on the handsome stranger standing next to the sofa. "What's going on?"

12

IT WAS nearly nine o'clock and I was wrung out.
I needed a break and so did Eve. I let Ted explain to Jamie
on the quiet what had happened to Omar and took the
opportunity—while Allie greeted her grandfather and was
introduced to Jamie—to order in some Chinese food. Then
I insisted that Eve come upstairs and change. If Ted and
Dad wanted to grill Jamie in our absence, that was okay
with me, but I didn't think Eve could take much more without some rest and at least a little nourishment. So despite
my misgivings about her, I played the good daughter. I ran
her a bath, poured in a generous amount of my special
stress-reducing bath bubbles, and insisted she soak until the
dirt and grime of her night in the hoosegow had dissolved.
When I judged her sufficiently clean and relaxed, I creamed
her face, washed her hair, adding about a ton of softening
conditioner, and wrapped her in my oversize terry-cloth
robe. In a very un-Eve-like manner, she acceded to my min-
istrations without a murmur. I insisted that she rest on my
bed, until the doorbell rang signaling the arrival of dinner.

By the time I escorted her downstairs, she was physically much improved and at least somewhat emotionally revived. I had to force-feed the wonton soup, but I succeeded in getting three-quarters of a bowl down her along with a little rice. This is the type of thing for which motherhood prepares you well. Everyone else wolfed down the food as if there'd never be another egg roll. For about ten minutes there was no talk and no tears, only the normal sounds of hungry bellies being happily stuffed. The best indication of Eve's state of mind was that she never once commented on Matt's slurping his soup.

"He used to take Jamie fishing—Omar, I mean, even though he was much older than Jamie was," she said softly, as I got up to clear the table. "His sister, Louise, she was my best friend. I never thought Omar couldn't be trusted, or I wouldn't have gone there." Her mouth twisted with bitterness. "I thought he'd help us, because he knew how Frank was, you know. He'd seen my bruises. He'd seen him knock Jamie around." She looked over at Jamie, her face reflecting a host of emotions as memories flooded back. "Do you remember the day you caught that big fish and I took your picture holding it?"

Jamie hesitated. "You mean the time—"

"When you wouldn't give it to Frank to have his picture taken, and Omar and he got in that big fistfight after he threw the fishhook at your back and you all ended up in the emergency room?"

"Yeah," Jamie said. "His ego wouldn't tolerate his being outdone by a nine-year-old kid, even his own. It was at the lake with the Indian name, wasn't it? Lake . . ."

"Webster Lake. The Indian name was some long—"

"Lake Chargoggagogg-manchauggagogg-chaubunagun-gamaugg."

She looked at him in wonder, as though he'd just explained the theory of relativity.

Jamie laughed. "It's the kind of name sticks in a kid's mind."

"I thought Omar was on our side, but he betrayed us."

"I can't believe it," Jamie muttered. "All these years I thought it was Louise who—"

Eve's voice was suddenly sharp. "No. Louise loved me. She would never have—she was my best friend."

He looked puzzled. "But my father told me—"

"He lied. He lied when the truth would have served him better. It was Omar."

And now Omar's dead, I thought, my heart sinking. As a motive for murder, it certainly worked for me.

I wondered if Ted's thoughts were running along similar lines, but if they were he didn't let on.

"Did you ever see Omar again?" he asked Jamie.

"Never. We lived in Toronto at first, so I never saw anyone from our old life, not even my father's family. We moved around a lot. I can't even remember how many new names I had or how many times I changed schools. We didn't come back to the States till I was fourteen."

"Did your father ever remarry?" Ted asked.

Jamie's voice was expressionless. "There were . . . women, but he never remarried, at least not while I lived with him."

"How long since you've seen him?"

"Eighteen years. I ran away when I was sixteen. I hope he's dead. If he isn't it doesn't matter. He's out of my life."

"You mean he never tried to get in touch with you in all that time?" Dad asked.

Jamie shrugged. "If he did he never found me. If there was one thing I learned from him, it was how to disappear. I lived on a commune in California for a while after I took off. When I was nineteen I joined the Marines."

"Why didn't you try to get in touch with your mother before this?" I asked. "I mean, once you were grown I would've thought—"

"The sonofabitch told me she was dead." He glanced at Allie and Matt, who were staring at him, openmouthed. "Sorry."

"They've heard worse, unfortunately. Okay, kids, it's late. Eat your fortune cookies, then wash and brush your teeth, and go to bed. I'll be up in a little while." I handed them each a cookie, out of habit broke one open for myself, and pulled out the little strip of paper.

That the birds of worry fly above your head you cannot change, but do not let them build nests in your hair.

Hey, I got the wrong cookie. I wasn't the one with the nest in my hair. I was tempted to slide it over to Eve but restrained myself. I crumpled it up and threw it away.

Ted and I went upstairs to pack his things, leaving my dad alone in the living room with Eve and Jamie. We'd decided that Ted would move back to his apartment for as long as it took to get everything settled, so Dad and Eve could have the master bedroom. I'd bunk with Allie, and Jamie could sleep in Matt's room while he was here. I didn't know for how long that would be, but I calculated it couldn't be for more than a few days.

"We could sleep on the studio couch downstairs," I said, wrapping my arms tightly around him. "I've kind of gotten used to sleeping with you."

"Look how long it took me to convince you," he teased. "And now you just can't wait to—"

I stopped his mouth with a kiss. It was a long, thoroughly satisfying kiss that, if we hadn't been so tired, would've had us locking the bedroom door for an hour or maybe three.

"It'll be too hectic," he said, finally releasing me. "Hopefully, we'll have them all on their way home within the week."

He picked up a shirt and started to fold it. I watched, amused, as he suspended it in midair, tucked the sleeves under with one hand, then kind of rolled it up. As he placed it in the suitcase, he regarded the crumpled heap in perplexity.

"Damn," he said. "That didn't work."

"Observe and learn." I took it out, laid it out on the bed, and did it the right way. It always amazes me that such a competent man can't figure out how to fold a shirt.

"Isn't it fantastic, what's happened?" I exclaimed as I completed the job. "I'm so happy for Eve."

"Pretty amazing. Not too often someone comes back into your life after a quarter of a century. Think you'd recognize Matt after twenty-five years?"

My instinct was to say I'd recognize my son if he shaved his head, grew a beard down to his belly button, and joined a monastery. But would I? A young boy's voice changes when he grows to manhood, so there are no clues there. There are the eyes, though. Those don't change. And the shape of the mouth. And that indefinable something that makes an elephant reject an orphaned baby because she knows it isn't hers.

"I'd like to think I would." I placed the shirt carefully in his overnight case and reached for another. "You know, I've never considered Eve the maternal type. She's always been so fussy and critical of the kids and me, but I'll bet that was because seeing us reminded her of him—of everything she'd lost." I shivered. "I can't even imagine how I'd deal with something like that."

"You don't have to worry. Rich is cool with his life just the way it is."

"So long as I don't stumble over any more dead bodies."

"That'd be a plus all around."

I added two more shirts and a few pair of socks while Ted went into the bathroom for his shaving kit.

"You notice how Allie couldn't take her eyes off him?" I called.

"What?"

"I said did you see how Allie couldn't take her eyes off him?" I repeated, raising my voice. "I think he may replace Alec from last year's *Mikado* production as the object of her affection. At least in the older-man department."

He laughed. "You're lucky he lives in Boston."

"Yeah, teenage crushes are hell to deal with."

"The upside is Eve'll get to see a lot of him now, provided the mess she's gotten herself into here can be straightened out fairly soon."

"I can't believe the transformation. Every time she looks at him, she positively glows."

"I'm afraid the glow may dim a little by tomorrow. Unless the boys in the city find evidence in that apartment that points to someone else." He came back with the kit and placed it in the suitcase, tried to close it. "Sit on this, will you?"

I plopped myself down on the bag. "But remember, she never got the information about Jamie's whereabouts. God knows she hated Omar enough to kill him, but why would she shoot him before she got what she'd come for? And where's the gun?" I added.

"A wild guess. In her handbag?"

"Which she didn't have with her when she climbed down the ladder. I was there, and it wasn't. And the police never found it, which means," I concluded triumphantly, "that someone—the killer probably—took it." I didn't want my father's nutsy wife to be a killer any more than I had wanted my children's sonofabitch father to be one.

He finally managed to get the bag zipped and dumped me onto the bed. "Make sure Eve and Jamie are ready at nine," he said. "I'll take them to the precinct, and then I'm gone for the rest of the week. The Tenafly homicide's going to keep me pretty busy for a while."

"I thought the guy next door did it."

"Complications. He may not have acted alone."

"How about I move into your apartment and take over the investigation, and you stay here and cope with this insanity?"

He grinned. "Your family, sweetheart."

I sighed. "My dad isn't the problem."

"I'll call Holbrook. She'll handle everything. She'll come out tomorrow and talk to Eve and Jamie. Eve isn't hiding anything anymore—so far as we know, at least—so Holbrook won't be working with her hands tied." He kissed me and picked up his bag. "Go to bed. Things won't look so bad in the morning."

"Ted?"

"Yeah?"

"You don't really think Eve killed Omar, do you?"

He paused at the door. "My gut tells me no, but I've been wrong before. Rage is a damned powerful emotion, and hers has been building for a long time. It could have exploded if he pushed the wrong buttons."

"But," I protested, "we know Eve. She may be a pain in the butt, but can you picture her pulling a trigger?"

"Could you say for sure how far you'd go if someone stole Matt or Allie?"

I opened my mouth and closed it again.

"Anyway, it's too soon to speculate. There's a lot we don't know yet about this guy Omar. He may've had accomplices, or maybe he was into drugs or God knows what other crap. Let's let the boys in the city do their job before we start jumping to conclusions."

13

MY ASSISTANT, Ruth-Ann, was already in the office reception area when I came charging in a little after ten, breathless from having taken the three flights of stairs two at a time. She had my first patient, an adult ADD (Attention Deficit Disorder), hooked up to the computer and had started the program. I peeked into my office, checked that Mrs. Thomassy was focused on the monitor and that the lights were flashing more green than red, which meant the protocol was set correctly. Then I quietly pulled the door closed.

"Thanks, Ruth-Ann. Sorry I'm late. We had a little excitement at the house."

"It's okay. I didn't mind so long as Doris and the gang wasn't your first."

"They're coming tomorrow. I promise I'll get here on time." I took off my coat and hung it on the coatrack, started for the file cabinet, stopped, turned around, and gave her a long, appraising look. Something was different. It wasn't the thick, shiny black hair that she always wears parted in the middle and pulled back in a bun, a style you have to have perfect features (which she does) to get away with, and it wasn't the makeup, which is always minimal, a touch of pink lipstick and a bare suggestion of eye shadow. Then it hit me. She was wearing a skirt that ended just below her knees. My rather meager understanding of the Orthodox Jewish dress code for women told me that was a no-no.

"What's with the skirt?" I inquired.

"Excuse me?"

"Haven't you lost a few inches?"

She deliberately misunderstood me. "I'm still a hundred fifteen pounds."

"You know what I mean."

Every time I look at Ruth-Ann I feel good about what I do. She's my greatest success story. When she first came to my office as a patient, she was grossly overweight. You couldn't see the perfect features. You could barely see the long black eyelashes peeking out from between the layers surrounding her soulful brown eyes. Getting to the source of her problem took perseverance on my part and courage on hers, but eventually the weight she'd been hiding behind began to come off, and today Ruth-Ann is a quite beautiful, well-adjusted young woman. Her work clothes generally consist of a high-neck white blouse buttoned to the chin and a full mid-calf-length dark-colored skirt. Today's outfit was a marked exception. The skirt was skipper blue, straight, and stopped just below her knees. It sported a small slit in the back. Her pink blouse had one button open at the throat. It was hardly the costume of today's Generation Xers, but neither was it that of a modest Orthodox Jewish woman. Was there a rebellion going on here?

"Have they relaxed the rules?"

"Who?"

"Whoever makes them."

"I just decided to try something new."

"Oh. Okay." I dropped it.

"What was the excitement about?" she asked.

I filled her in while I checked my appointment book and started pulling charts. When I'd finished telling the story, my eyes were moist all over again and so were Ruth-Ann's.

"It's like a movie," she murmured. "A fairy tale. It gives me goose bumps."

"I know. It makes me cry just talking about it."

"Whoever killed the man in the apartment's still out there, though, right? They don't know who it is?"

"Right."

"You think the son's in any danger?"

I looked up from the file. "What do you mean? Why would Jamie be in danger?"

"I don't know," she replied, her expression thoughtful. "Just . . . the murder and everything, sounds like something that horrible father would be involved in."

"Jamie hasn't seen or heard from him in years. He could be dead."

"What if he isn't? A man who could take a child from his mother and never let them see each other again, I'd think he'd be capable of anything."

I slid the file drawer closed. "Well, I agree with you about that, but there's no motive. People don't go around killing people for no reason."

There was a slight pause and then she said softly, "I don't think my parents would agree with you about that."

Ruth-Ann's parents are Holocaust survivors.

"Come on, Ruth-Ann. This is completely different."

"Is it? Evil is evil." She took the charts from my hands, sat down at her desk, and began busily arranging them in order of the patients' arrival times. "Is he handsome, the son?" she inquired, avoiding my eyes.

"Well," I said, "if you like the Greek god type . . ."

"Will he be coming to the office?"

"Shame on you, Ruth-Ann," I teased. "Your father would never approve."

Her face colored. "I wasn't . . . I didn't mean . . . it's such an unbelievable story. I just wanted to meet—"

"I was kidding. He won't be coming today. Eve and he are meeting with her lawyer. But maybe I can arrange something before he goes back to Boston."

"Okay," she replied, keeping her face bent over her work.

"I've gotta go see how Mrs. Thomassy's doing. Grab the phones, will you?"

"Okay."

It flashed briefly through my mind that something was going on with Ruth-Ann, that I should have a talk with her. *I'll get to it later in the week,* I thought.

Despite what I'd expected, Ruth-Ann did get to meet Jamie that very afternoon. I'd just finished my last patient, Tanya Johnson, a thirteen-year-old African-American girl whose mother drives her all the way from Hackensack religiously twice a week for Attention Deficit training. Tanya's the same age as Allie, with the same budding (or maybe not so budding) interest in the opposite sex. I was cleaning the gel out of the ear sensors with a Q-Tip, so my back was to her when she opened the door to the waiting room.

"Who's the hunk's got Ruth-Ann actin' like the sisters?"

"What?"

"Ruth-Ann. I've never seen her gigglin' and carryin' on before."

My serious-minded Ruth-Ann, giggling and carrying on? What changes had this new attire wrought, or was it the other way around? I dropped the leads and followed Tanya out to the waiting room. Jamie was perched on the arm of the chair next to Ruth-Ann's desk, his head bent toward her, regaling her with a tale that had her giggling as though Robin Williams were sitting there cracking jokes. And Tanya was right. Ruth-Ann's cheeks were flushed a rosy pink, and her eyes were sparkling in a way I'd never seen before. Eve was huddled in one of the waiting-room chairs next to an attractive young woman who I guessed to be in her late twenties or early thirties. She had long straight blond hair, legs to match, a snub nose, and that ultraslim build that does not allow for more than a thousand calories a day to pass the lips. Her charcoal-gray suit skirt ended top-thigh, about eight inches higher than Ruth-Ann's. There was a briefcase at her feet, a notepad in her lap, and a cell phone in her hand. My brain didn't have to work overtime to tell me this was the lawyer Ted had hired for Eve. Ted had said he'd run into her a few times and she was good. It went through my mind that he'd better be referring strictly to her professional attributes; then immediately I admonished myself for the disloyal thought. Ted wasn't Rich, and I'd promised myself I'd get rid of all that old baggage. She rose to her feet and started toward me as I closed my office door.

"Ms. Carlin? I'm Vivian Holbrook."

My fingers were still sticky from the gel on the sensors. I pulled a tissue from my pocket, swiped at them, and held out my hand. "Sorry," I apologized. "Professional hazard."

"It's okay," she replied pleasantly. "I have to get back to the city, but I wanted to bring you up-to-date and get your version of events before I left."

I glanced at Tanya, who had stopped by the coatrack, her hand seemingly frozen to the post as she stared at Jamie.

"Tanya," I said. "Your mom's probably waiting."

"I'm goin'." She grabbed her coat and backed out the door. "Lucky Ruth-Ann," she whispered as she passed me. "He's a hottie."

Did she say *honey*? "A what?"

She flashed me a glance as if to ask what planet I'd been living on. "Hottie. He's hot."

"Oh." *Hot* I knew. *Hottie* hadn't yet made it into my children's vernacular, but I was sure the day wasn't far off.

If there was one thing Ruth-Ann didn't need in her life, it was a "hottie," especially one who'd knocked around the way Jamie had. "Excuse me for just a minute," I said to Vivian Holbrook. I walked over to Ruth-Ann's desk. "Hi, Jamie."

He smiled warmly. "Hi," he said. "Nice setup you've got here. Piermont looks like a fun town."

"It is. Friendly. You get to know your neighbors. Ruth-Ann," I said, turning to her. "Jamie and I need to talk to Eve's lawyer. I didn't finish cleaning the sensors. Would you mind . . ."

She jumped to her feet. "Oh, sure. Right away." She blushed even deeper. "Nice to have met you, Jamie," she murmured, not looking at either of us.

His eyes followed her trim figure as she walked into my office. "Same here," he called after her. And to me, "Nice girl. Classy. She worked for you long?"

I'd better nip this in the bud, I thought. *Backgrounds're about as compatible as the Capulets and the Montagues.*

"She's Orthodox," I whispered to him after she'd closed the door.

He looked puzzled. "Orthodox what? Greek?"

"Jewish. Her father's a rabbi. They're very strict." And it was mean of me, but I couldn't resist. "You know, when she gets married she'll have to shave off all that beautiful hair and wear a wig."

He stared at me. "You're kidding. Why?"

"I'm not sure, but I think it's so she won't be attractive to men other than her husband."

"She won't be attractive to her husband either."

"He's supposed to love her for who she is on the inside."

"Well," he muttered, shrugging his shoulders. "I guess it works for birth control."

"Ms. Carlin? Can we talk?"

"Coming." I pulled two of the chairs around so that Jamie and I were facing Eve and Ms. Holbrook. Jamie positioned his so that the back of his chair was toward them. He straddled the seat and hooked his arms around the splat. Eve was looking so distressed, I felt compelled to lean forward and give her arm a sympathetic pat before turning to Ms. Holbrook. "What would you like to know?"

"For starters," she replied, "I'd like to ascertain exact times with you regarding when you arrived at the crime scene. It could be important. I've just been explaining to Mrs. Carlin that there is a possibility she'll be indicted for the murder of Omar Kassel."

I caught my breath. Holbrook had spoken seriously but matter-of-factly, as though what she was saying was merely an uncomfortable bit of information she thought we should have. I'd been aware this might be coming, but somehow I hadn't really believed it in my gut. Hearing it said aloud caused me to break out in a cold sweat. I glanced at Eve. Her hands were tightly clenched in her lap. Jamie wasn't saying anything. No indignant protests from that quarter. Did he think his mother had killed Omar? He probably hadn't a clue. His memory of her was sketchy. The truth was, he didn't know what she might or might not be capable of.

"They won't hold her," Holbrook continued. "It's clear she's no threat to society. I don't think the judge will set bail unreasonably high, and my understanding is your father will be able to pay it."

What did this lawyer consider not unreasonably high? My experience with lawyers was that their idea of high contained a few more zeros than my idea of high. I started thinking what her little trip out here to the suburbs might cost and decided to talk fast.

"I got there at twelve twenty-five," I said. "I remember specifically because I was late. I'd gotten stuck in traffic and I was constantly looking at my watch."

Holbrook began writing on her legal pad. "Did you see Mrs. Carlin climbing down the ladder as soon as you drove up?"

"No, not immediately. I spent about twenty minutes making inquiries in the area. Eve had been in the bookstore about half an hour before I got there. The woman from The Black Orchid can verify that. And," I added emphatically, "a man saw her a little later looking for the number on the building. The police must've checked that out. So if Omar was killed much earlier, it's clear Eve couldn't have had anything to do with—"

"Time of death hasn't been determined yet, but, unfortunately, it's never accurate to the exact hour."

I knew that. I caught myself biting my nails, an old habit I thought I'd conquered. I made a conscious effort to keep my hands in my lap.

"I'm afraid from what you're telling me, the police will find that Mrs. Carlin's presence at the scene of the crime falls within that time frame. And, of course, it doesn't look so good that she ran away and failed to notify them."

Major guilt. I'd been a coconspirator in that. "She was in shock," I protested weakly. "You have to understand, when she saw that body all she could think of was to get out of there."

"Look," said Holbrook. "I'm on your side. But if I'm going to help Mrs. Carlin, we have to face reality and deal with the facts as the police will perceive them. Then we look for evidence to counter their conclusions. Which brings me to the missing handbag—"

Eve's moan coincided with the ringing of Vivian Holbrook's cell phone.

"Excuse me," she said, clicking it on and bringing it to her ear. "Holbrook here."

It's a new world. It would never occur to me to answer my phone, "Carlin here." Who else would anyone be calling if they dialed my number? And if I'm answering my phone, of course I'm here. I looked at the long legs and the abbreviated skirt and decided I was definitely getting old.

She rose and walked over to the window to be out of earshot. All we could hear between pauses was an occasional "uh-huh . . . right . . . uh-huh."

A minute later Holbrook joined us, and she was actually smiling.

"Good news. We have a new development that could help your mother," she said to Jamie. "I just had a call from my partner. An alarm has been put out for Mr. Frank Garrett. It seems something was found on the body that—"

Jamie's face went as white as the paper on Holbrook's notepad. "Where is he?" he whispered.

"I don't know," the lawyer answered. "What's the matter? This can only help our case. If there's evidence that he and this Omar Kassel were both involved in the plot to get money from your mother, it's possible they'll find evidence that he was involved in the killing. Your mother will be—"

Jamie's voice rose to a shout. "I won't see him. No way. No way am I ever going to lay eyes on that sonofabitch motherfucker again." He looked wildly around, then made for the door. "I have to get out of here," he mumbled. "I need—I need air."

"Jamie," Eve pleaded, jumping to her feet. "It's all right. You don't have to see him if you don't want to."

"They may not even have picked him up," I added. "They probably don't know where he is."

Jamie wasn't listening. "No . . . I can't . . . I'm outta here. I've gotta . . . think. I'll see you later."

And he was gone, the door slamming behind him. In the stunned silence that followed, his footsteps echoed eerily up the stairwell as he raced down the three flights.

No one spoke. Then Holbrook's eyes came to rest on Eve. "Did your ex-husband abuse him when he was a child?" she asked, her voice hushed.

The floodgates opened again. "He beat him," Eve sobbed. "Over nothing. I told you. He was a very cruel man. That's why I—"

"That isn't what I meant," Holbrook replied.

"What did you mean?" I asked, although I thought I knew where she was heading.

"That outsize reaction. Just the thought of having to see his father again evoked such a terrified response."

"But Jamie's a grown man now," Eve protested. "Frank can't hurt him anymore."

"It doesn't matter how old he is," Holbrook said. "It's what it dredges up."

"Wait a minute," I interrupted, not wanting the words said. "Let's not jump to any—"

But Holbrook was not to be silenced. "I'm no psychiatrist, but I've seen enough child-abuse cases to recognize the symptoms. He was sexually abused by that father. Probably for years."

"Nooo," Eve wailed.

"Has to be it." Holbrook shook her head. "He couldn't deal with facing him again. Classic."

It was then I looked up and saw Ruth-Ann standing in the doorway to my office. The expression on her face was one of such naked horror, I flew out of my chair and went to her. "Ruth-Ann," I began. "This isn't—"

"He was raped, wasn't he?" she gasped, grasping my hands. "And by his father. Oh, my God, by his father."

Talk about dredging up nightmarish memories. Ruth-Ann had been raped by a neighbor when she was sixteen. She'd never told her parents, believing she must have done something to bring it on, and had eaten her way into a size twenty to ward off future attacks. We'd unearthed the memory through alpha-theta training, and Ruth-Ann's progress from that time on had been steadily upward mentally and downward weightwise. I didn't want to see a regression.

"Ruth-Ann," I said. "Jamie's situation is nothing like yours. He's had a bad time and he's come through it. He's a little upset now, but he'll be all right."

"I could help him," she murmured. "We both could. We could do alpha-theta with him, help bring the traumatic memories to the surface. . . ."

Oh, Lord.

"I think the problem may be that he remembers what happened too well," I whispered, putting my arm around her and leading her to the door. "You go on home now and try not to think about this." *Fat chance.* "Don't worry. Eve and I will figure out what to do."

I snagged her coat off the coatrack, opened the closet door, grabbed her handbag, and thrust them at her. "I'm sure he'll be at the house by the time we get there. I'll tell you all about it tomorrow." And I ushered her out before she had a chance to say anything more. One nervous wreck at a time was absolutely all I could handle.

14

VIVIAN HOLBROOK SPENT less than ten minutes more with me and the other nervous wreck, and then she left for the city. I could see she found this new wrinkle about Jamie fascinating and was anxious to find out if this monster of a father had been picked up yet. It would certainly make her life easier—to say nothing of Eve's—if it turned out that Frank Garrett was the killer.

Eve had gone off the deep end again. Her situation was disturbing enough, but now she didn't know where Jamie had gone, if or when he was coming back, and she was consumed with guilt over the possibility that her attempt to escape her husband's tyranny had resulted not only in her son's kidnapping but in his sexual abuse as well.

"I should've stayed with Frank," she sobbed in the elevator. "Anything would've been better than what happened."

"You'd've both been dead," I said. "You did what you had to do. There was no way you could have known he'd snatch Jamie."

"He's scarred for the rest of his life because of me," she wailed as we walked to the car.

"He seems pretty together to me," I replied. "And whatever scars he carries were inflicted by his father, not by you. Besides, Holbrook may be way off base in this theory of hers."

"What if he never comes back? What will I do?" she moaned as I buckled her seat belt.

I wasn't so certain I knew the answer to that, but I plugged determinedly on. "He will. He's expended too much time and energy tracking you down to lose you now. Did he tell you how he found you at my house?"

"No."

"He followed you to the airport the day you came here, found out which flight you were on, and took the same flight. He was on the plane with you Saturday, but he was too nervous to approach you. Believe me, he's not going to let you go out of his life over this."

"Where do you think he's gone? He doesn't know anyone here. He has no car."

I braked and pulled over to the curb in front of The America Shop. "What's the matter with me? You're right. He hasn't gone home. He's probably walking down by the pier to clear his head. I used to do that all the time when I was going through my divorce." I took a quick look around, didn't spot any of the local gendarmes, and made a fast U-turn. "It's very peaceful watching the gulls," I chattered on. "Once I saw an owl perched on one of the stanchions. And I used to watch the lights of the cars going across the Tappan Zee and walk and walk till I'd figured out what to do about whatever was bothering me. I'll bet that's just what Jamie's doing." I pulled into the bank lot and brought the car to a halt. "I'll bet we find him down here. Stay in the car while I have a look."

"But I want to—" she began.

"You need to watch for him in case he heads back to the office. You can see the entrance to my building from here. Lock the door after me." I was out of the car and moving before she could unbuckle her seat belt.

The sun was sinking fast and the wind was getting blustery. A sharp hail stung my skin like the bites of tiny insects. Walking down to the pier, I wasn't shielded by trees or buildings, and I could feel the chill piercing through my car coat. I suddenly realized Jamie hadn't taken his jacket. The way our luck was running, I figured pneumonia would be next. For some crazy reason the hail beating on my skin reminded me of the ten plagues that God visited on the Egyptians when Pharaoh wouldn't free the slaves. What were they? Blood, gnats, something—flies maybe, or frogs, or both—murrain, darkness, hail, something else—oh, yeah, locusts—and the final punishment, death of the firstborn. I don't know what any of us had done to bring on the plagues, but we'd already had blood and hail and darkness. And Jamie was Eve's firstborn!

Snap out of it, I told myself. *Ruth-Ann's rubbing off on you.* I didn't even know what murrain was, I had no slaves— although my children might take exception to that—and Jamie wasn't going to die, despite the concern Ruth-Ann had expressed earlier about his being in danger.

I began calling his name. "Jamie," I yelled. "Where are you? It's freezing. You forgot your coat. You'll catch your death."

Stop obsessing about death.

There was movement in the shadow of the massive millwheel sculpture. I squinted, trying to make out whether it was a person or an animal. A person. One figure became two, one form melting into the darkness. I stopped. "Jamie?" I called. "Is that you?"

"It's me."

"Who was that with you?"

"I'm alone."

You are now.

I hurried toward him. "Are you all right?"

He stepped out from under the steel arm. "Sorry I ran off like that. It was the shock. I'm okay now. I just had to be by myself for a while."

But you weren't.

"Your mother's worried to death." *Stop with the death thing.* "She's waiting in the car."

He came up to me. "I haven't thought about my father for years. Thought I'd never have to see him again."

"You don't have to if you feel that way."

"Well, I won't be hanging around. I'll head back up to Boston in the morning and wait for my mother and your dad to come home."

"The police may want to talk to you."

"Why would they? I haven't seen Omar since I was a kid."

"Maybe you're right." I wasn't going to try to convince him to stay. It was probably a good idea for him to go home. The sooner this whole mess was cleared up and out of my hair and my home, the happier I'd be.

"I guess you have a job waiting for you," I remarked.

"I took a couple of weeks' vacation time, but I don't have to use it all now."

"I never asked you. What do you do?"

We were still about ten or fifteen yards from the car, and before he could answer the door flew open and Eve practically tumbled out. She threw her arms around Jamie, repeating his name over and over. *He must be worn out with all the emotionalism,* I thought. I was getting pretty tired of it myself. Still, as compared with the outburst that had greeted his arrival, this was, on a scale of one to ten, about a four, a manageable number. And to give credit where it's due, through it all Eve never once brought up the conclusion that Vivian Holbrook had drawn.

"I thought I saw someone with you when I saw you by the sculpture," I said, when we were back in the car and headed for home.

Jamie was quiet for a moment, then he replied, "Ruth-Ann had parked her car in the lot behind the gas station. She saw me by the sculpture and came over to see if I was okay. She thought it'd upset you, seeing her with me, so she took off when you called out to me."

I was embarrassed. These were, after all, two grown people, and I really had no right telling them who they could or couldn't see.

"It's nothing personal against you, Jamie. It's just—I think Ruth-Ann's kind of rebelling against the rigidity of her upbringing right now, but . . . well, she's still a product of that upbringing, and your backgrounds are so different. Why complicate both your lives?"

"Besides," Eve chimed in, "you live in Boston and she lives here. Why get involved? There're lots of beautiful girls in Boston."

Jamie laughed. "I'm not getting involved with anyone. Why would I? I've just found my mother, and she's the only woman I want in my life right now."

I could sense Eve beaming.

The roads were slippery, and I concentrated on my driving, keeping my speed to well below the limit. Even so, we made it home in less than half an hour. I was surprised to find the house dark and my dad's car gone. Horty began barking as soon as he heard my car pull in the driveway, an indication that he was waiting to go out. As soon as I opened the kitchen door, he bounded past me.

"Where's Dad?" I asked Eve. "And the kids? They're supposed to be doing their homework."

"Oh, I meant to tell you," Jamie said. "Your dad took them to Comp USA. Matt wanted a new modem, and Allie went along for the ride."

I guess I was more tired and overwrought than I thought, because I did overreact.

"Matt shouldn't be hitting his grandfather up for a modem," I snapped. "They're expensive. And it's a school night. They should've called me before they decided to go."

"Gosh, I'm sorry," Jamie said. "It was my suggestion. I thought it'd be nice for your dad to have some time alone with the kids while we were with the lawyer. Of course, we should've called and asked you first."

"What's the matter with you, Carrie?" Eve scolded. "It gives your dad pleasure to be able to buy things for the children now that he can. Why do you want to be a spoilsport?"

It came back to me in a rush—what I didn't like about this woman. My entire life had been turned upside down trying to keep her out of trouble, and had I heard one word of thanks? No. I was a spoilsport because I wanted my own children to abide by my rules.

I thought about doing a relaxation exercise but decided liquor is quicker and headed for the wine bottle. "Anyone for a drink?" I asked, struggling to keep my tone neutral.

Jamie came to the rescue. "Let me make them. Why don't you go upstairs and rest a while? You've had a long day."

"Thanks, but I have to make dinner and feed the animals and—"

"Let me help, then."

I smiled at him gratefully. "Okay. You can start by opening the wine. It's in the rack on the wall opposite the kitchen table. Open the red. Fix yourself whatever you like."

Jamie went into the kitchen, and I took Eve's coat from her and started to hang it next to mine in the front closet.

She followed me into the foyer. "Don't you think you drink too much, Carrie?" she queried. "I remember when you were going through your divorce, your father was very worried."

The plastic hanger broke in my hands.

"Did you know," I retorted through gritted teeth, "that one glass of red wine a day is good for the heart? Have you been seeing to it that Dad has some every day?"

Jamie appeared, glass in hand, before she could answer. "Here you go. Mother, would you like some?"

Eve's eyes filled, and she looked at me with such wonder that suddenly I wasn't angry anymore. "He called me *Mother*," she said.

If someone had stolen my child, I reflected, sipping the wine, I suppose I'd be a royal pain too. Being a nag was her way of getting her mind off her troubles. She needed to fuss, and my dad liked being fussed over, so what the heck, maybe it really was a match made in heaven.

"Go for it, Eve," I said. "We'll drink to new beginnings." I smiled at Jamie. "And to your son."

By the time we heard the key turn in the front door, the cats were fed and curled up between us on the couch, Horty was by my feet, the stew was bubbling happily in the Dutch oven, and we'd managed to bury—for the moment—the hatchet and all thoughts of murder and mayhem. None of us, not even Eve, was feeling any pain.

I looked up to see my father coming through the door, holding fast to Allie's hand and leaning heavily on Matt. His face was gray and beaded with perspiration. He was rubbing his left arm.

"Mom," Allie whispered, her voice trembling. "Grandpa doesn't feel well."

We were on our feet before she'd finished the sentence.

"Don't fuss," Dad whispered. "I just need to lie down."

Jamie shoved Matt aside, grabbed Dad around the waist, and half-carried, half-dragged him to the couch. "Get a blanket, Allie," he ordered her.

Glad to surrender responsibility, she took off up the stairs.

My mouth had gone dry, but my body was suddenly drenched with sweat. I knelt by the couch and began mopping the perspiration from Dad's forehead. As I did, I saw his eyes roll up into his head.

"He's losing consciousness!" I shouted frantically. "Dad!" I cried. "Dad!"

"David!" Eve screamed, falling to her knees beside me.

Roughly, Jamie jerked her to her feet. "Call 911! Carrie, help me get him down on the floor."

Together we managed to roll him off the couch. He'd stopped breathing. I was trembling from head to foot as we crouched over his inert body.

"Dad!" I shouted again and began shaking him, a memory from a long-ago CPR course taken after his first heart attack coming back to me.

No response.

What was the next part? Mouth to mouth. Oh, God, it had been too long. I couldn't remember how.

"Move away."

And I watched, relief flooding through me, as Jamie tilted my father's head back, brought his chin forward, pinched his nose, and administered two quick breaths. Through a haze of unshed tears I saw him check my father's pulse, then go back to doing mouth to mouth. He continued the process, pausing every few breaths to check his pulse. But terror gripped me anew as I realized Dad wasn't responding.

"Do compressions," I cried.

There was a brief moment when Jamie looked up at me and hesitated, and I thought Dad was gone and Jamie was giving up.

"Don't stop!"

He moved to the chest and started the compressions, counting, "One and two and . . ." The effort produced beads of sweat on his forehead. I leaned forward and mopped his brow. And then Eve was there, in control now. "I'm all right. I can do the head," she said. "I know how."

I was hardly aware that the children had come to stand beside me, my emotions swinging wildly from agonized suspense to admiration as I watched mother and son, working in unison, slowly bring breath back to my father's body and color back to his face.

Matt squeezed my hand. "Mom?" he whispered. "Is Grandpa going to die?"

In the distance I heard approaching sirens. "No," I breathed, my eyes fastened on Jamie. "I think he's going to make it."

I followed the ambulance to Englewood Hospital. Eve rode with Dad, and Jamie stayed home with the children.

Eve and I sat together in the waiting room while Dad was in the emergency room. I gave up on my nails, chewing them to the nub. Eve was silent and composed.

She's like two different people, I thought. Elaine/Doris/Patty/ Gloria leapt to mind. Maybe we all have other people living inside us. Maybe it just depends on the circumstances who comes to the fore at any given moment.

When the doctor appeared in the doorway, his face somber, my heart began pounding so loudly I thought everyone in the room could hear it. My knees nearly buckled under me as I rose to my feet and followed Eve.

"Mrs. Carlin," he said, addressing Eve. "Your husband is all right. We've stabilized him."

"Thank God," we murmured simultaneously.

"Whoever did the CPR saved his life."

"My son," Eve said proudly.

"We've had some rather . . . traumatic things happening in the family recently," I managed to say. "Do you think that could've brought this on?"

"It may've been a factor," he replied. "But it seems Mr. Carlin has been remiss about taking his medication. His blood levels were extremely low. Is he forgetful or just resistant?"

"I always put his pills by his plate," Eve said. "I was away for a couple of days, but he's never forgotten before. . . ."

"My father's very responsible," I added. "He's never been forgetful."

"You know," the doctor said gently. "when an elderly person has had open-heart surgery, there is occasionally some oxygen deprivation. It tends to make them forgetful. Sometimes, when we love someone, we blind ourselves to the changes that are occurring. In Mr. Carlin's condition, missing his medication even for a day is much worse than tapering off. With his history he should never miss a dose. My suggestion to you would be that from this point on, you watch him very carefully."

Eve and I were silent as I drove home, both of us trying to make sense of what the doctor had said. Was my father becoming forgetful? It didn't seem so to me, but I didn't see him often enough to accurately assess that. If, as Eve had indicated, he'd come to rely on her to see that he took his medication, I suppose he might have missed a dose or two during her absence and in the turmoil of the past few days' events. My father had always been mentally sharp and had stayed physically active despite his heart condition. So far as I knew he still played golf and walked every day. I had to struggle with this new image of him. It occurred to me I've never thought of him as elderly. These days, sixty-eight isn't old. Could the surgery have made the difference? If so the change certainly hadn't been readily apparent. Maybe it was the kind of thing that crept up slowly. Finally, I had to ask.

"Have you noticed a change in Dad since you first met him, Eve?"

"Not really."

"You'd be the one who'd notice. You see him on a day-to-day basis."

"Anyone could forget to take their medication with what's been going on," she snapped. "But your father is as mentally competent as he ever was."

I stopped at the light by the Closter Exxon station. "What made you start putting his pills by his plate?"

"No particular reason. Just to be helpful. I always did that for Charles when we were married."

I let it drop, but I resolved to have a talk with Dad when he was feeling better.

We were on Piermont Road, almost in Norwood, when Eve spoke again, an edge of excitement coloring her voice.

"I have a suggestion."

"What's that?"

"I want to be your sidekick."

"Excuse me?"

"You know, your helper, your partner in crime-fighting." I almost hit a tree. "What're you talking about?"

"Don't be coy, Carrie. You've solved murders in the past. What you've done before, you can do again. And if you can do it, I can do it."

Anything you can do, I can do better.

She appeared sane, but clearly she'd flipped. This thing with my father had unhinged her. "Eve," I said. "You're talking nonsense. Don't you have enough on your head?"

"Yes. That's why we have to do this. You seem to have the feel for it, and I can provide background information. We'd be a team like—like Batman and Robin."

Try Beavis and Butt-head.

"This isn't a TV show. Omar isn't going to get up and go home at the end."

"Don't you think I know that? But what's happened is because of me, and now it's made David sick. I want the killer caught before anyone else gets hurt, and I think I can help."

I looked over at the determined face. Gone was the emotional nervous wreck of this morning, nowhere to be seen, the nag who'd accused me of being an incipient lush. In their place was the CPR-certified, super-efficient gray lady, ready to take on the Joker. This woman changed personalities more often than I change clothes.

"Unless there's something you haven't told us, I don't think there's anything you can do."

"We. We have to work together on this if we're going to pull it off. Now, I've thought of a plan."

I concentrated on the road, trying to tune her out. I was still trying to deal with my father's near brush with death. I couldn't believe that after the day we'd had, his wife was gung ho to play Batman. And with me as Robin. No. It was the other way around. I was the crime-fighter. I was supposed to be Batman.

"We'll use me for bait," she went on. "The killer wants money. That's the reason Omar contacted me in the first place."

"Do you have any particular fish in mind, or are we just casting and taking whatever bites?"

She leaned toward me, straining at her seat belt, her face animated. "It's Frank, don't you see? We need to flush him out because the police won't find him if he doesn't want to be found. He's a Svengali when it comes to disappearing. We could do a—what do they call it? A setup to trap him—"

I didn't attempt to keep the sarcasm out of my voice. "A sting operation?"

"Yes, that's it. Now, as far as we know, he has no idea that Jamie is back. So we'll place an ad in the Boston papers, something to the effect that anyone with information about the whereabouts of Jamie Garrett should write to a post office box that we'll rent here in Norwood or Piermont. Then we'll arrange to meet him and I'll have a tape recorder in my handbag. . . ."

And when he confesses, we'll spray him with pepper spray, tie him up, and Ted will ride in on his white horse and cart him off to jail. And we'll all live happily ever after.

"Eve," I said. "I'm tired and I can feel every nerve end tingling. I know you mean well, but if I agreed to your plan and Frank didn't kill us, you can be sure Ted would. So let's not talk about it anymore."

Frowning, she sank back against her seat. I let the silence hang heavy between us, hoping that I'd heard the last of the world's most unlikely dynamic duo.

When we arrived home, Ted's white Miata was sitting in its usual spot in the driveway, looking like it knew this was where it belonged. I found myself hoping he'd stay over. My father's sudden illness had reminded me how fragile his life was, how at any time I could get a call telling me he was gone. I didn't see my dad very often these days, but just knowing he was there, only a phone call away, was a sustaining force in my life. Granted, on occasion Eve would get a little overprotective and tell me he was sleeping or make up some other feeble excuse to save him from having to deal with what she'd considered, at least until now, my outrageously unstable life. But eventually I'd get through, and that reassuring voice would come booming over the line. Ted was becoming another such force, and much as I'd fought it I realized I was coming to depend more and more on his level head. Considering his profession, that was a scary thought. The call I dreaded receiving could come from that quarter as well.

Before I could insert my key in the lock, he'd opened the door and wrapped me in his arms.

"How is he?" he asked.

My reply was muffled as the tears I hadn't allowed myself to release until now spilled over. "He'll be okay." I sniffed. "Somehow he missed a dose or two of his medication, but they've stabilized him."

When I lifted my head off Ted's chest, I saw that Jamie's arm was around Eve. "Can I get anyone anything?" he asked.

"How about chamomile all around?" I said. "The box is in the top right cupboard. Where're the kids?"

"Here." Two pairs of feet came pounding down the stairs. "Is Grandpa going to be okay?" Allie asked anxiously.

"He's going to be fine. He must've forgotten to take his pills this morning, that's all."

"No, he didn't," Matt said. "He asked me to get them off your night table when he was in the bathroom, and I did."

"Well, he obviously forgot to take them. We'll just have to make sure they're put by his plate while he's here, like Aunt Eve does for him at home."

"How long does he have to stay in the hospital?" Allie asked.

"Just till they get his blood levels back to normal. Go on back upstairs. I'll be up in a minute."

Allie glanced at Ted, then back at me. "You going to be sleeping in my room tonight?"

I flashed Ted a questioning look.

"I'm afraid you're stuck with her, Allie," he replied. "I'm working."

"You are?" I asked, surprised.

"Yeah, tell you about it later." He reached down and threw Matt over his shoulder. "Come on, you sack of potatoes. Time to cash it in."

Matt giggled as Ted charged up the stairs, making roaring engine noises.

I put my arm around Allie's shoulder as we followed them up the stairs. The chaos wasn't letting up, and I was worried about her. "You okay, honey?"

"I was so scared when the ambulance took Grandpa away. I thought he was going to die, but Jamie told me about this friend of his who had a bad heart, and a couple of times they took him away in an ambulance and Jamie was afraid he was going to die, but he didn't. He said they do wonderful things today with heart patients."

"He's right. There've been big advances in the last few years." That made twice today Jamie had come to the rescue.

"And then Matt came down and we ate dinner and Jamie told us funny stories about when he lived on the commune, so it kind of took our minds off things. He was great," she said. "It's hard to believe he's Aunt Eve's son."

I smiled back. "She's not so bad. I think losing Jamie made her . . . well, peculiar. I think now she has him back, she's going to be a whole new person."

Fifteen minutes later I was spooning stew onto Ted's

plate. Jamie had eaten with the kids, and Eve had finished
her tea and the few mouthfuls of stew Jamie had insisted
she swallow before Ted and I came back downstairs. We
passed her on the stairs and tried to convince her to join
us, but she pleaded exhaustion and disappeared into my
bedroom. Within minutes Jamie went upstairs, claiming he
wanted to take a long shower and retire early. I stopped him
before he went into the bathroom.

"I haven't had a chance yet to thank you. You saved my
dad's life." I felt myself choking up. "You were wonderful. I
don't want to think about what would've happened if you
hadn't been here."

"Gotta take care of my new family," he said, and hugged
me. I hugged him back. I'd never had a brother, and it
felt good.

I was famished. I react to extreme stress by not eating at
all—and to the aftermath by gorging myself. It's a peculiar
anomaly, but it seems to keep my weight where it ought to
be and my electrolytes in balance.

"So, what's going on? How come you're here?" I asked
Ted between mouthfuls.

He forked a piece of potato into his mouth and swallowed before answering. "How about because I missed you
and you're such a good cook and I was hungry?"

"That's lovely, but now tell me the real reason."

His face grew serious. "Actually, something came up I
thought you should know about, but this doesn't seem to be
the time, what with your dad—"

"About what?" The piece of meat I'd been chewing got
stuck in my throat, and I had to swallow hard to get it
down. I grabbed for my water and drank. "About Eve?" I
asked when I'd stopped coughing.

"I'll come by tomorrow. I think you've had enough for
one day."

"Ted, don't do this to me. What is it?"

He sighed. "Homicide in Fort Lee. Woman was shot in her bed at the Welcome Motel."

That was a little close for comfort, but I didn't get the connection. If I were to pick a local hangout to have a murder, of course, the Welcome Motel would be right up there. It's known for changing sheets several times a day without missing a beat. The clientele runs more to upscale executives looking for an afternoon quickie with the girlfriend than to prostitutes and johns, but the establishment isn't fussy.

"That's awful," I murmured, "but what's it got to do with us?"

"I'll get there." He got up and closed the kitchen door. I bit off what was left of my nails.

"Our first guess," he said as he sat back down, "was it was a john. But there was no sex, and the woman was shot in the head, execution style."

"Could be her pimp," I said as a chill ran down my spine.

"Lady wasn't a prostitute. She'd been dead for a couple of days. Her purse was gone, so at first we thought robbery was the motive."

I put my fork down. My appetite had vanished. I was back into my superstress phase. "But now you don't."

He reached for his glass and took a long drink before he spoke, and then he didn't answer me directly. "What do you know about your dad's will?"

"What?"

"Your dad's will. Who inherits? You and the kids? Did he do a prenup?"

"Of course. We get everything except the lottery money. Whatever's left of it when he—when he—"

"Goes to Eve, right?"

"That's only fair," I said defensively, while my heart

pounded wildly. "She's his wife. She was with him when he bought the ticket."

"How much would you say there is left of it now?"

"I don't know."

"Would you say there's a lot more now than there will be if he lives another fifteen years or so?"

I was starting to feel sick to my stomach. "Are you saying that Eve did something to—"

"No. I'm just saying money changes people, and two people are dead."

Money is the root of all evil.

"But to infer Eve would . . . she's crazy about my dad. She watches his diet like a hawk, she puts his pills out to be sure he—"

"That was before the lottery win."

I could hardly breathe. "What . . . what's this woman in the motel got to do with it?"

"The woman was registered. Her name was Barbara Storey."

"Doesn't ring a bell."

"Barbara Storey was Eve's friend Louise's stepdaughter. We got a match on the bullet. She was shot with the same gun that killed Omar Kassel."

15

I DIDN'T SLEEP well—so what else is new?—but morning arrived anyway. Normally I take Wednesdays off, but two of my Thursday patients had asked to be switched, so I'd done some juggling and made Thursday my errand day. I didn't say a word to Eve or Jamie about the homicide before I left. I found myself avoiding conversation with Eve, afraid she'd bring up the dynamic duo again, which, based on the seeds Ted had planted in my mind last night, put that scenario in the never-to-be-considered category. I figured I'd let Ted do his thing without interference from me. Still, I had a hard time seeing Eve as a Bonnie Parker plugging anyone who got in the way of her acquiring enough capital to live in a way to which she'd never been accustomed even when she was married to the dentist. I pointed out to Ted that she'd spent very little time out of my sight over the past few days. I'm not saying she couldn't have made it to Fort Lee and shot her old friend's stepdaughter the night she took my car, but she would've had to be pretty speedy, and why would she have done it? So far as Ted knew she'd never even met the stepdaughter, because Louise wasn't married at the time they were friends. And what about Louise? I'd asked him. Where was she now? Had she been notified about her brother's death? And now her step-daughter's? Ted wasn't talking.

"I guess you should take a look at Eve's last husband's death certificate, see if he really did die of pancreatic cancer," I'd muttered as he was about to leave.

"Occasionally we cops do think of these things ourselves, you know," he'd said as he closed the car door. "I realize we're pretty slow on the uptake, but give us a little credit."

Deep down I didn't believe Eve was a serial killer. Still, no way was I going to leave my dad alone with her until I was certain.

Jamie offered to come with me to the office so he could borrow my car and pick Dad up at the hospital around one. On the way I very casually asked him about Omar's sister, Louise.

"Isn't it odd that she was Eve's best friend and yet it was her brother who betrayed her by calling your father?"

"I don't think it was Omar who called him. In spite of what my mother said, I think it was Louise."

"Why? Why would Louise do that?"

"Jealousy."

"Jealousy? What was she jealous of? The beatings?"

"I was a kid. I don't remember much. Just something Omar said to me once kind of sticks in my mind."

"What was that?" I glanced over at him. He wrinkled his brow, trying to recall the exact words.

"He said . . . he said Louise thought my mother was one of the golden children."

"I don't get it."

"You know, spoiled, one of those people to whom things

come so easily they don't appreciate what they have. She thought my mother didn't know how to handle my father, that she sometimes provoked the attacks."

"How could she call herself Eve's friend and say that?"

He hesitated. "When you're a kid you see things, but you don't put it together until years later."

"What do you mean?"

"Louise was an attractive woman, sexy, you know? And my mother—well, she was pretty in her own way, but not like that."

"Are you saying—"

"I think Louise and my father had something going."

"But that doesn't make sense. Then why wouldn't she have been happy to see you and your mother disappear? Eve was playing right into her hands."

He shook his head. "I think maybe unconsciously she wanted things to stay just the way they were. My father was a violent man, and we served a purpose. Louise got the best of him. He used to go over there after—after he'd blown off steam at home."

"My God. That's sick."

"Lots of people are into sick relationships." He shrugged. " 'Course, I could be adding two and two and getting five."

"Where is she now?"

"Haven't a clue."

We were silent for most of the rest of the drive, both of us consumed by our own thoughts. When we stopped at the light in Rockleigh, I asked him about his friend, the one he'd told Allie about.

"There was no friend," he said. "I made him up. I hope you're not mad. Allie was so scared, and it was all I could think of to say to make her feel better."

"Of course I'm not mad."

"I didn't mean to lie, but—"

"You did make her feel better. I'm grateful."

We arrived at the little bridge by the Baptist church, and two minutes later I pulled into my office driveway.

Gloria of the Elaine/Doris/Patty/Gloria quartet was waiting outside my door when we arrived. She took one look at Jamie and was smitten. The stunned expression on his face when this stringy-haired behemoth started coming on to him would have had me on the floor in hysterics if I wasn't such a consummate professional.

"Hi there," she said, her cutesy voice dripping with promise. "And who're you?" Batting her eyes, she sidled up to him, reached out a huge calloused hand, and squeezed his biceps. "Man, you are one sexy stud. What say we ditch the shrinkette here and go someplace quiet?"

Leave it to Jamie. He overcame his shock and his aversion and rose to the occasion. "What'd you have in mind?"

"Use your imagination."

I felt compelled to jump in before Gloria got him down on the couch. "Jamie, this is Gloria Wiszneskie. She's my first patient today. I hate to spoil your fun, but we have work to do."

Jamie winked at me. "Sorry," he said to Gloria. "Can't argue with the boss."

"Gloria, please go in my office and start practicing your breathing," I directed. "I'll be right with you."

"Don't go 'way, big boy," she tittered as she backed into my office.

Jamie grinned. "Man, that's some interesting roster of patients you've got here," he said.

With as straight a face as I could manage, I replied, "We'll be finished in about three quarters of an hour if you want to wait. Of course, Gloria's only seventeen, which makes fooling around with her a felony, but if you—"

"Seven- . . ." His voice trailed off. It was the first time since I'd met him that Jamie appeared totally at a loss for words.

"On the other hand, maybe you'd rather take a walk over to my friend Meg's café. It's just down the street, and she makes wonderful blueberry muffins."

"Seventeen! You're shittin' me."

"Scout's honor. Don't be late picking up Dad." I waltzed into my office, suppressing my own giggles. These days I take my fun where I can find it.

By the time I'd closed the door, Gloria was gone and Doris was in the chair, a mean scowl plastered on her face. I was tempted to send her back out just to see Jamie's reaction but decided he'd had enough of a shock for one day.

"This is my time slot!" she growled.

"I know," I replied pleasantly.

"Who's the fuckin' cowboy?"

"Actually," I began, "he's—"

"What's a new patient doin' showin' up durin' my time?"

"He's not a patient. He's my stepbrother."

"Oh." Somewhat placated, she considered that. "Well, he's too cute. I don't like him."

Sometimes, when things go beyond the realm of all reason, I just can't help myself. "Gloria does," I answered smugly.

"Huh," she snorted. "Gloria's brains're in her—"

"I know," I interrupted hastily. "But Gloria's young. Let's cut her some slack."

"Cut that whore slack, she'll end up preggo."

My ears hurt and I was sorry I'd started this. I longed for Elaine to come out. "I wouldn't worry about it," I said. "Jamie's not going to be here long. He lives in Boston."

"Good thing."

"So, Doris," I said, reaching for the leads, "Dr. Golden has asked me to do some brain-wave training today and record your waves both before and after the session. If you're not in the mood, maybe Elaine would like to work."

But Doris stayed, cursing and grumbling all the while about constantly having to save her other selves from themselves. I was moving the head sensor from the center of her head to the right side when the sound of a chair going over in the reception area made me jump. Then there was silence, followed by the murmur of male voices. I glanced at my watch, although I was certain my next patient, Bill Strobe, wasn't due yet. Ruth-Ann wasn't coming in until noon, so there was no one to handle the outer office. I figured Bill must have come early, run into Jamie before he left, and they'd gotten into a conversation.

I continued with Doris, concentrating on recording and printing out her brain waves, trying to ignore the escalating pitch to the voices coming from the other room. I pulled the brain map from the printer. "Oh, look, this is good. Your high beta is down from the last time we checked—"

"No!" someone shouted.

I jumped to my feet.

Doris's eyes lit up. "Fight," she said.

"Don't be silly," I said as I reached into my desk drawer and palmed the extra canister of pepper spray I keep there for emergencies. "Excuse me a minute. Try to keep focused on the screen. I'll be right back." I hit the key to start up the monitor and slipped out the door, closing it behind me.

"Yell if you need me," she called through the door. "I'll throw a bucket of water on 'em."

The scene before me stopped me in my tracks. The chair Jamie had been sitting on was overturned. Fists clenched, Jamie faced a tall man who was slouched in the doorway wearing a dark jacket and a ski cap pulled down low over his forehead. His complexion was florid, with lines deeply etched around his mouth and eyes. The broken veins on his nose and the jagged scar on his cheek suggested this was the face of a man who might still have been good-looking had he not been in a few too many barrooms and a few too many brawls. The posture of both men reminded me of a couple of bantam roosters warily sizing each other up before a cockfight. Jamie looked pale, an involuntary twitch pulling at the left corner of his mouth. The expression on his face was grim, but the man was smiling. He was a good twenty-five or thirty years Jamie's senior, heavyset, with a pronounced belly that protruded over his belt. Jamie could have taken him easily, but I guessed instantly what had held him back. His eyes darted from the man to me. "Carrie," he said in a hoarse voice. "This is Frank Garrett." Then he added, as if uttering the words caused him physical pain, "My father."

Garrett held out his hand. "Ms. Carlin," he said pleasantly.

I ignored the hand and turned to Jamie. "What's been going on out here? What does he want?"

Garrett bent over and righted the chair. "My boy Jamie here and I have been getting reacquainted. We've been what you might call estranged for fifteen or twenty years." He laughed. "My showing up like this was a real surprise. Threw him for a loop. But we're fine now."

I reached for the phone. "Mr. Garrett, the police are looking for you in connection with a—"

"They found me." He smiled. "That's how I found Jamie."

I hesitated. "Aren't you . . . didn't they want to . . ."

The smile grew broader. "Hold me? I guess they did, but they couldn't. At least not for the murder of Omar Kassel. I was in Florida when old Omar bought it." He winked. "Got a lady friend who'll back me up."

My hand dropped to my side. "That's not my business, but this office is. I have a patient inside, and your being here is disturbing my session. Please leave."

"Tsk, tsk, aren't you the feisty one? Well, Jamie and me have a lot to talk about, so we'll get out of your way. Is there a place around here we can get a drink?"

"I'm sure Jamie has no desire to drink with you," I said stiffly.

"No? Jamie, she right about that?"

The tone carried menace and I saw real fear in Jamie's eyes. His reaction yesterday to the possibility of having to see his father again, and Vivian Holbrook's words explaining it, came back to me full force.

"It's all right. I'll go," Jamie said finally. "We . . . have some things to . . . discuss."

I moved to Jamie's side and took his arm. "You don't have to go with him if you don't want to."

"It's okay. I won't be long."

"Atta boy," sneered Garrett, stepping aside to let Jamie precede him. "Nice to have met you, Ms. Carlin. I'm sure we'll run into each other again, you being my son's new stepsister and all."

"Jamie," I called after them. "You can get a drink at Meg's Place. Come back here when you finish."

He didn't reply, and I closed the door. The man made my skin crawl. Worse, he scared me. But what frightened me most was that Jamie had not been able to stand up to him. What kind of hold could the father have over the son after all these years?

I reached for the phone and called Meg.

"Wait on them yourself," I told her after I'd described the scene in my office. "Try and hear what he says."

"You want me to spy?" Meg replied. "What would your father say?"

"Wait'll you see this guy. He'd say, 'Go for it.' "

"Hey, Carlin," came the coarse voice from my office. "I'm done. Get rid of lover boy and come back in here. Golden ain't payin' you to let a machine do your fuckin' job for you."

I sighed. If four-letter words were struck from the English language, it's my belief Doris would go mute.

In my few moments of free time between Doris's departure and the arrival of Bill Strobe, I called Ted to see if he knew about Frank Garrett, but he didn't answer his page. I left a terse message asking him to please call me. I thought about phoning Eve to warn her, but she was at the house alone and I didn't want her getting this particular bit of news when no one was with her. Then I remembered Ted had planned to stop by to talk to her this morning. Ideally he'd be there when I called, so I tried the house and got our machine. Frustrated, I called Meg again.

"I can't spy if I'm on the phone talking to you," she scolded. "I'll call you when they leave."

"Just tell me if you've heard anything so far."

"All I got so far is Rudolph wants bourbon and water and Jamie ordered a beer."

"His name's Frank."

"With that nose, Rudolph's more appropriate. Guy must have pickled kidneys."

"We should be so lucky. Leave a message in case I can't pick up," I said, and hung up.

Bill Strobe was waiting for me when I went out to the waiting room. Bill's an ambitious young executive with Price Waterhouse, into self-improvement. He does brain-wave training like the astronauts at NASA do, to improve his memory and to enhance his already considerable creative powers. He's an absolute pleasure to work with, primarily because he's so focused and motivated that he improves at every session. All I have to do is hook him up and watch him go.

I schedule him after Elaine/Doris/Patty/Gloria whenever I can. It restores my belief in what I'm doing. Today, as I sat behind Bill watching him doing alpha-theta training, listening to the music and the computer beeps, my eyes closed and I felt myself, like Bill, falling into a dreamy alpha state.

I am sitting on a mossy slope in a peaceful meadow beside a running brook. The air is sweetly scented with the aroma of pine trees and mountain laurel. All around me I see rows of oversize multicolored blossoms—tulips, black-eyed Susans, mums, and daisies. I pick one, watch in delight as two others grow in its place. I pick another and the same thing happens. I pick a third and a fourth, laughing as the flowers multiply around me. And then faces appear on the blossoms—Frank Garrett's bulbous nose in the center of a black-eyed Susan. Terrified, I toss the bunch I'm holding in my hands into the brook, as if the stems were covered with thorns. But then all the blossoms have faces—the young Omar's as it had appeared in the photograph, Jamie's smiling little face as he'd looked in the picture, Eve's, Jamie as an adult. And I try to get up, but the vines twist around my legs, binding me, and I start tearing at the flowers and tossing them into the brook. But the more I pick, the more grow back, until the brook is choked with flowers and they're choking me, and when I try to push them away I see that the stems are covered with thorns, and my hands are bleeding. . . .

With a start I came back to the present, my hands actually hurting, my heart pounding. I sat up quickly. The beeps had stopped, but when I glanced at Bill I saw his eyes were still closed, a circumstance for which I was inordinately grateful. It gave me time to compose myself. I knew where the dream had come from—a guided-imagery exercise I use with my panic-attack patients, in which I suggest they imagine themselves sitting in a meadow by a mountain brook. As they sit there feeling peaceful and relaxed, they notice flowers growing all around them. In the exercise I suggest they pick a blossom, put their problem on the blossom, and toss it into the brook, letting it float away forever. Big problems, big blossoms; little problems, little blossoms. And because the place is magical, as the blossoms are picked they replace themselves.

I wondered why this exercise, meant to evoke serenity, had become so distorted as I'd relaxed into an alpha state. Probably because murder was not a problem one could easily put on a blossom and toss away. And now there were two murders. I was certain Frank Garrett was connected with both of them. Not just because I hadn't liked his face or his manner, although that was true. My reaction had more to do with what I knew of his past, with the timing of his visit, and with his effect on Jamie. I tried to fit the puzzle pieces together. Garrett knew Omar. They'd been together in the photo with the young Jamie, and the men had probably maintained contact over the years. Assuming they'd concocted a plot to get money from Eve in exchange for information about Jamie's whereabouts, they'd've been pretty pissed off when Jamie foiled their plan by showing up. But why would Frank have killed Omar? It wasn't Omar's fault that Jamie had returned; how could he have known that Jamie would see us on television and make the connection that Eve was his mother? What did Frank think he had to gain by coming back into the life of a son who clearly feared and detested him? And by extension coming back into Eve's life? He must have believed my father would pay him to leave them alone. Over my dead body would he ever see a dime from my family. And what role had the dead woman in the motel played in the plot?

My ruminations were interrupted by Bill opening his eyes and turning to me with a happy smile on his face as he began to talk about his experience. He'd seen himself as an astronaut in a rocket ship on his way to the moon. Good for him. That's how it's supposed to work. *A man's reach should exceed his grasp*, and all that.

16

A T ELEVEN-FIFTEEN I still hadn't heard from Meg, and Jamie hadn't come back to the office. If everything was all right, Dad was going to be discharged from the hospital by early afternoon, and I was worried that Jamie had been so traumatized by the sudden appearance of his father that he might have forgotten he was to pick Dad up. My next patient wasn't due till one and, while I usually do paperwork whenever I have a break, I decided to take an early lunch. I left a note for Ruth-Ann, deliberately omitting any reference to Jamie, and instructed her to get Kate Neilson hooked up and start without me in the unlikely event that I was late.

When I walked into Meg's Place, I found Jamie and Meg sitting at a corner table, deep in conversation. Frank Garrett was nowhere in sight, which immediately lightened my mood. The café was hopping with a full lunch crowd, and Betsy, Meg's usually unflappable waitress, was scurrying from table to table looking decidedly harried. I pulled up a chair opposite Jamie.

"You okay?" I asked.

I don't know why I expected him to smile and say, "Sure, I'm fine. I told the evil genie to take a powder, and he's out of my life forever," but I did. Wishful thinking. And about as far off as I could get, because he gave me a twisted smile and said, "I can't believe that sonofabitch is back in my life."

My heart skipped about four beats. "Back in your life? What're you talking about? You don't have to—"

"I do. He needs me."

"He needs you?" I was sounding like Polly the parrot, screechy voice and all, but I was so stunned by his words that I had to repeat them to make sure I'd heard right over the din of the lunch crowd. "Are you nuts? What kind of father was he to you all those years when you needed him? Tell him to go to hell!"

He shook his head. "I can't."

I looked at Meg, who shrugged her shoulders helplessly and got to her feet. "Betsy looks about ready to drop. I'd better go rescue her and let you two discuss this by yourselves."

My ally was leaving. "Meg, wait," I said, desperately reaching for her arm. "Tell him—" But she shook her head and sidestepped my grasp, disappearing into the kitchen.

I could feel the anger rising in me, but I wasn't sure who I was angry with—Garrett for having the chutzpah to show up, Jamie for being a wuss, Meg for abandoning me, or God for allowing people like Frank Garrett to exist at all. I took a couple of deep breaths and exhaled slowly, following to the letter the advice I give my patients for non-life-threatening situations.

"Okay," I said quietly when I'd cooled down. "Tell me if I'm missing something. This man was so abusive to you and your mother that she took you and ran away from him. Then he kidnapped you. He lied to you when he told you Eve was dead. He was responsible for taking precious years out of both your lives, years that can never be recouped. You had to live on your own when you were little more than a child because you couldn't take the abuse, but now he makes you feel needed, so all is forgiven?"

He grabbed both my hands in his. "Carrie, it's not like that."

"Tell me where I've got it wrong."

"He's sick."

"I'll say."

"I mean physically sick."

I hesitated. "With what?"

"Cancer."

I took my hands back. "I don't believe it. He looked pretty damned healthy to me."

"Looks can be deceiving. He told me he was two hundred thirty pounds just a month ago. Now he's down to two ten."

"So he's seeking absolution from the people whose lives he ruined? Well, I've got a little secret for him. It's not that easy to get into heaven."

"He wants to meet with my mother and apologize," he said softly.

"I would guess your mother isn't interested in an apology. Not unless he can give her back those years he stole."

He sighed. "It doesn't seem like much for a dying man to ask."

"As opposed to what? Asking her to nurse him in his final hours?" Something in his expression set off alarm bells in my head. "He wouldn't dare!"

His eyes avoided mine, settled on a painting on the wall. "No."

The realization hit me like a punch in the stomach. "You?" I asked, horrified. "He wants *you* to take care of him?"

"It wouldn't be for long," he said. "The cancer's weakened his heart. He could go"—he snapped his fingers—"just like that."

"No! It'll kill your mother. You don't owe him this."

"I don't expect you to understand."

"I'm trying. But all I can see is that you're allowing that selfish bastard to victimize you and your mother again."

He couldn't meet my gaze. "You don't know what it's like. Your relationship with your father is so different."

"You'd better believe it. Because my father was so different."

"But this is the only father I have. He raised me—"

I shot him a look of such outrage, it stopped him cold.

"Okay, living with him wasn't the greatest, but there were some good times. And now he's dying."

I started to answer and caught myself. Sometimes I think I'm in the wrong business, because I'm supposed to listen and not judge. I hear the wildest stories from clients, and I keep wanting to set them straight. It's all those maxims I was raised with: *Leopards don't change their spots; If you lie down with dogs you get fleas; What you see is what you get;* et cetera. I have patients—battered women—who keep going back for more, who tell me their children want their father in their lives, no matter what he's done. Maybe there's something in us all that needs a father, and if he isn't perfect we'll take whatever nature sticks us with. It isn't that I have no forgiveness in me. It's just that I believe in right and wrong, and some things aren't forgivable. In this situation, however, I could see I was making no progress. I opted for passing the buck.

"You know what, Jamie? This isn't my call. You're going to have to talk it over with Eve. And if I were you I'd approach it very carefully, and I'd pick a time when my dad isn't around."

"You're right." He tossed his napkin on the table and got to his feet. "Speaking of your dad, I'd better get going. What time are they springing him?"

"Call the hospital first. He has to wait for his doctor to sign the discharge papers." I waved at Meg, who was placing two delectable-looking salad plates in front of a couple two tables away. "Can Jamie use the phone?" I called.

"Sure. Tell Betsy I said it's okay," she instructed him, coming over to join me.

I glanced at Betsy as he approached her. Her pale face turned bright red, and she dropped an entire stack of clean napkins. *Good thing she wasn't holding a stack of dishes,* I thought, amused. "You needn't have bothered. Looks like Betsy would give him her virginity on a platter if he crooked his little finger."

Meg laughed. "Whatever it is he's got, they should bottle it and sell it. I'm surprised some gorgeous young thing hasn't snapped him up by now."

"I guess trusting a woman comes kind of hard when you think you've been abandoned by your mother."

"I thought he was told she was dead."

"He was, but who knows what really went on in his head all those years?"

"You convince him to give the old man the boot?"

"Couldn't get through." My eyes wandered to the jeans-clad figure as he leaned across the counter and replaced the phone, his smile of thanks causing Betsy to blush again. He said something else and, still mute, she pointed in the direction of the men's room. "He tell you what that SOB had the gall to ask?"

She nodded.

"Bizarre. He hates the man, but he's ending up doing exactly what he wants."

"The guy didn't look on his way out to me."

"Me either." Being in one of my mildly stressed-out, therefore-I-need-to-eat phases, I noticed my stomach rumbling. "Let me have one of those great-looking salads you brought that couple. Gotta be back at the office by one."

Meg signaled to Betsy. "Bring Ms. Carlin the eggplant-and-mushroom salad special, please, Betsy," she said when the girl arrived.

"And lots of bread and a Coke," I added, thinking I'd better stoke up. With Garrett's appearance on the scene, a cannot-push-food-down-my-throat phase could set in at any time.

Betsy scrawled on her notepad and retreated. I waited till she was out of earshot, then I leaned forward and whispered, "Did you hear any of their conversation?"

"Not much. When I took their drink order, Jamie seemed okay, more pissed off than upset. The father knocked off three drinks while Jamie nursed his beer. Then Garrett asked for coffee, and when I brought it I heard him say something about getting the information from Somebody Heidelberg, and that was when I saw a big reaction from Jamie."

"What kind of reaction?"

"Shock and then, I guess, fear."

"That must've been when Garrett told him he was dying."

"I guess."

"Strange. Did you ask him about it when you were talking just now?"

She raised an eyebrow. "I didn't think my being sent by you to eavesdrop would go over big."

Keeping an eye out for Jamie's return, I reflected on Meg's tidbit of information. "How'd they seem when Frank left?"

"Tense but calm."

"Heidelberg must be Garrett's doctor."

"I'll bet it's cancer of the liver," Meg said. "From the boozing. He polished off those three drinks like they were apple juice. Didn't order any food."

"You don't get cancer from boozing. You get cirrhosis."

"If he is dying," Meg said, "that kind of eliminates him as a suspect, doesn't it?"

"I suppose, if he can prove it," I said reluctantly. "But if the best alibi he can come up with is only the word of some lady friend . . ." I shrugged.

Betsy brought my lunch just as Jamie returned.

"Dr. Kaplan was called out on an emergency," he said. "No one will take responsibility for discharging your father till he gets back."

"Oh, man, Dad'll be fit to be tied," I groaned.

"I'll keep checking. Meanwhile, if it's okay with you, I'll run back to the house and have that talk with my mother."

"Jamie, think about what you're doing," I begged. "You just found her. Don't let this man give either of you more pain."

"Don't worry. Everything'll work out. You'll see." He patted my arm as though I were the one needing comforting, then picked up his jacket.

"I finish at five," I called as he got to the door. "If you can't be back by then, let me know so I can—"

"If you're not back by then, I'll bring her home," Meg interrupted.

He gave a half wave and left. I wolfed down my salad and two rolls in ten minutes flat and still felt empty.

"What an extraordinary thing for him to be willing to do after all that man's put him through," Meg said, as we got up from the table.

I glanced at the check Betsy had delivered with my Coke, dug in my wallet, and dropped ten bucks beside my napkin.

"I'll say," I muttered, reaching for my coat. "Hard to believe such a sweet apple fell so far from that miserable, rotten tree."

* * *

When five-thirty arrived and Jamie still hadn't shown up, Ruth-Ann offered to drive me home. I had a feeling she was hoping to see Jamie, a meeting *I* was hoping wouldn't happen, but I accepted the offer because I knew this was Meg's busy time. I called her, told her I had a ride, and Ruth-Ann and I headed for her car. It was almost dark, and a wicked wind cut through the fabric of my car coat as though it were stuffed with paper instead of down. I was shivering as I belted myself into the passenger seat, but it wasn't only the cold that was causing the chill. The intrusion of Frank Garrett into our lives boded, I was certain, no good.

"Is Jamie going back to Boston tonight?" Ruth-Ann inquired casually as she pulled out of the driveway.

"I don't think so," I replied shortly.

"I thought because he didn't want to run into his father—"

"He ran into his father."

"He did? When?"

"This morning. In the office, before you came."

She was silent for a minute. "Is he okay?"

Dear God, all I needed to add to my already overfull plate was a distracted, lovesick assistant pining for a hopeless love. I had to do something.

"Ruth-Ann," I said sternly. "Jamie is a wonderful young man, but he's got *tsouris* up the wazoo. Besides, he's thirty-four, too old for you and he's *traif*." *Tsouris* is Yiddish for troubles like you wouldn't believe. *Traif* means nonkosher, as in pig's knuckles or clams on the half shell. "If you let yourself fall for him, you're going to get nothing but grief."

"Who said anything about falling for him?" she asked, indignant. "I just wanted to know if he was okay." •

"Well, he's not."

We sank into an uncomfortable silence for the rest of the drive home. I could feel Ruth-Ann's annoyance with me seeping through her pores. I was about to apologize for butting in and giving unwanted advice, when we turned the corner into my street and I saw the flashing lights. For an instant I stopped breathing as my father's pinched face—gray with pain, the way he'd looked yesterday leaning on Matt's arm—flashed across my mind.

"That's my house!" I gasped. "My dad—"

Ruth-Ann slammed on the brakes, and we screeched to a halt two feet from the ambulance. I was out of the car without being aware I'd opened the door. A cop emerged from behind a patrol car and grabbed my arm.

"Ma'am, you can't go in there. There's been—"

"This is my house! Let go of me!" I shoved him out of my way and sent him reeling into his rear fender as I took the three brick steps to my porch in one giant leap. The front door was wide open, and I ran smack into two white coats pushing a gurney. A sheet was drawn up over the figure lying on it, concealing the face. Through blinding tears my peripheral vision picked up Jamie and Eve sitting on the couch, their faces pale and drawn. I think I screamed my father's name as I fell to my knees and ripped the sheet from the still form. And looked down at Frank Garrett, the sneer permanently wiped from his lips, the scar on his cheek, so visible in life, blending into the pasty whiteness of his death mask.

17

AN HOUR LATER the police and the ambulance finally left. When I'd collected my wits from wherever they were scattered, I called Meg, explained the situation, and asked her to please pick up the children—Allie from Chorus rehearsal and Matt from Chess Club. She'd insisted on taking them to her house for the evening, for which I was grateful. One less problem for me to have to deal with.

When I explained I'd thought the dead man was my father, the cop whose arm I'd nearly broken in my frenzy to get into the house had agreed not to arrest me for assaulting an officer. He'd even taken it upon himself to phone the hospital to inform them that Mr. Carlin wouldn't be picked up until morning. The reception clerk had started giving him a hard time, evoking hospital and insurance-company policy, and got a verbal dressing-down for her trouble. I thanked him profusely, aware that if I'd called, they'd probably have told me the allowable stay for a cardiac event was one night and then put my poor father out on Engle Street.

Apparently, Jamie hadn't moved from the couch where

he'd been sitting since the cops took his statement. He was holding his head in his hands and mumbling softly to himself. Ruth-Ann sat quietly by his side, timidly reaching over every so often to pat his knee in mute sympathy. Eve sat unmoving on his other side and appeared to be still in shock. One of the paramedics had given her something that was supposed to calm her down, but the results weren't apparent—unless catatonic was what they were aiming for. Once I'd realized it wasn't my father lying on that gurney, I'd recovered quickly.

"Why?" Jamie whispered. "Why did he have to come here to die? Why couldn't he have stayed where he was for one more damned day?"

I wanted to say I was glad he was gone, even if we had to deal with the fallout, but I wasn't quite sure what Jamie's reaction would be. The man was his father, and Jamie had already demonstrated that, despite their history, an emotional tie still existed.

"He was sitting drinking coffee, and he just keeled over?" I asked.

"Like I said to the cops, when I got here, he and my mother were screaming at each other. I'd told him not to come until I'd had a chance to explain things to her, but he obviously didn't listen. I finally got them quieted down while I went to make coffee. After I brought the coffee we got to talking and I think he was about to apologize, tell her, you know, how sorry he was about what he'd done, when . . . when all of a sudden he said he felt nauseous and dizzy. Then he dropped the mug and . . . and went into kind of a convulsion and began to gasp, like he couldn't get his breath. His heart was going a mile a minute, and his eyes rolled up in his head. Mother called 911 and I tried CPR, but it didn't help. He was gone before they got here."

"He wasn't apologizing," Eve said, her voice barely audible. "He was gloating."

"I think you may have misunderstood—" Jamie began.

At that, Eve seemed to revive, her bosom heaving, her voice suddenly high-pitched and harsh. "I didn't misunderstand anything. He wanted money in exchange for not taking you away from me. I wasn't going to let him get away with it. Not again."

Jamie went to her and knelt by her chair. "No way. No way would I have left you," he said.

But you were going to, I thought. *That was exactly what Frank Garrett had planned, and if God or the devil hadn't intervened, he'd have succeeded.*

For the first time I became aware of the mug lying on the rug and the coffee stain near it that would probably never come out. My gaze shifted to Eve—to this fussy little woman with the flyaway hair—and I tried to imagine her pointing a gun at someone and firing it. Unbidden, an expression we all use so carelessly crept into my mind. *I'd kill for this or that,* we say, without meaning it literally. I'd already seen two sides of Eve's personality: the imperious, pettifogging nag, and the efficient, take-charge gray lady who knew CPR. Was there a third? Another *Three Faces of Eve?* Did Eve have a killer living inside her? Had she killed Omar in an attempt to extract information about Jamie? Would she have killed to keep him? My instinct told me no, but my intuition, of which as a biofeedback professional I'd always been so proud, had been somewhat out of whack these past few years. When you consider that I thought the sun rose and set on a lying, cheating egomaniac for most of my adult life, maybe I should consider another profession.

And what about Frank? Dead or not, he wasn't out of the running as a suspect. Eve had said he'd demanded money not to take Jamie, so maybe he was in on the plot with

Omar. If he was dying, though, why would he have needed money? Maybe for the search for a medical miracle? Then why kill Omar? Why kill that woman in the motel—Omar's stepniece? Unless they were all in on the plot and something had gone terribly wrong.

I leaned over and picked up the mug. "I'll just clear this stuff away," I murmured.

Ruth-Ann spoke for the first time. "I know you feel bad because he was your father, Jamie," she said. "But he wasn't a good man, and if he was dying anyway, isn't it better that God took him quickly?"

"That's true," I added from the doorway. "Cancer deaths can be prolonged and terribly painful."

"God had nothing to do with it," Eve rasped. "If He had, Frank Garrett would have suffered the tortures of the damned. Which, if there's any justice, I hope he is at this very minute."

Personality Number Three. The killer. I walked into the kitchen. I was weary. Body and soul. I didn't like the direction my thoughts were taking. I wanted this to be over. I wanted everybody to go away. I wanted Eve to go back to being Personality Number One, the health-police lady, and go back to Massachusetts, where she could feed my dad foods containing vitamins A through Z and fuss over him to his and her heart's content. I wanted Jamie back in Boston so she could fuss over him and so Ruth-Ann would eventually get that tortured, lovesick look off her face. I wanted my household back to normal and Ted back in my bed. . . .

If you want something done, do it yourself, came my father's voice from inside my head. *Thank you, Dad.* If I wanted all those things to happen, I was going to have to figure out who had killed Omar and his stepniece. And if I was going to accomplish this while I was still relatively sane, I was going to need help. I was going to have to enlist Jamie's aid, get him to dredge up buried memories. If I could get him to do alpha-theta training, something might come back to him. I wanted to know more about the friend, Louise Kassel Storey. I was going to have to get Ted to find out where she lived now and what her relationship with her brother and stepdaughter had been. And I was going to have to trust that, when we finished digging and discovered who it was that had committed these terrible murders, it wouldn't be my father's beloved wife.

Horty had followed me into the kitchen and was standing by the back door, whining. I put the three mugs down on the counter next to a saucer full of something that looked like wet chewing tobacco, which one of the cops must have left, and opened the door to let him out. Luciano, Placido, and José came barreling in. Lucie jumped up on the counter, Placido rubbed up against my leg, and José sat by the fridge and began yowling for his dinner.

"Okay, *okay*, chill," I muttered. I grabbed a large can of Friskies mixed grill, pulled off the cover, and began dividing it among three cat dishes. Lucie wandered over to the saucer and started batting at the contents. "Get away, Lucie, that's not food." I dropped the spoon, scooped him off the counter, and dumped the sodden mess into the garbage.

Horty began making such a racket, I made for the door, certain Shadow had gotten into our yard again. He was halfway in, balanced on the fence that divides the yards, back arched, fur bristling, snarling and spitting. Horty, floppy ears as erect as he could manage, was loudly defending his honor and his territory from the safety of the deck, several feet above ground.

"Horty," I yelled. "Shut up. Come and have your dinner." I grabbed him by the collar and was about to pull him inside when I noticed a nondescript dark blue car round the corner, ride slowly up to the end of the block, turn around, and wend its way back down the street, as though casing the neighborhood. I watched for a minute, wondering if that's what was happening, when my attention was caught by the license plate. I probably wouldn't have noted it if I wasn't involved with a detective who rides around all day in an unmarked police car. Unlike Ted's brown Chevy, this vehicle displayed New York plates. But like his, they were municipal plates: M679. It pulled up to the curb in front of my house and parked directly behind Ruth-Ann's silver Civic. With quickening heartbeat, I watched as two men, whom I recognized as the plainclothes detectives who'd brought Eve home Sunday night, emerged and walked up my front walk.

"A search warrant?" I asked angrily. "I don't understand. What is it you're looking for?"

"Look, we don't want any trouble. Just stay out of our way and we'll be out of here in no time."

No time. I'd seen enough TV shows to know that *no time* was sufficient time to wreck my house totally. Where the hell was my significant other when I needed him? I tried throwing around a little weight.

"You do know Lieutenant Brodsky of the Bergen County Prosecutor's office lives here," I said.

"Yes, ma'am," the older one, a tall, lanky guy who identified himself as Sergeant William Carmine, said politely. He had one blue eye and one brown eye, which totally disconcerted me when I attempted to look directly into them. *Maybe he does that on purpose,* I thought, *wears a colored contact lens to confuse the criminals he interrogates.* I switched my focus to the other detective, a short, stocky guy with a crew cut and a pronounced overbite. The ID he flashed at me read Detective Julio Segura.

"Well, I don't think he's going to appreciate this one bit."

"He's aware of the warrant, ma'am," replied Sergeant Carmine coolly.

"He's—" *Why hadn't he called and warned me?*

Horty began to sniff Segura's shoes and gave a low growl, as though sensing that these guys were trouble. Segura stepped back.

I chided Horty halfheartedly. "Sit, Horty." He obeyed, plopping a hundred and ten pounds of himself right on Segura's foot. "Sorry," I said, not sorry at all, but I nudged the dog aside.

"Don't you have to have probable cause to invade someone's privacy?" Jamie snapped. "My mother's had a very traumatic day. On what grounds have you—"

"The judge agreed that we have probable cause, sir," replied Carmine. He held out the warrant. I glanced at the signature. *Judge Carleton P. Davis.* It looked real enough, but it could've been signed by Judge Judy and it wouldn't have made any difference. These guys were going to pull apart my house looking for God-knows-what evidence to implicate Eve. Heaven help us all if they found something.

Segura was losing patience. "If you'd please get your dog out of our way, we'll be out of yours as soon as we can."

Eve spoke up for the first time since the detectives had arrived. "Let them search. I haven't done anything. They're not going to find whatever it is they're looking for."

I took Horty by the collar and pulled him close to me.

"Why don't you folks go sit in the kitchen while we have a quick look around?" said Sergeant Carmine. "We'll tackle the kitchen last."

And they took off their coats, rolled up their sleeves, and went about the business of trashing my house. I couldn't accuse them of rudeness, which was probably the only perk my being Ted's significant other was going to afford me.

Well, maybe that was why they didn't slash open my uphol-
stery or my mattresses, but the perks stopped there. All my
closets and drawers got an early spring cleaning.

When they'd finished in the living room, Eve and Jamie
went back and sat on the couch. Horty and I followed the
detectives upstairs and into my bedroom. I stood leaning
against the doorjamb, petting Horty, hoping the low growl
in his throat was making them nervous, while mentally de-
vising ways I was going to get back at Ted for not having
done something to stop this. He probably couldn't have
stopped it even if he'd tried, but that was irrelevant. I was
pissed. He didn't know how to fold a shirt? Well, by God,
next weekend he was going to learn. He was going to fold
every goddamned shirt, every jersey, every sweater those
SOBs shook out and cavalierly tossed onto my bed. He was
going to roll up every pair of socks they unrolled, restack
every book. . . .

Carmine was pulling something out of Eve's coat pocket.
"Is this your coat, ma'am?"

"It's my stepmother's."

"What's this?"

I looked at the object dangling from his hand. "Looks
like a key ring to me."

"Interesting that your stepmother feels the need to carry
pepper spray."

My stomach did a flip-flop, but I walked nonchalantly
over to him and took a closer look.

"I'll be damned. That's mine."

"Yours? You carry pepper spray?"

"I work late sometimes. So far as I know, pepper spray is
legal."

Segura grinned. "Guess that's what comes of being involved with a cop. My wife carries it too."

I tried to keep my expression impassive. No need for

them to know that this was my other key ring, the one Eve had in the handbag that had disappeared. "I forgot I'd lent that to her." I held out my hand. "I suppose that's one good thing that's come out of this stupid search."

Carmine palmed the ring. "I hope you won't mind if, before we leave, I check that one of these keys opens your front door."

"Be my guest," I said haughtily, and sank down on the bed, my mind in a turmoil. I didn't follow them when they went on to search the kids' rooms. Whatever mess they made in there would hardly be noticeable.

How had the key ring gotten into Eve's pocket? If she had the key ring, she must have the handbag. But I'd seen her climb down the ladder without it. The only way she could have gotten it is if the killer had given it to her. Unless . . . unless she'd put the keys in her coat pocket the day of the murder and forgotten about them. I went over to the coat and dug my hands around in the pockets. They were wide and deep. She could have fit a Luger in them.

Or a thirty-eight, whispered a little voice in my head. Why hadn't she given my key ring back to me? Best-case scenario, she'd simply forgotten.

What seemed like hours later but probably wasn't, the two detectives appeared in my doorway. I smiled sweetly. "Find any dead bodies? Smoking guns? Any marijuana plants?"

"Sorry to have upset you, Ms. Carlin," Segura said uncomfortably. "Just doing our job. I'm sure Lieutenant Brodsky would understand."

I stood up. "Yeah, well, I'll try to remember that when I'm up all night cleaning up this mess."

The three of us and Horty trooped back downstairs. I didn't follow them into the kitchen. I didn't want to watch them taking apart my refrigerator. I just stood in the foyer fuming, listening to the sounds of dishes clattering and of cans and boxes being removed from my—okay—not-so-neat cupboards. When the two men emerged, Segura was carrying a large brown paper bag. I looked at it curiously.

"Are you going to tell me what you've taken?" I said as Sergeant Carmine fit my key into the front door lock.

"Whatever we've taken will be returned to you at a later date," he said, and handed me my keys.

I couldn't imagine what they had in that bag. "Maybe you'd like to tell me what you were looking for. In case I find it, I could call you."

Carmine's brows drew together as he stood in the open doorway letting the cold air make me shiver. He scowled down at me. "Out of deference to a fellow detective, we've gone easy on you, Ms. Carlin. But this is a homicide investigation, and it might be a good idea if you took it seriously and cooperated."

"You wouldn't believe how seriously I'm taking it, Detective," I snapped back. "My entire life and my family's lives have been horribly disrupted. I'd just be a lot more cooperative if you were spending your time looking for the real murderer instead of hounding my stepmother. Good night." And I slammed the door behind them.

I stood with my back against it, breathing hard, clutching the key ring tightly in my hand, my heart thudding against the walls of my chest. I was furious, even though I knew these detectives were doing exactly what Ted would be doing in their position. I forced myself to walk into the kitchen, surveyed the chaos in dismay. I wanted to sit down on the floor amidst the cans and boxes strewn there and cry.

I stooped down and gathered up several cereal boxes. There were cornflakes and bread crumbs on the floor. I put the boxes on the counter next to the sink and reached for the broom.

"Let me help."

I turned to see Jamie standing in the doorway.

I managed a smile. "I won't say no. This could be an all-nighter. Where's Eve?"

"Believe it or not, she dozed off on the couch. I straightened up in there."

"Thanks."

"What can I do?"

I pointed. "Clean dishes in the middle cupboard, glasses on the right, cans and boxes on the closet shelves. I'll load the dishwasher. I'd like to get the place halfway back to normal before I call Meg to bring the kids home."

We worked in companionable silence for a while. The physical work was good for me. It kept me from thinking. As Jamie swept up the last of the spilled crumbs, I reached out and touched his arm.

"Jamie, if we don't figure this thing out pretty soon, they're going to arrest your mother on circumstantial evidence."

"I know," he replied. He walked over to the window and stood there looking out. I followed his gaze. There were no stars. Only the trickle of light cast from the spotlights on the side of my house and a lone street lamp pierced the darkness.

"You see something?" I asked.

"No. I was just thinking."

"About?"

"What they were looking for."

"The gun."

"Yeah."

"They didn't find it."

"Of course not. Who would be stupid enough to hide the murder weapon in the place they're staying?"

I felt a jolt like an electric shock run through me. "Are you saying you think Eve—"

He turned. "No, no, I didn't say that. I know she had every reason to hate Omar, but from the little I've seen of her, I think she'd have found it hard to actually pull the trigger."

Treading carefully, I said, "She's kind of in the place I was a couple of years ago."

"What place was that?"

"Where all the evidence pointed to me but I didn't do it."

His eyebrows shot up. "What was it you didn't do?"

I took a deep breath. This was not a time of my life it gave me great pleasure to recall. "Knock off my husband's plaything."

He laughed. "Bet you didn't grieve over her demise, though."

"Would you think I was horrible if I said I didn't?"

"Not at all. All's fair in love and war."

That wasn't one of my father's favorite maxims.

"So you don't agree with the NYPD," he commented.

"Honestly?"

"Yeah."

"I go back and forth, because . . . because despite the evidence it's awfully hard for me to imagine Eve on the Most Wanted list. I guess she's probably mentioned to you that she and I haven't always . . . well, I think we find each other hard to take. But we both love my dad, so . . ." Ted's words of last night came back to me: *That was before the lottery win.* I pushed them away. "Anyway, for that reason and for the care she's given him, she deserves the benefit of the doubt from me."

He smiled and silently applauded me. "Good for you, Carrie."

I sat down at the table and continued. "Okay, then. Let's try to come up with another possible scenario. I want you to think back. Way back. What else can you remember about your mother's old friend, Louise?"

He went to the refrigerator and poured himself a glass of Coke. "Only what I told you this morning."

"How long had she and your mother been friends?"

He shrugged, came over, and sat across from me. "I don't know. You'd have to ask my mother."

"You said you thought Louise was jealous of your mother. You thought she betrayed her by calling your father that night. Well, what if in her twisted thinking she blamed Eve for her losing Frank when he took off with you, something she never expected would happen when she made that call? Then all these years later she hears about the lottery, the way you and Frank did, and thought, *Damn, the golden girl always lands on her feet.* What if she and Omar and her stepdaughter cooked up this plot together? What if she was actually the instigator and then decided she wanted the whole pie?"

He took a swallow, drummed his fingers on the table, and stared off into space before he spoke. "You're stretching things, because first, Omar was her brother, and second, if she actually did kill him, she killed the goose that was laying the golden egg."

"No, because Eve's the golden goose, not Omar. If you hadn't shown up and spoiled—wait a minute, how would she have known where you were? How did any of them know?"

A sheepish look passed over his face. "My fault. After I saw you all on television, I couldn't think of a good way to contact my mother, so I thought I'd take a stab at letting her find me on the off chance she might still be looking. I went on the Internet and linked up with several of those missing-persons and child-find Web sites. I certainly wasn't concerned about anyone else finding me at this late date, but I guess I should've been. I made it easy for them."

"Looks like everybody found you *except* your mother. So what do you think about my theory?"

"I don't buy it. I think Louise did make that call, but I think my father got in touch with Omar, or the other way around, and I think they had a fight and he killed him."

That didn't account for the woman in the motel, but it wasn't an implausible theory, and if that was the case Eve's worries were over. Provided we could prove it. "What would Frank have needed Omar for, though? Why wouldn't he have contacted your mother himself?"

"That's easy. I think he knew she would never have met with him. She wouldn't have believed anything he told her. He needed an intermediary."

"But if Louise was the one who called him that night, she'd be the logical one for him to use as a conduit. Eve would've trusted her more than she would have Omar."

"But my mother told me she never kept in touch with Louise. Her supposed best friend. Think about why that was."

I *was* thinking. I was thinking the answer lay somewhere deep in Jamie's subconscious. "Listen," I said with mounting excitement. "Would you be willing to try a little experiment?"

He peered at me warily from under hooded lids. "What kind of experiment?"

"I do alpha-theta training," I began.

"What the hell is that?"

"It's kind of like hypnosis, but not really. What happens, though, is sometimes I can lead you—get you to bring up memories that your conscious mind has buried. Like if you saw something that happened between your mother and Louise—or maybe Louise and Omar, or Omar and your father—that you pushed down into your subconscious. Sometimes they're painful memories and—"

"It wouldn't work." He polished off the Coke and got to

his feet. "I'm a lousy subject for hypnosis. I've tried. I'm one of those people they can't put under."

"Well, this isn't exactly—"

There was the sound of a key turning in the front door, and then Ted was standing in the archway.

"Hello," he said. "What's this I just heard about Jamie's father dropping dead in our living room?"

Suddenly, all the emotions that had been churning around inside me since Frank Garrett had walked into my office this afternoon congealed into one poisonous dart and found a target. "What's this *I* heard about your giving your okay to my house being searched?"

Jamie's eyes shifted from Ted to me and back again. "I seem to be in the way. I think I'll just go see if my mother's awake."

18

TED CLOSED the door and waited till Jamie was well out of earshot. "I'm sorry. There was nothing I could do. They had a warrant."

"You could've called."

"I did call. No one answered. I left a message on your machine."

In all the confusion I hadn't thought to check my messages. Knowing he'd made the effort should have diminished my anger, but it didn't. "Well," I said, "you should've kept trying. Or you could've called me at the office."

His eyes turned slate-gray and he fired his own dart. "I could have, but occasionally I do have a few other things to do besides trying to ward off your crisis of the day."

The dart pierced whatever armor of control I had left. I could actually feel my nerve endings fraying. I didn't care that he hadn't done anything wrong and that he had a right to be annoyed with me for attacking him. I was exhausted and frazzled and fast running out of resources to deal with even the most infinitesimal of altercations, and here was the one person I'd been counting on to understand, returning my poison darts instead of deflecting them. My voice went up a few decibels.

"Oh, so everything that happened today was my fault? That bastard showing up at my office and then having the temerity to drop dead in my house was my fault?"

He sighed. "Of course it wasn't your fault."

"But I'm a magnet, right? Trouble finds me."

"I didn't say that, although it's not far off the mark. If you—" He stopped himself and reached for me. "I didn't mean that. Let's stop this stupid argument before we say things we'll regret. Why don't you—"

I was too far gone. I spun out of his grasp. "Stupid? Now I'm stupid?"

What is the matter with me? What am I doing?

"Goddammit, Carrie, I don't want to fight with you. Suppose you just calm down and fill me in on what happened."

"Calm down? Stop patronizing me." If I'd stuck out my tongue and stamped my foot, it wouldn't have surprised either of us.

"Look," he said, his voice becoming dangerously glacial. "You are not the only one who's had a bad day."

"Bad?" I cried. "Try horrendous! Try unbearable!"

"Try," he said, in a manner so infuriatingly, icily quiet I wanted to smack him, "following your own advice and taking some deep breaths. This is not a life-threatening situation."

That did it. He was throwing my own words back in my face at a time when they were the last words I wanted to hear from anyone, especially from him. I lost it. "Do you know that those bloody NYPD dicks nearly wrecked my house tonight and then left the mess for me to clean up?" I shrieked. "I've been violated! How dare they do that? How do those pigs get away with doing stuff like that to a private citizen in this country?"

I'd struck a nerve. He grabbed his jacket from the chair where he'd tossed it and headed for the back door. "You'd better be damned glad we 'pigs' are out there doing this fucking job, saving your pretty little ass from all the—"

"And do you know," I yelled, unable to stop, "that less than two hours ago I looked straight into the face of a dead man who I'd been talking to just a couple of hours before that? You may be used to that sort of thing, but I'm not. And do you know I thought it was my father lying dead on that gurney? Have you any idea what that felt like? Do you know that every day I think about the call I'm going to get telling me it *was* him on a gurney . . . and . . . and about the call I'm going to get one day telling me it's . . . that . . . that . . . someone . . . that you—" My voice broke and I started sobbing, racking sobs that seemed to come from a place so deep inside me I wasn't aware till now that it existed.

There was an agonizing pause as he stood at the door with his back to me and I thought he was going to walk out and never come back, and I wanted to say, "Don't go, I love you," but I still find it hard to say those words to him, and the stubborn part of me was still mad, and I was crying so hard I couldn't get words out anyway. But then his arms were around me and I was sobbing against his chest and he was stroking my hair and murmuring comforting, soothing things, like, "It's okay, everything's going to be okay." And I relented and bought into it for the moment because I wanted to believe that everything was going to be okay, although I couldn't see how. But it helped for a few minutes to trust that somehow this man, whom I was coming to care for and rely on so much it scared the hell out of me, could in some miraculous way keep the monsters at bay, as my father used to do when I was a child.

But minutes later I pulled away. I wasn't a child and no
one could keep my monsters at bay except me—not even
me sometimes, and certainly not a man. I'd learned that the
hard way, so I hiccuped a couple of times and got a grip on
myself.

"Sorry," I murmured shakily, reaching into my pocket for
a tissue. "I guess I needed to have a tantrum, and I can't have
one in front of my dad or Eve or the kids, so you got elected."

He gave me a wry smile. "Not too many people can push
my buttons like you just did and get away with it, but I
guess we're all entitled to a tantrum now and again. Just
glad you didn't have your pepper spray handy."

Which reminded me of the key ring that was burning a
hole in my pocket. "Actually, I do," I said without thinking.

"What? I thought you told me Eve had it."

"She did, but . . ." If I told Ted about the NYPD detectives finding it, would he feel compelled to pass the information about where it had been on to them?

"But what?" he asked impatiently.

"Uh . . . nothing."

"Shit. Not nothing. Give."

"No, honestly, I . . ." *Honestly?*

Honesty is the best policy, came the little voice inside my
head. *Shut up, voice.*

I sniffled a couple more times, blew my nose, and changed
the subject. "Have you found out anything more about
Omar, or the sister and her stepdaughter?"

He made a rude gesture.

"Come on, Ted."

"You ever hear of tit for tat?"

I considered my options, decided it might be safer to go
with the little voice. I pulled the key ring out of my pocket

and held it out. "Those bird-dog detective pals of yours found my key ring in Eve's coat pocket."

"And you didn't tell them she'd had it in the handbag she left behind on Sunday."

"No."

"Why am I not surprised?"

"I didn't because I figured she'd probably put it in her pocket without thinking and forgot she had it. And because I think they should be looking at other possibilities," I protested. "Like—"

"You think. Christ, Carrie, this is a homicide investigation. How about letting the pros draw their own conclusions?"

"If I'd told them that Eve had this key ring with her when she found Omar, they'd think she has the handbag and maybe the gun and—"

"And they might be right."

I could feel my gorge rising again. "They'd probably have started slicing up my furniture looking for them. And just because Garrett had some kind of attack and died doesn't eliminate him as a suspect. I didn't want to add to the evidence piling up against Eve, even though—"

"Even though if it looks like a duck and it quacks like a duck . . ."

I started to laugh, but it was mirth bordering on hysteria. "It's a golden goose."

He stared at me as if sure I had gone over the edge. "What the hell does that mean?"

"If you sit back down I'll tell you." When he did, I gave him my golden-goose theory.

"Interesting," he said, "but Louise Storey has an alibi for the afternoon of her brother's murder."

Disappointment washed over me. "Where was she?"

"At a concert. She has the ticket stub."

"That doesn't prove anything. She could've—"

"Give it up, Carrie. So far her story checks out. Anyway, I don't think Eve's the golden goose."

"Who, then?"

He reached for my hand. "Your dad. The lottery ticket was in his name. Eve only becomes the golden goose if your dad . . . isn't around."

The room blurred. It was so quiet I could hear Lucie purring from ten feet away.

"If you're right, then my dad's in danger," I breathed.

"If I'm right."

"So you really think Eve—"

"There's another possibility, you know."

"Who?"

"Jamie."

"Jamie! He saved Dad's life!"

"Shh."

"But what are you basing that on?"

"Following the money. He'd inherit from Eve."

"So why'd he help Dad? If what you said is right, he'd be better off with Dad . . . out of the way."

"Yeah. That's the hole in my theory."

"And you might as well put me in there. If I knocked off Eve, all the money would come to me."

"True. Guess I'll have to keep my eye on you." He pocketed the key ring and started to get up. "Which most of the time, when your mascara isn't running all over your face, is a pleasure."

"Hey, not so fast," I said, reaching in my pocket for a tissue to repair the damage. "I told you about the keys. I still want to know what you found out about Louise."

He sighed, but he sat back down and rattled off the information as though he had the report in front of him. "Living in Hartford, Connecticut; was married in '78 to a guy named Harold Storey, who died three years ago. He was a widower with a daughter, Barbara, and a son, Ron. He was fifteen years older than Louise, had worked for AT&T, retired when he got sick in '93. Lou Gehrig's Disease. Things were rough financially, but she apparently took good care of him. Her relationship with her brother, Omar, was almost nonexistent. Says he left home soon after Jamie was kidnapped, moved out of state, and they saw very little of each other."

"What about the stepdaughter?"

"She was out of the house long before her father died. Both kids were. Louise says she wasn't close to them. Another thing that shoots down your conspiracy theory."

"If she's telling the truth. How did she react to the double murder?"

"Report says with shock but not grief. These people weren't a major part of her life anymore."

"Did she know about Eve and Dad winning the lottery?"

"Apparently not. Said Eve never returned her calls and she hasn't seen or heard from her since the night Jamie was kidnapped."

"Don't you think that's strange?"

"It's for Eve to explain. But not right now." He picked up his jacket and put it on. "Call you tomorrow. Don't discuss anything with Eve or Jamie. Let's just cool things for a day or two."

"But what—"

"I'll tell you when I know something. You working tomorrow?"

"I took Thursday off this week. I'll be able to pick Dad up."

"Good. Keep your eye on him."

I'd certainly intended to do that, but his saying it made me nervous.

"Where're the kids?"

"Meg took them to her house." I glanced at my watch. "I'd better call her."

"Wait till I leave. I'm going out the back. I don't want to run into Eve or Jamie right now."

"Okay."

He pulled me to him then, his lips brushing my eyelids, sliding down to my earlobe, and ending up almost angrily bruising my mouth.

"You can be a real scary lady sometimes," he whispered, releasing me. "Don't fuck us up."

As I worked on dousing the flames kindled by that kiss, I reflected that was the last thing I wanted to do. I watched as he walked to his car, thinking I liked his walk, the way all the motion seemed to come from his hips and those long legs.

"Hey, Brodsky," I called softly, cracking the door open.

He paused with his hand on the car door and turned. "Yeah?"

"You've got a cute ass."

"All the better to jump you with, my dear."

I laughed. "That a promise?"

"An IOU." He grinned and folded himself into the Miata. "Ted?"

He stuck his head out the window. "What now?"

"What about the son, Ron or Don, whatever his name is?"

"Ron. Haven't located him yet. Buzz you later."

I watched the Miata's taillights until they disappeared and the icy wind drove me back indoors.

We all went to bed early. I don't know about the others, but I slept as though I'd been drugged. It was pure exhaustion, physical and emotional. Meg had fed the kids at the café, which pleased them no end because Matt got his long-overdue death by chocolate and Allie pigged out on Meg's famous apple brown Betty drowned in whipped cream. These are not desserts they normally find in our refrigerator. They're lucky if I manage a birthday cake on the appropriate occasions. Meg had seen to it that their homework was done, so all I had to do was give them the barest outline of what had happened and send them to bed with the vague promise that everything was going to be all right. I doubted they believed me, my record of late not being one to inspire confidence, but they went without a murmur. Matt was completely recovered from his virus and no one else seemed to have caught it, which was at least one positive mark in the ledger.

I woke at six-thirty, refreshed, determined to keep my cool and to see to it that everyone else kept theirs when I brought Dad home.

When I arrived in his hospital room at ten o'clock, he was dressed and waiting for me, looking a whole lot better than he had in the ambulance. His complexion had lost the terrible gray cast that had so frightened me, and his eyes were clear, their old sparkle firmly in place.

"It's like getting out of jail," he muttered as we emerged from the hospital into the glare of the morning sun reflecting off the mounds of snow piled up at the sides of the driveway.

"Wait here. I'll bring the car around."

"I'm not an invalid," he admonished me. "I can walk."

"We're having a cold snap, Dad. With the wind-chill factor, it's below zero. Maybe you shouldn't be exposed to—"

"You're dead a long time, sweetheart. Don't bury me while I'm alive."

Nothing to say to that. We walked to the visitor's parking lot in silence. By the time we got to the car, our faces were bright red and we could see our breath. I blasted the heat and waited until we were on Piermont Road, halfway to Norwood, before I brought up the subject of his pills.

"Eve puts them by my plate at breakfast," he said. "I told the doctor that. How could I forget to take them?"

"Since she's been away, though, do you think you may have missed a day or two? I know if my birth-control pills didn't have dates on them, I'm sure I'd screw up. Sometimes I get so busy, I can't remember what I've—"

He interrupted my babbling. "Look," he said, slightly annoyed. "I don't know what happened that I got destabilized. Maybe the dosage needs correcting. But I am a long way from being in my dotage, and I am not so busy or so addle-brained that I can't remember whether or not I took my medication."

I let it drop. We passed the farm in Closter where I used to go for sweet corn in the summer, and I chitchatted about how most of the land had been sold off for housing, so now they have to bring the corn in from outlying farms and it's expensive and not as good.

"The price of progress," Dad said.

We were almost home by the time I got around to telling him about Frank Garrett.

"God almighty, that must've been terrible for all of you," he exclaimed. "Is Eve all right?"

"She's . . . recovering. Jamie's been great with her. It was rough on him too, first seeing that SOB again and then having him drop dead in front of him."

"It must be pretty clear that devil was the one killed that Omar fellow, though," Dad said. "They were in it together to get money from Eve."

I didn't answer, and Dad went on. "Got his just desserts, I'd say. The police shouldn't be bothering us anymore."

"Well," I began. "I don't know that . . ."

"We'll get out of your hair by the weekend."

"I don't think you should plan to go quite that soon, Dad."

"Why in hell not?"

"Well, for one thing, Eve's still up on a breaking-and-entering charge," I murmured. "Her lawyer's working on cutting the red tape, but I wouldn't count on leaving by Sunday."

I kept my eyes on the road, but I could feel his piercing glance.

"What aren't you telling me?"

"She's not completely in the clear yet. There's no real proof that Frank killed Omar, and so far there's no motive that we know of for him to have committed the murders—murder," I amended quickly.

"The lust for riches. Greed. The worst of the seven deadly sins."

"If it can be proven, but they're both dead, so it complicates things. There's also no proof," I added, "assuming there was a conspiracy, that he and Omar were working alone, that they didn't have accomplices."

I turned the corner into my street and pulled into my driveway behind a rusted-out maroon Chevy Malibu.

"Who's here?" I muttered, like Mama Bear, annoyed that someone was parking in my space. I opened my door and ran around to help Dad with his bag.

"I can carry it," he said. "You expecting company?"

"Nobody I know of."

"Well, let's go see."

I dashed up the porch steps, fit the key into the lock, and pushed open the door, holding it ajar for my father. "Hi. We're home," I called out.

The only response was an excited yip from Horty, who came bounding out to greet us. I gave him a quick pat on

the head and, shedding my coat and gloves, followed my
father into the living room. Jamie was straddling the chair
by my desk, arms draped over the back. Eve was sitting on
the couch, her hands folded tightly in her lap, her face
flushed a dull cherry red.

I've gotta get her to the office, I thought. *Her diastolic must be triple
digits.* My eyes shifted to the person who I gathered was the
cause.

Standing by the bay window was a delicate-boned
woman, a few inches taller than I am, who I judged to be
in her late fifties or very early sixties. She was wearing a
tailored royal blue blouse and skirt, with pearls adorning
her neck and ears. Her dark hair was laced with swirls of
gray and cut chin-length, setting off the earrings and
framing her face. She brought to mind an image of how I
believe Vivien Leigh would have looked had she lived to
portray an aging Scarlett O'Hara.

19

PLUCKING HER COAT from the window seat, she bolted for the door, almost colliding with us as we crossed the threshold. Dad reached out an arm to steady her as she skidded to a stop. "Whoa there," he said.

"Excuse me," she gasped. "Could I get by, please?"

Startled, I started to move aside, but some instinct inspired Dad to hold his ground.

"Where's the fire?" he inquired with a smile, not budging from the doorway.

"I . . . was just leaving. I'm very late."

Who was this woman and what was she doing in my house?

Eve was on her feet and flying across the room. She threw her arms around Dad, pressing her cheek up against his chest as though counting the heartbeats. I assume there were enough of them to satisfy her, because after a few seconds she lifted her head, and her hands fluttered over his face like a blind person's—checking, I suppose, that he still had two eyes, a nose, and a mouth. Could these be the actions of a woman who'd just tried to off her husband?

"David, thank God you're back," she cried. "Are you feeling all right?"

"Good as new," he replied, wrapping his arms around her, completely unruffled by her fussing. "You seem to be losing your guest. Aren't you going to introduce us before she runs off?"

"Oh, yes. This is Louise Kass—I'm sorry. Louise Storey. You remember. I told you about her."

I caught my breath, locked eyes with Jamie. I wondered if he was reconsidering what I'd said.

Always the gentleman, my father courteously held out his hand. "Nice to meet you."

Reluctantly, Louise proffered hers. "I really must go," she said. "I have—"

"I'm Carrie Carlin," I jumped in, determined not to let this opportunity pass. "Eve's stepdaughter."

She mumbled a greeting, her eyes sliding past me to the door.

"I'm afraid my car is blocking yours," I rushed on. "I'll have to move it. But why don't you stay for a while? I'm sure you and Eve have a lot of—"

"No, no, I can't. I just wanted to see Eve again, and now that I have, I must go. I have to be somewhere."

What had happened while I'd been out? Something had clearly upset her. More than upset. Frightened her. Had Eve or Jamie accused her of being involved in the conspiracy, if indeed there was one? I shot a pleading look in Jamie's direction, hoping he'd come up with some way to detain her, but he only shrugged his shoulders and glanced away. What to do? I couldn't tie her to a chair.

Dad stood aside and allowed the woman to scurry past. No good-byes to Eve and Jamie, no apologies for her haste.

She was getting away and I had to figure out how to stop her. I grabbed my car keys from my handbag and, coatless, took off after her, all the while plotting how to convince her to talk to me. By the time I came down the steps, she was already in her car, the engine springing to life. I hurried over and knocked sharply on the window. I could see that she was debating whether or not to ignore me, but my car stood between her and the open road, so she gave in and rolled the window partway down.

"What is it?"

"I'd really like to talk to you. I have some questions that I think you could—"

She shook her head emphatically. "I have to leave. I have an important appointment. Please move your car."

Standing on the wet driveway with the north wind spitting icy particles in my face and only my sweater between me and the elements, I was fast developing frostbite, but I didn't move. Even if this woman wasn't the killer or hadn't been directly involved in the extortion plot, I was certain she knew things that no one else alive knew, and I wasn't about to let her ride off into the sunset. "Why did you come here today?"

"I told you. I wanted to see Eve again."

"You can't have spent much time. Why leave before you've had a chance to get reacquainted? I'm sure Eve would like—"

Her eyes darted to the house and back to me. "My brother and my stepdaughter have been murdered," she said, her voice taut with tension. "I'm here because they want me to identify the bodies. That's where I'm going now." Unable to suppress a shudder, she gripped the steering wheel so tightly her knuckles turned white. I shivered in sympathy while my own were turning blue from the cold.

"It was a terrible mistake, my coming here," she whispered.

"Why?" I leaned in closer to the car, hoping some of the heat would escape out the window. "Did Eve say something to upset you?"

For a minute I thought she was going to open up, but all she said was, "Please move your car. I haven't anything to tell you."

I was jiggling up and down now, hugging myself in an effort to retain body heat. "Where're you staying? I'll come to you. Ten minutes of your time and I promise I won't bother you again."

She saw I wasn't going to move even if it meant pneumonia, and that translated to her not going anywhere either. I was losing feeling in my toes, which were starting to solidify into one huge block of ice.

"The Radisson," she whispered finally.

"In Englewood?"

She nodded.

"I'll come tonight around eight."

There was a long pause as she studied my face. "Come alone," she said.

It dawned on me that just yesterday I'd been casting this woman in the role of murderer. "Let's meet downstairs in the restaurant," I said.

She nodded and rolled up the window. I raced to my car and backed out onto the street, watching through my fogged up windshield as she tore down the street, taking the corner curve practically on two wheels. I knew it was a gamble as to whether or not she actually would be there at the appointed time.

Back inside the kitchen, I grabbed Matt's soccer jacket off the back of a chair where he'd tossed it and wrapped myself in it. It was fully five minutes before I stopped shivering. Kicking off my shoes, I sat on the floor and began rubbing my toes to get the circulation going. I couldn't decide which part of me was worse off: my ears, my nose, or my feet. I could hear the low rumble of voices in the living room, was thinking about crawling in there so I could get the straight poop on what had scared the woman to death, when the door swung open. I looked up and saw Jamie standing in the doorway.

"You okay?" he asked.

"I'll let you know when I can feel my feet again," I replied. "What did you two do to that poor woman? You didn't accuse her of murder, did you?"

He shook his head. "Maybe I hurt her feelings. I didn't recognize her when she came to the door. It's been a long time, and she's changed."

"She's still attractive."

"I suppose seeing me here could have thrown her. She was only expecting to find you and my mother."

"I don't think that was it. And I think maybe I was wrong about her. She didn't strike me as the type who could shoot somebody."

"I'd guess shooters probably come in all shapes and sizes, but I agree with you. She's too skittish." He smiled. "Definitely more the poison type." He came over and knelt by me. "Here, let me do that." Gratefully, I surrendered my half-frozen foot. He began massaging vigorously, which left my hands free to defrost my ears. "You were out there quite a while. You talk to her?" he asked.

"I nearly froze to death begging her to stay, but she said she couldn't, she had to—to be somewhere. Tell me what happened when your mother saw her. It must've been a shock."

"She came only a few minutes before you got here. At first they seemed glad to see each other, but then she started up about my mother not keeping in touch and how she shouldn't have blamed her for what Omar did. She said

Omar was always trouble." His hands paused and he looked up at me, his glance faintly accusing. "Then she told us about her stepdaughter having been murdered. Did you know?"

I squirmed under his gaze. "Ted asked me not to say anything. What did Eve say when Louise told her?"

"Well, you can imagine. She got pretty upset. That's when she told Louise about my father's dying, and all of a sudden Louise said she had to go, she had to identify the bodies. Come to think of it, I'll bet that's what got to her."

"That and the fact that she had to go look at two corpses."

He started massaging again, his hands moving up past my ankle, rubbing my calf gently. I leaned back against the cabinet doors, closing my eyes, enjoying the return of sensation to my extremities, when out of the blue I felt a surge of heat course through my body. I froze with shock. My eyes flew open as, flustered, I pulled my leg away and jumped to my feet.

"Thanks," I said, avoiding his eyes. "That's fine. They're fine. I'm okay now."

Get a grip, girl.

I could feel my face burning, and I limped over to the broom closet and made a big thing out of hanging Matt's jacket where I never hang coats.

"You believe Louise about Omar making the call to Frank?" I called from the safety of the closet.

"No," he replied after a long minute. "I still think she made the call."

"You may be right. She sure shot out of here like the place was about to blow."

"I told you. Guilt."

I couldn't stay in that closet much longer without it looking peculiar, so I came out, closing the door behind me. When I raised my eyes he was smiling at me in such a friendly, nonsexual manner that I was ashamed of myself.

My horny body had misunderstood the signals, and I needed Ted to come home. That's all there was to it.

I started for the living room. "C'mon. Let's see how the reunited couple are doing."

I didn't linger long. Eve and Dad began bombarding me with questions about what I'd known and when regarding the murder of Louise's stepdaughter, and I had a difficult time telling only half a story. Ted hadn't wanted anyone to know Barbara Storey was killed with the same gun that had been used to do in Omar, so I danced around the subject, saying only that it was an ongoing investigation and so far the police were baffled.

My dad's no dummy.

"Of course it's the same person," he said. "Any fool would know that. Uncle and niece were in it together, probably along with Garrett. They had some kind of disagreement and Garrett killed them. Case closed. There should be no question about Eve's innocence now."

"Well," I hedged. "It's not quite that simple."

"Nonsense. It's Ted's case, isn't it? The woman was killed on his turf. You talk to him. We want to go home. It's time for this craziness to end."

"I'll talk to him," I responded meekly.

Today was my day to get all my errands done, and I found myself torn between a reluctance to let Dad out of my sight and the need to keep my household running smoothly. Forget smoothly. Just to keep it running. I decided to allocate jobs. Determined not to leave Eve alone with Dad, I asked her if she'd mind doing the food shopping for the weekend. I explained that the doctor had said

Dad should rest and I needed to stay home to do the laundry and sundry other necessary but unpleasant household chores. Fortunately, we had an extra vehicle, Dad's beautiful new Buick having resided in my garage for the past couple of days. Time for it to earn its keep. She looked annoyed, but she was hard-pressed to refuse, and I sent her off with a long list that included cat food, dog food, kitty litter, and enough groceries to feed the entire Kosovo refugee population. I asked Jamie if he would please take my car to the gas station to have it inspected, get the oil changed, and have the tires balanced. I figured that should keep them both busy for at least an hour or two. Besides, it wasn't all bad. It was like having two little elves doing my work for me. I was tempted to ask Dad to balance my checkbook but decided that would be pushing it.

By the time they returned a couple of hours later, I'd put in my last load of wash and was getting ready to pick up Matt to take him to his orthodontist's appointment, his very first. I invited Dad to come along, using the excuse that his presence would make the trauma of getting fitted for braces easier on his grandson.

"Poor kid," Jamie said as we were donning our coats.

"Why?"

"The other kids'll make fun of him."

"No they won't. Nine-tenths of the kids wear them. And Mattie's teeth are coming in crooked. He'll thank me one day."

"I guess I was lucky. I've never had a problem with my teeth."

"You *were* lucky. I had to wear them for two years."

"Bitching every inch of the way," Dad added.

I gave him a hug. "But now I'm thanking you."

"Better late than never," he said, smiling.

*　*　*

The long day finally ended. By seven-thirty, six people and four animals had been fed, Dad had taken his medication under my watchful eye, and the kids were upstairs doing their homework. Mattie's orthodontist's appointment had been relatively stress-free, although he complained loudly about gagging on the goop-filled trays they stuck in his mouth in order to take impressions. I didn't blame him. You'd think they'd've made some improvements since my day.

I couldn't wait to get everyone set so I could be on my way to meet the mysterious Louise Kassel-Storey, and I was getting exhausted with the effort of keeping Eve and Dad apart. Finally, in a flash of brilliance, I convinced Eve to take a relaxing bubble bath in my bathroom while I was out, so it would be free for me to take mine when I got home, and I got Jamie and Dad involved in a chess game. I figured that would keep Eve and Dad separated till I got back.

"I have to pick something up at the office," I called to no one in particular. "I'll be back in an hour or two." I got a couple of grunts in response. I bundled up in my down car coat, pulled the hood over my head, and slipped out into the frigid night.

I drove slowly to avoid skidding on the slick road surface. The Radisson was on Van Brundt Street in Englewood, just before the junction leading to Route 4, a drive that took more than a half hour from my house. I pulled into the turnaround drive at eight-ten, parked in the lot, and made it into the open lobby restaurant in less than three minutes. There were several businessman types having dinner together, a few couples, and a raucous group of teenagers celebrating something at a long table in the corner. I walked through the restaurant, hoping to find Louise seated behind a post or hidden behind one of the glass-brick dividers, but she wasn't there. I crossed to the reception desk and asked the clerk if there was another restaurant other than the Carlyle in the hotel. There wasn't, so I went back and checked the restaurant again, then went into the ladies' room, peered under all the stall doors, but came up empty. Maybe she's fallen asleep, I thought. After all, she had a pretty difficult day. I plodded back to the desk and asked if they'd please ring Louise Storey's room. The clerk looked on the computer for her room number.

"Oh, Ms. Storey has checked out," he said.

"Checked out when?" I asked, my heart dropping into my shoes.

"A couple of hours ago."

She'd never had any intention of meeting with me.

"Are you sure?"

"Yes, ma'am."

I knew it was fruitless, but I had to ask. "Would you mind checking again? I was supposed to meet her."

He shrugged, clicked his mouse again, and shook his head. "Sorry."

"Thank you." Defeated, I started to walk away.

"Excuse me. Ma'am?"

I hate being called "ma'am." It wasn't so long ago that everybody called me "miss." I turned back. It was another reception clerk. "Yes?"

"Are you Carrie Carlin?"

"Yes."

"Ms. Storey left this for you." He held out a white envelope about the size of the average birthday card.

I thanked him, grabbed it and hurried over to one of the lobby chairs. I tore off my gloves and, with unsteady hands, ripped it open. Reaching inside, I pulled out two photographs. The top one was very similar to the color photo of Jamie I'd seen earlier this week. He looked to be a little older, and he was holding a soccer ball instead of a fish. I studied it, trying to think what about it disturbed me, because the child looked happy and was smiling into the camera. Finally, disappointed because I couldn't pin it down and it told me nothing I didn't already know, I put it aside and held the other one up to the light. Almost immediately, my dinner did a flip and started rising up into my throat. The photograph was of a young boy lying facedown on a bed. He was nude, his back and buttocks covered with angry red welts. A handwritten tight scrawl across the top read, *For Jamie, as a reminder to always do as he's told.*

20

MY MIND WENT numb. I don't know how
long I sat there staring into space, clutching the photograph in hands gone clammy with shock, unable to make
my eyes focus on that obscenity. When my brain finally
came off hold, questions started zooming around in my
head, questions without answers. Why had Louise left this
horrible picture for me? What did she think I could do about
it? You don't go to a child-welfare agency complaining about
abuse committed twenty-odd years ago by a man already
dead. *One picture's worth a thousand words.* The quote from
Pauline Kael that Ted had used in an entirely different con-
text the day Eve's letter arrived came back to me. So what
were the thousand words Louise was trying to communi-
cate to me? I forced myself to look down at the picture
again. Maybe this boy wasn't Jamie. His face was buried in
the pillow. There was no way to tell who the child was.
Maybe that beast of a father had shown him a picture of another brutalized child in order to frighten him into submis-
siveness but hadn't actually committed this atrocity. Then I

saw the scar. Just above the waistline, a jagged white raised comma—probably the injury from the fishhook, I suddenly realized, that had sent him to the emergency room, marking him like a cattle brand, like a Holocaust survivor's tattoo, burned forever into his skin, burned forever into his soul.

I wanted to cry, but my eyes wouldn't produce tears. I wanted to rail at a God who would allow such a monster as Frank Garrett to live and breathe, who would allow such agony to be inflicted on a helpless child, but I knew this wasn't God's doing. These barbarities were the work of aberrant men, and they went on every day of the week.

How could I show these photographs to Eve? I couldn't. I could only thank God that Louise hadn't. Perhaps that had been her intention when she came to my house this morning, but something had stopped her. Maybe it was seeing Jamie and Eve together; maybe she'd realized that seeing the photos could only add to the pain of two people who were desperately trying to come to terms with the issues raised by their long separation. Jamie surely didn't need to view them. He bore the scars. Aside from the physical scars, what invisible scars did Jamie carry from those years with his father?

I flew out of the chair, thrusting the photographs into my purse, pulled my hood up over my head, and dashed out to the parking lot. Something Ted had said last night came back to me, electrifying me as though someone had jabbed me with a cattle prod. Ted had suggested that Jamie might have had a motive for the killings, but Ted was way off base as to what that motive might have been. I had a more realistic one. Abusees become abusers. Omar was dead. Barbara Storey was dead. And Frank Garrett was dead. *Vengeance is mine, sayeth the Lord.* What if it was payback time?

I was barely out of the lot before the logic of that reasoning fell apart like a puzzle whose pieces were jammed into the wrong places. Barbara Storey hadn't been in Jamie's life—probably they hadn't even known each other—and Frank Garrett had expired from a stroke or a heart attack. I felt deflated but relieved. Jamie had every reason to want the people who had destroyed his childhood and probably his trust in humanity dead and buried, but he hadn't killed them. Any more than I had killed the bleached-blond siren whose song had lured my hedonistic husband into her arms.

So who did that leave? Who else might be motivated by revenge? There was Louise herself, of course. By leaving these photographs was she attempting to point the finger away from herself and toward—who? Eve? I kept pushing that thought away, but if revenge was the motive, Eve certainly topped the list. Was I harboring a killer in my home, a fiendish black widow? I glanced at my watch. It was eight-forty. I hit the accelerator, going fifty on Dean Drive, ignoring the squeal of my tires on the wet pavement. An image of a panicked Eve looking like Big Bird in a fit, scrambling down the ladder the day I'd rescued her from the brownstone on Eighty-first Street, played across my mind. That bizarre figure—as murderer, as someone who'd just blasted a man off the face of the earth—just didn't compute for me. Besides, no killer with half a functioning brain would be caught dead in that very recognizable red hat she'd worn that day. Where was the hat? Where was her handbag? Did she remember putting my keys in her coat pocket that day? Maybe she'd wanted to keep the pepper spray within reach. That made sense. In any case, we needed to talk.

At the junction of Westervelt and Dean Drive, lights from an oncoming truck momentarily blinded me and I slammed my foot down on the brake. The car went out of control, skidded across the courtyard of the Coldwell Banker building that divides the roadways, careened onto the exit ramp of the Exxon gas station, wobbled crazily back onto the road for another block, jumped the curb, and ended up facing in the wrong direction, bumper against a fence in someone's front yard. For a minute or two time stopped. My hands were stuck to the steering wheel, and my heart was banging against my ribs like a pendulum gone awry. I don't know how long I sat there before I stopped shaking and my heartbeat resumed something resembling its normal *lup-dup, lup-dup.* I managed to unglue my hands from the wheel, checked my arms and legs to make sure nothing was broken, took a deep breath, and looked around to see if I'd killed anybody. All was quiet. No moans or screams broke the stillness of the night. The truck had gone merrily on its way, oblivious to my situation, and fortunately for me there apparently had been no cops, other cars, or witnesses to my stupidity. From what I could see, the frozen ground had preserved the lawn, and no visible damage had been done to the property. As I read the sign directly in my line of vision, it registered that I was not in someone's yard; I was on the lawn in front of a professional building, and the irony of where I'd come to rest momentarily startled me. A funeral home. I'd come to rest against the fence of the local funeral home. How's that for a message from above? I'd been speeding on an icy road surface, my mind a million miles away, and luckily had gotten off with only a warning.

Speed is only good for catching flies, came my father's stern voice in my head.

When you're right, you're right, Dad, I answered the phantom voice, and very cautiously backed out onto the road. I crawled the rest of the way home, hanging on to the steering wheel as though it were a life preserver, wondering if I'd ever again be able to relax while driving in treacherous road conditions. There's nothing like a near miss to give you religion. I started to think that maybe the message-sender was trying to send a dual message. Two people had been murdered. There was a killer on the loose who would have no compunction about annihilating anyone who got in his or her way. Maybe the message-sender was warning me to tread with caution on the treacherous road of life.

Except for Horty and Placido, Dad was alone in the living room when I came bustling in, still pretty shaken up but able to maintain some surface composure. Horty raised his head from Dad's foot and thumped his tail on the rug at the sight of me. Placido didn't budge from his lap.

"I see I'm being replaced," I commented, as I hung up my coat. "Where's everybody?"

"Kids're in their rooms, Eve's gone to bed, and Jamie's in the shower," he replied, putting down his pen. "Ted wants you to call him at the precinct."

"Okay. Is Eve asleep? I wanted to talk to her."

"Dunno. You can look in and see. Anything wrong?"

"No, I just wanted to check something with her. When did Ted call?"

"Just a few minutes ago."

I came over and sat beside him, reached for his hand. "You feeling okay, Dad?" I asked.

"I'm all right, Cookie."

Cookie. His old term of endearment for me when I was a little girl. So much more comforting than Rich's ultimate sobriquet, "Nudnik," or even Ted's more affectionate "Curious Georgette." I rested my head against his shoulder. "What've you been doing?"

"Just making some notes for Eve's lawyer."

I sat up. "Did Holbrook ask you to do that?"

"No, but I thought I'd make up a list of character references just in case. Ted didn't say what he was calling about, and after we hung up I got a little worried."

"Oh, I'm sure he just called to say good night," I said offhandedly. "He always does that if he's working late." That was a bald-faced lie, but I felt the tension leave Dad's body, and I was glad I'd said it. "Who won the game?"

"I did. The old brain still works pretty good, you know."

"I never doubted it for a minute."

"Yes, you did. You thought I was getting senile, forgetting to take my pills."

"No, Dad. Honestly, I was just trying to figure out what happened. . . ."

He smiled and patted my knee. "Well, you don't have to worry anymore. Eve's back on the job."

Why didn't that make me feel better? I jumped to my feet. "I'm going to look in on Eve and the kids, then I'd better go call Ted."

"If Eve's still awake, tell her I'll be up in a little while."

"Okay." I took the steps two at a time. As I reached the top of the stairs, Jamie was coming out of the children's bathroom. He was wearing only a towel slung around his hips, and I couldn't help sneaking a glance at his rugged physique. "Hear you lost the chess game," I called teasingly over my shoulder.

"That's one smart old guy," he retorted, disappearing into Matt's room. "You should've warned me."

"Can't outmaneuver a Carlin," I called back. "We come from a long line of smart guys."

"I'll keep it in mind," came the laughing response.

I knocked softly on the door to my bedroom. When there was no reply, I pushed it open and peeked in. The lamp on the night table was still on. Eve had fallen asleep with a book in her hands. I tiptoed over to the bed, removed the book, and reached across her to switch off the light. In doing so my eye fell on the title of the book: *Children in the Crossfire*. I stood still for a moment, studying the cover on the book, which depicted a man's arm grabbing a small child. *The Tragedy of Parental Kidnapping* was written under the title. I looked down at Eve. Her face smoothed over in innocent sleep, she looked younger than her sixty-plus years. What had the tragedy of a parental kidnapping done to this woman? What had it made her capable of? Had it created a monster, made her capable of murder? Would it do that to me? I turned off the light and sneaked out of the room, the book clutched tightly in my hand.

I spent an hour in the bathtub in the children's bathroom flipping through the chapters. The book was a study of the effect of child-snatching by the noncustodial parent on the children and on both parents. As in any war, there were no winners, and the effect on the psyches of the children themselves was devastating and long-lasting. I wondered how Jamie had survived it so well. Then I thought about that photograph and about his reaction when he'd seen his father, how easily he'd succumbed again to his father's bullying, and I changed my mind. He hadn't survived unscathed.

"Mom, did you drown?" Allie's voice outside the door.

"I was reading, honey. I'll be right out."

"Ted's on the phone."

I'd been so absorbed in the book I'd completely forgotten to return his call. I hadn't even heard the phone ringing. "Tell him to hang on. I'm coming," I called. The water temperature had dropped about ten degrees, and I hadn't noticed that either. I grabbed a large fluffy towel and wrapped myself in it.

Allie was standing outside the bathroom door, holding the cordless phone. "You're all shriveled up," she said with a grin.

I glanced at my fingers as I took the phone. She was right. I'd need a whole bottle of body lotion tonight.

"Hi," I said into the receiver as I followed her into her bedroom. "Sorry I didn't get right back to you. I was—"

"Who's with you?" he asked curtly.

"Allie just handed me the phone," I replied, surprised at his tone.

"Make some excuse, and go someplace where you're alone."

There went my heart again. I was becoming a walking example of the damaging effects on the body of constant stress. I closed my eyes and took a couple of deep breaths. "Allie," I said in the casual voice I was learning to use in crises. "Would you hand me my robe, please?"

"What's the matter?" she said as she complied. So much for my acting ability.

"I have to go downstairs and get something for Ted. The bathroom's all yours." I threw my terry-cloth robe onto my still-wet body and fled barefoot from the room, closing the door behind me.

"What's going on?" I whispered into the phone as I ran down the stairs.

"I'm with Vivian Holbrook."

Thrilled to hear it. "Oh?"

"Where are you?"

"On my way to the kitchen."

"Where's Eve?"

"Asleep."

"And the others?"

Why was he asking me this? "Dad's in the living room, and Jamie's in Matt's room. What's going on?"

There was a deep sigh on the other end of the line. "Don't wake Eve, but you'd better prepare your dad."

Dread, like a choking fog, settled over me, cutting off my air supply. "For what?" I gasped.

"There's a good possibility Eve's going to be picked up and charged."

"What're you saying?" I almost shrieked, slamming the kitchen door behind me. "What're you talking about?"

"Shh. Try and keep calm. Viv and I are trying to come up with a way to head it off."

Viv? "But why?" I whispered, shoving the green monster back into its box and clamping on the lid. "What happened?"

"We got preliminary results on cause of death. Garrett didn't have cancer like he told Jamie."

"So what? So the sonofabitch lied to get Jamie to go with him. That doesn't surprise me."

"Listen to me. No cancer. He didn't die from the disease."

"Well, of course not. You don't just keel over from the disease. He had a heart attack or a stroke or something."

"Carrie, he didn't have a heart attack or a stroke."

I wanted to hang up. I didn't want to hear what was coming, but I had to ask. "What . . . what did he die of, then?"

"Nicotine poisoning."

"So he was a smoker. He smoked himself to death. He—"

"Smoking was the one vice he didn't have. It's beginning to look like he was murdered."

21

I DIDN'T SAY anything to Dad. He was going to
need a good night's sleep to be able to face what tomorrow
might bring. Needless to say, I didn't sleep. I lay in the twin
bed in Allie's room, trying not to wake her with my tossing
and turning. My mind jumped from one cataclysmic event
to the next, the way a TV remote flips through channels.
Eve's words the day Frank Garrett had died, when she told
me he'd demanded money in exchange for not taking Jamie
away, played over and over in my brain like a song whose
melody you can't get out of your head: "*I wasn't going to let him
get away with it,*" she'd cried. "*Not again.*"

Not again, not again, not again.

The preliminary report indicated Garrett may have died
from nicotine poisoning. So how had she done it—forced
him to smoke about a thousand cigarettes? It didn't make
sense, and Ted hadn't explained how the M.E. had arrived
at that conclusion. I remembered the saucer with the hunk
of wet tobacco I'd tossed. It had looked like chewed chewing tobacco. Maybe Frank had chewed tobacco and, aware

of her ex-husband's habits, Eve had mixed some kind of poison in it. But Ted had said he'd died of nicotine poisoning. Not arsenic poisoning. Not strychnine. Not rat poison, which would have been more fitting.

The photograph of the child, Jamie, his back striped with the effects of a belt lashing, flashed in front of me, and I thought, *This man deserved to die.* He deserved to die from the kind of beatings he'd inflicted on his small son, but not at Eve's hand. Not now, so many years later when mother and son had just found each other.

I turned over, punched my pillow, and buried my head in a futile attempt to block out the ugly images, then tossed some more. Finally I sat up and squinted at my watch. Women's watches never have those little buttons you push to make them light up. I crawled out of bed and went into the hallway. Three-twenty. I had car pool tomorrow and five patients to unstress. How was I going to manage either one with no sleep? What if they arrested Eve tomorrow? How would my dad react? With him just coming home from the hospital, his condition not completely stable yet, it could precipitate another attack. *I should have told him tonight,* I thought. *Given him time to absorb the shock. But then he'd be up all night too.*

I tiptoed back into Allie's room and tripped over Horty, who barely grunted as I fell over him and onto the bed.

"Mom?" Allie murmured sleepily. "You okay?"

"I'm sorry, honey. I'm having a little trouble falling asleep. I'm going downstairs. Go back to sleep." I gathered up a comforter and my pillow, stepped around Horty, and made my way down to the couch. Not bothering to open it, I lay down and attempted a Schultz progressive muscle-relaxation exercise. I closed my eyes, began at the top of my head, and slowly relaxed each individual muscle all the way down to my toes. After some time I got my body pretty much under control, except for the knot in my chest that wouldn't allow sleep to come. *I'll do the safe-place thing*, I thought, and forcing my eyes shut, put myself in my old tree house. But Eve was there again, tossing away the lottery money. I went to diaphragmatic breathing and deep-breathed to the point of hyperventilation. No good. There was nothing for it but to hit the bottle. I got up, padded barefoot upstairs to the bathroom, fished around in my cosmetics case, and pulled out my little bottle of Bach's Rescue Remedy. It's become a running joke with Meg and me that I, a biofeedback practitioner who preaches mind over matter and self-healing, am occasionally forced to resort to herbal remedies. *Desperate situations require desperate remedies*. Hey, it's not like resorting to drugs.

I put four drops in a quarter cup of water, tiptoed back downstairs, and sipped it slowly. Call me crazy, but I could feel the knot loosening. I began to drift off.

I am walking down a path. On either side of the path are tall trees, poplars and leafy oaks and giant pines, and in between the trees are stone benches and larger-than-life-size statues on pedestals. The statues are of Greek and Roman gods and goddesses, beautifully sculpted by masters, graceful figures in flowing robes, heads crowned with wreaths of flowers—Juno; Diana, goddess of the hunt, with her bow and arrow; beautiful Aphrodite. And perfectly proportioned male gods in robes and loincloths—Zeus; Poseidon, with his trident; Apollo. I walk over to the statue of Apollo and circle it, admiring the skill of the sculptor, the way he'd carved each sinewy tendon in the leg, caught the curl of the hair, the fold of the loincloth, the curve of the back as it tapered down from the muscular shoulders. I reach up and run my hand over the curves, feeling the smoothness of the cold marble, and suddenly the muscles ripple as the statue comes to life under my touch. And the cold marble is warm skin and the loincloth is a towel and the figure turns and smiles down at me, reaches out a hand to hoist me onto the pedestal. . . .

"Did you sleep here all night?" Dad was standing over me, gently shaking me awake.

My eyes flew open. I sat up, disoriented, flustered, not quite certain where I was. "What . . . what time is it?"

"Six-fifteen. You look exhausted. I feel terrible putting you out of your bed."

Coming fully awake, I sat up. "Don't be silly," I said. "The bed in Allie's room is very comfortable. That's not why I slept here. I came downstairs so my tossing and turning wouldn't disturb her." I swung my feet onto the carpet, stretched and yawned, trying to ignore the uneasy feeling in the pit of my stomach. "I've gotta get up. I have car pool."

"Get dressed. I'll make coffee."

Ted, come home. I think I'm starting to fantasize about Jamie.

The coffee was perking and smelled wonderful when, still bleary-eyed from lack of sleep, I staggered downstairs. Dad had let Horty out and fed the cats, so we sat together drinking the real stuff (I usually settle for instant in the morning), and I allowed the caffeine to clear my head. On my second cup I told Dad as gently as I could about the possibility of Eve's arrest. He didn't say anything, just sat there with his hands wrapped around the mug as if the warmth from the coffee could somehow counteract the cold fear within.

"I'm sure it's a mistake," I said, offering what comfort I could. "If Garrett died of nicotine poisoning, how could that possibly implicate Eve? Ted and Vivian Holbrook have been—"

"How good is this lawyer Holbrook?"

"Ted's worked with her before. He thinks she knows what she's doing."

"How old is she?"

An infant. "I don't know—twenty-eight, twenty-nine."

He slammed his mug down, the hot liquid splashing out and splattering, a muddy river snaking across the table. "Won't do. I want a big gun. I've got the bucks."

I reached over with my napkin and began mopping up. "I have a couple of names that Meg gave me when I was—you know, when I was in trouble, but why don't we wait until—"

"No." He got to his feet and began pacing the floor. "She's not going to spend one night in jail. I won't have it. It's insane to think she killed anybody. The police aren't doing their job. What the hell has Ted been doing all week? Where is he? Why hasn't he—"

"He and Holbrook were up half the night trying to find a way to keep the wolf from the door."

"Hey, what are you two arguing about?" A smiling Jamie, looking sexy as hell in cowboy boots, jeans, and a pullover, stood in the doorway.

"Ted called last night with some bad news," I said. "It looks like your mother may be charged today."

The smile faded. "For chrissake, why? Don't they get it? Frank killed Omar. It's as clear as—"

"It's not about Omar. They're saying your mother killed Frank. He didn't have an attack, Jamie. He didn't even have cancer. He was poisoned."

Jamie's face turned a sickly white, and he sank into a chair. I reached out and grasped his hand.

"I'm sure it's a mistake—about Eve, I mean. I know how it works. They're getting pressure to solve the other cases and they're looking for a scapegoat. Eve had motive and so—"

"But poison. How . . . how are they saying she did it?"

"Ted didn't give us the details."

"But . . . he had a heart attack. I was there. What kind of evidence have they got? What're they basing this on?"

"They haven't got a goddamned thing," Dad exclaimed

angrily. "It's all circumstantial. Carrie, get me the names of those lawyers."

"In a minute, Dad. Jamie, you were with Frank and your mother in the living room the whole time, weren't you?"

Jamie was silent.

"Jamie?"

"I . . . I went into the kitchen to make coffee, but I was only gone a few minutes. . . ."

"Was there any time after you brought the coffee she could've slipped something into it?"

"For God's sake, Carrie," Dad snapped. "What're you trying to do?"

"I'm trying to prove there was no way Frank was poisoned in this house. Jamie?"

It seemed forever till he answered. "She . . . she went to the bathroom. She was gone so long, I thought maybe she wasn't coming back, but when I went into the kitchen to get the coffee, she was there pouring it into the mugs."

"Jesus, God," Dad breathed.

"I won't tell them that," Jamie said quickly. "I'll cover for her."

"She didn't do it!" Dad shouted. "I don't know what happened to that guy, but I know that woman as well as I know myself, and she didn't do it!"

As well as I knew Rich?

"Mom?" Wide-eyed, Matt stood in the doorway, knapsack on his shoulders, staring at his grandfather. "What's the matter with Grandpa?"

I jumped to my feet. "He's had some upsetting news. Dad, you and Jamie go look through the Rolodex on my desk for those two lawyers' names. They're under the *A*'s, not the *L*'s. You can make the calls from there." I grabbed two bowls out of the cabinet and turned to my son. "It's just

going to be cereal and juice this morning, Matt, and I'm going to ask Mrs. Moscone to take car pool for me today,
okay?"

He nodded, but there was a familiar scared look on his
face. It was only a few months since I'd taken the kids out
of therapy, the result of the Erica episode. I could just
imagine Dr. Brubaker's face if they showed up in her office
again, victims anew of post-traumatic stress syndrome.
She'd have Social Services on my neck before I could say
Sigmund Freud.

"What happened?" Matt whispered when the two men
had disappeared into the other room.

I'm getting to be a pro at telling white lies and half-
truths, but my mind went blank. I scooped him into my
arms and hugged him instead.

"It's something to do with Aunt Eve, sweetheart. Nothing for you to be concerned about. We'll talk about it later."
I reached for the phone with one hand and the raisin bran
with the other. "Go tell Allie to bring down my purse so I
can give you lunch money. I have to call Mrs. Moscone."

The children were barely out the door when Eve came
downstairs. She was dressed in a ruby-red spangled sweater
and a hunter-green skirt, with a long rope necklace made
of huge beads that bobbed up and down on her chest like
candelabra bulbs as she breathed. She looked like a half-
decorated Christmas tree, which, all things considered, was
a definite step up from an organ grinder's monkey. All she
needed was a star on her head, and I was willing to bet there
was a hat in her closet that would fill the bill. But the way
Dad looked at her, she could have been Christie Brinkley
at the Academy Awards. What would happen to him if it

turned out she wasn't the person he thought she was? A lump rose in my throat as I stood in the archway and watched him take her arm and lead her to the couch.

She took the news better than I'd anticipated. I'd expected hysterics, but she just sat there clutching his hand, making me worry about her blood pressure as her face flushed the color of her sweater.

Jamie came in with a plate of toast and a steaming cup of coffee, placed them in front of her, and sat beside her. I couldn't imagine how she was going to choke down food, but I hoped she'd try. This might not be her last supper, but it was probably going to be her last decent breakfast for a while.

"I got hold of Brimfield," Dad said to me, referring to one of the lawyers whose name he'd found on my Rolodex. "He said we should call him from wherever they take her. He'll meet us there."

I nodded. I guessed Vivian Holbrook would probably be waiting as well. We were on our way to assembling a dream team. All we needed were Johnnie Cochran and F. Lee Bailey and we could go for broke. Completely broke.

The worst of it was how helpless we all felt waiting for the ax to fall. It was like knowing you're in the path of a hurricane. You've boarded up the windows and stocked up on candles, but beyond that, there's nothing to do but wait for the storm to hit.

We didn't have long to wait. Horty heard the car first and, as if sensing that doomsday were imminent, he howled, a long wolf call that jangled my nerves and had me rushing to the window.

Eve was shaking all over, and Dad looked ready to go for his shotgun if he had a shotgun, or for mine if I had one, which I didn't.

"It's only Ted," I called out in relief. "And Vivian Holbrook. It's going to be okay, Eve."

But it wasn't. Ted and Vivian had come to ask Eve to turn herself in.

"We decided it'd be easier on her if she came in voluntarily," Vivian said. "I'll stay with her while they book her."

God. While they book her.

"Things'll go better for her if she's cooperative," Ted added. He looked exhausted. He and Holbrook had matching raccoon rings under their eyes. My own were running a close second.

"I don't get it," Jamie kept repeating. "I don't get it. He had a heart attack. I was right here. I saw it."

"They'll want to talk to you, Jamie," Ted said. "You'd better follow Vivian."

"I won't have her kept there overnight," Dad roared. "How much is bail? I'll write a check—"

Ted cleared his throat. "I'm not sure the judge will grant bail, Mr. Carlin. You see, it's not just—"

"They've got nothing. Only circumstantial evidence. This is the United States of America. You can't hold somebody without—"

"Mr. Carlin," Holbrook interrupted. "They found her handbag."

A ringing started in my ears. I looked over at Ted, but he was looking at Eve. I opened my mouth, thought I shouted the word, but it came out in a whisper.

"Where?"

"In a Dumpster. Just a block from the Welcome Motel."

22

BELIEVE IT or not, after everyone left I actually went to work. There was nothing I could do for Eve other than to give her moral support, and she had my father and Jamie for that. I figured I'd just be in the way at the precinct, an assumption with which Ted all too readily agreed, and besides, I had five patients scheduled. So Vivian Holbrook drove with Dad and Eve in Dad's car, and Ted took off for parts unknown. Jamie came with me to the office so he could take my car and meet them at the precinct later.

We didn't say much on the way. It was as though, if we didn't talk about it, we could pretend it wasn't happening, but our minds were ahead of our tongues, refusing to buy into the charade. As I made the left over the bridge opposite the Baptist church, Jamie took the plunge.

"It was my fault for saying I'd go with him," he mumbled miserably. "It pushed her over the edge."

Hearing him say aloud that he thought his mother had done these terrible things, I felt the way I had the time I'd gone snorkeling and something had clogged my breathing tube. I didn't answer him until we'd driven the several blocks to my building. I pulled into the parking lot and left the motor running with the heater blasting, as much to keep out the internal chill as the external.

"If it's true that Eve murdered Frank—which I don't for a minute believe—then she shot the others, and that was before you came," I said. "You can't blame yourself."

He shook his head. "It was all because of me."

"That's ridiculous. It was an old vendetta. Whatever happened was caused by the kidnapping, and that wasn't your fault."

Our breath was fogging up the windshield and I cracked the window, letting in a stream of icy air.

"We just found each other," he muttered. "And now it's over."

"Come on, Jamie. You can't lose faith. You really think Eve murdered three people? All these years she's lived a quiet, normal life, volunteering in hospitals and feeding my dad fish oil and alfalfa sprouts, and suddenly she goes on a killing spree, knocking people off like they were mosquitoes?"

"If I hadn't seen her pouring the coffee into the mugs . . ."

"That doesn't mean she put something in it. Isn't it possible the poison was already in Frank's system? We don't know anything about his life since you ran away. Given his M.O., he certainly must have had enemies."

"That's for sure, the sonofabitch. I wouldn't even blame her if she had done it."

"Maybe he had a second wife who wanted to get rid of him. It could've been happening over a period of time. A lot of poisons are slow-acting."

"Not nicotine."

"What if it was an accident? He swallowed his chewing tobacco."

He looked skeptical. "I never heard of anyone dying from chewing tobacco. How would that happen?"

"I don't know. Maybe he was chewing and a piece caught in his throat, and he swallowed it by mistake."

"What makes you think he chewed tobacco?"

"Because there was a big disgusting wad of the stuff in a saucer in the kitchen. I thought one of the cops had left it there, but if Frank did—"

"What happened to it?"

"I tossed it."

"Oh. Too bad."

"Why?"

"Maybe they could've learned something from it." He looked at me hopefully. "If it could be proved his death was accidental, then it's possible I was right and it was my father who killed the others."

I cut the motor and opened the door. "Except it doesn't explain how Eve's purse got in that Dumpster. I keep thinking Louise is involved. She shows up, and all of a sudden they find Eve's handbag. Think about that." I started to get out of the car, when he stopped me.

"You know anything about her stepson?"

"Ron Storey? No. Ted was going to check him out, but I haven't heard anything. Why? You think he might be part of it?"

"Well, I'm thinking if the stepdaughter was in on it, and now you're saying Louise might've . . ." He shrugged. "I don't know."

Suddenly I had a brainstorm.

"How about coming up to my office with me and trying alpha-theta? It just might bring up a memory that would link her to all this in some way."

"I told you. I've tried hypnosis. It doesn't work on me."

"This isn't hypnosis. What I do is I bring you to a totally

relaxed state, so that experiences you've forgotten or re-pressed come back to you. It's called an abreaction. Some-times we suppress memories about things that happened to us that were too painful to deal with at the time. Bringing them to the surface allows us to heal."

"Does it work with everybody?"

"No. And sometimes it takes lots of sessions. It depends on how receptive the patients are and on their ability to re-lax into an alpha state."

He gazed out the window, contemplating the frost on the tree branches, considering my suggestion.

"And you think I might remember something from when I was a kid that might help my mother?"

"I really do."

"Well, it sounds crazy to me, but I'm willing to try. It'll take the police a while to process her. I probably have an hour to kill."

Enthusiastically, I grabbed his hand. "Great. I have to brain-map my first patient, but I'll make it fast."

"That's okay. It'll give me some time with Ruth-Ann."

It was a helluva moment to broach the subject, but he'd given me the opening and I was determined to take advan-tage of it. "I've been meaning to talk to you about her," I said. Reaching into the backseat, I picked up my briefcase and slid out. Jamie got out the passenger side, and we walked up the driveway and went in the front entrance.

"So," he asked. "What about Ruth-Ann?"

I pressed the elevator button, gathered my courage, and began my little lecture.

"She's got a crush on you, Jamie. You're not being fair to her. You should tell her you're not interested."

He lounged against the wall, a quizzical expression cross-ing his face. "Who said I'm not interested?"

"You told me . . . I thought I'd explained about her . . .

and after this is over, you're going back to Boston," I finished lamely.

He looked at me with narrowed eyes, as if to ask what
business this was of mine. But after a pause he said, "Okay,
okay, I'll talk to her." And glanced away.

I knew I'd said the right thing, but I'd obviously hurt him.
I should've butted out. He was a young man; he was bound
to have sex and romance on the brain. And Ruth-Ann was a
grown woman, capable of making her own decisions. Anyway, who was I to talk—I, who had erotic fantasies about
statues?

The elevator door opened and we got on. I stared at the
ceiling while we rode up to the third floor in silence.

Ruth-Ann looked up from her desk as he trailed me into
the office, her smile broadening at the sight of him, edging
with relief on seeing me. I understood the relief. Elaine/
Doris/Patty/Gloria was straddling a corner of her desk. She
was wearing tight black stretch pants, which looked as
though they'd been painted on her lumpish thighs, and an
olive-green man's shirt tied under her bust, revealing a roll
of fat like a cream-filled doughnut around her waist. Her
hair was tied back in a ponytail, and she was made up like a
Forty-second Street whore with too much rouge, bright red
lipstick, smudged purple eye shadow, and black mascara. I
knew immediately that it was Gloria who was out and that
she believed she was a dead ringer for Uma Thurman. Catching sight of Jamie, she slithered off the desk—which is
quite a feat when you're toting around her bulk—sashayed
across the floor, and rubbed up against him.

"My, my," she cooed. "Look who the cat dragged in."

I guessed I was the cat, the cat on the hot tin roof.

"Hiya, handsome." She emitted a cutesy giggle and wound
her arms around his neck.

Ruth-Ann rose to her feet. "Gloria," she said, her voice

uncharacteristically sharp. "Ms. Carlin has a busy schedule today. Come into the office and let's get started."

"I'll hook her up, Ruth-Ann," I said. "Jamie wants to talk to you. Come on, Gloria. We have to do a brain map for Dr. Golden today."

But she didn't move, and it seemed as though Jamie was playing along just to get back at me. I began to wish I'd kept my big mouth shut about Ruth-Ann. He favored Gloria with an inviting smile. Encouraged, she ran her hands up his back, allowing them to creep under his sweater.

Embarrassed and hurt, Ruth-Ann averted her eyes. "I'll do it. It's my job." She grabbed Gloria's chart off her desk and escaped into my office.

"Gloria, quit that, and either let Ruth-Ann hook you up or go home," I snapped, my annoyance at Jamie overriding my professionalism.

Gloria dropped her arms, made a little kissy noise with her mouth, and backed away. "See ya later, lover boy," she tittered, and minced into my office.

I frowned at Jamie. "Why'd you encourage her? What did you think you were doing?"

He shrugged. "You told me to discourage Ruth-Ann. Just following orders."

"I didn't mean for you to stick a dagger in her heart. Don't we have enough problems with your mother on her way to jail, without reducing Ruth-Ann to tears?"

"Sorry. Guess I'm a little uptight."

"Join the crowd." I opened a drawer in my file cabinet and pulled the charts of my four other patients, then turned back to him. "How else do you suppose Garrett could have gotten the nicotine if it wasn't from the chewing tobacco? Did he wear a patch, do you know?"

"You mean the kind to help you stop smoking?"

"Yeah."

"No idea. But wouldn't they have found that at autopsy?"
Of course they would have. "Yes," I muttered.

Minutes later Ruth-Ann opened the office door and beckoned to me. "She's got that funny look on her face," she whispered, pulling the door shut behind her. "I think she's Patty now. She says she feels sick and wants to go home."

"Damn." I dumped the files on top of the cabinet and started for the office. "Jamie, I'm sorry. This could take some time. She gets like this now and then when she's Patty. We may have to put things off."

"It's okay. I should be going. My mother . . ."

"Wait a minute." I stopped at the threshold. "I don't see why I can't do you first. Ruth-Ann, take Patty into the back room. Tell her I said I want her to lie down and rest."

Ruth-Ann nodded. Moving quickly, Jamie crossed the room and caught her by the arm.

"Ruth-Ann," he said, turning her around and placing his hands on her shoulders. "I'm sorry if I upset you. When Carrie and I finish, I'd like to talk to you."

Flushing, she raised her eyes to his. "Okay," she murmured. "I'll wait for you." She opened the door and disappeared into the office.

I smiled. "Thank you. That was much better."

He shrugged. "So, what do we do now?"

"After Ruth-Ann gets Patty into the other room, I'll hook you up to the computer. We'll begin with a relaxation exercise and go from there." I was eager, now that he had done the right thing vis-à-vis Ruth-Ann, to smooth things over between us. I searched my mind for something to say. "Did I tell you about my crazy dream last night?"

"No."

"You were in it."

He cocked his head, intrigued. "No kidding. What was I doing?"

"You were a statue of Apollo in a garden."

"Apollo, the Greek god?"

"God of light, purity, and truth."

He laughed. "Don't know if I can live up to that."

"You have in Eve's eyes." I cracked the office door and peeked in. "They're gone. Come on."

He followed me inside. "What's next?"

I pointed to the recliner. "Sit. Start taking slow deep breaths from your diaphragm. Like this." I demonstrated, placing my hand on my diaphragm so that he could see the slow rise and fall.

He followed my instructions, and within seconds his eyes closed and his breathing became regular and even.

"You're a fast learner," I said approvingly. *This could work*, I thought, my excitement mounting. I reached for the leads hanging on the hook by the computer. "I have two sets of sensors," I explained. "One set I attach to your ears and to the top of your head. They record your brain waves. The other set I'll attach to your fingers and to a muscle on your back. Those record muscle tension, skin temperature, and electrodermal response.

His eyes opened. "What's that?"

"Your fight-or-flight response. Works kind of like a lie detector. If you're not telling the truth," I teased, "I know it immediately."

I was surprised to see his body stiffen.

"I thought this was about bringing up repressed memories."

"It is," I replied soothingly. "Don't worry, I promise not to ask you about your sex life."

At that he seemed to relax again, although I noticed a tightness in his shoulders that hadn't been there before. *Men*, I thought. *As if I'd be interested in his sex life.*

I flipped on my Healing Waterfall tape and walked behind

the chair. "Close your eyes," I said. "Listen to the music. Let yourself go with it." I removed an alcohol pad from its wrapping and began rubbing it on his earlobes.

"Carrie?"

I reached for the gel. "What?"

"Didn't Apollo kill the Cyclopes?"

"I think so. Relax your shoulders."

"Why do you suppose that was, if he was such a good deity?"

I scoured my memory for the Greek mythology stored there. "It was something about their making the thunderbolts that Zeus used to kill Apollo's son."

"Ah," he said. "Justifiable homicide."

"There's no such thing."

"They were responsible for his son getting killed. You don't think they deserved to die for that?"

I was having a hard time attaching the ear clip to his lobe, and I didn't like the direction the conversation was taking. "It was Zeus who ordered the killing."

"The Cyclopes made the thunderbolts."

"By that reasoning, we should kill all the gun manufacturers."

Actually, not a bad idea.

"In Greek mythology the gods were all-powerful," I said. "They had the power of life and death. Now, can we get back to . . ."

"Wouldn't you like to have the power to even the score and know you couldn't be punished?"

"I suppose there are times we would all like that, but in reality . . ."

He twisted around to look at me, pulling loose the clip I'd just attached. "Wouldn't the world be a better place without the bad guys?"

"I wouldn't want to be judge, jury, and executioner." I

reached for the dangling clip. "If I was, I'd be no better than the people whose fates I was deciding."

"You're a hypocrite, you know. You wished your husband's mistress dead a thousand times, but you didn't have the guts to do it."

"What can I say? I'm not a killer."

"From my perspective, Apollo was right on."

My heart skipped a beat. Was he telling me he'd taken it on himself to be judge, jury, and executioner of the people who had ruined his and his mother's lives? That he'd evened the score? The tube of gel dropped from my hand, and as I bent down to pick it up, I heard him laughing.

"Gotcha," he chortled, looking down at me. "Oh, Carrie, Carrie, you should see your face. You've decided I'm the big bad wolf."

It took me several seconds to recover. Slowly I got to my feet. "That wasn't funny. You scared me."

"I'm sorry. I was getting back at you for that lie-detector stuff. Go ahead. Finish hooking me up. I promise I'll be good." And he flashed a smile. A toothpaste-ad smile. Perfect teeth. Evenly spaced.

Where's the space between the two front teeth that you saw on the photographs of young Jamie? asked the little voice in my head. Hadn't he just yesterday mentioned that he'd never had orthodonture?

I was rattled. I re-attached the ear clip, picked up an alcohol pad and the muscle sensors, and pushed him forward in the chair. "This attaches to your latissimus dorsi muscle," I said, all business. "I'm going to clean the area first with alcohol." I tore the paper off the pad, leaned forward, and pulled up his sweater.

And saw his back. Apollo's back. Apollo of the rippling muscles—Apollo of the smooth back. The smooth back of my dream, the figure in the loincloth—in the towel—

smooth, unscarred—UNSCARRED! It hit me like Zeus's thunderbolt! WHERE WAS THE FISHHOOK SCAR?

And the thunderbolts kept coming.

How had Jamie known Garrett died of nicotine poisoning? I hadn't told him. How had he known that nicotine poisoning was fast-acting? It isn't common knowledge. I hadn't known. How would Eve have known which mug Jamie was going to hand to Frank? She couldn't have. Only the killer would have known.

The killer who had no scars.

The killer who had no conscience.

The killer with the perfect smile, who was sitting in my chair.

The killer who couldn't be Eve's son!

He sat back and looked up at me. "Anything wrong?"

I stood up, willing my hands to stop shaking. But my breath was coming in short gasps and my legs were wobbly. They didn't want to carry me to the safety of the waiting room, where I could get to the phone and call 911. For an instant our eyes met. "Forgot something," I gasped. "Be right back."

Heart beating like a trip-hammer, I reached for the knob and jerked the door open, forcing myself to walk slowly out of the office. I pulled the door shut and made a mad dash for the phone on Ruth-Ann's desk. But before I could lift the receiver, I felt his grip like a vise on my wrist.

"Hell," he said, and there was regret in his voice. "Why couldn't you have let it alone?"

I attempted to bluff, struggling to keep my voice steady. "Let what alone? What are you talking about?"

"Give it up, Carrie. You're a rotten poker player."

I knew that.

I attempted to withdraw my hand. "I don't know what you're talking about. And you're hurting me."

He shook his head. "Shit, what am I going to do with you?"

"We'll talk later after I finish with Patty."

His grip on my wrist tightened, and he began pulling me toward the outside door. "We'll talk now."

I wanted to yell for Ruth-Ann to get her pepper spray, but I was afraid to put her in danger. Still, there were three of us and only one of him, and if I went quietly, I was pretty sure I would end up like the Cyclopes.

"Let me go," I hissed, "or I'll scream."

"No, you won't," he replied, reaching into his boot with his free hand and drawing out a gun—big, black, and looking to my terrified eyes like a cannon.

"Because if you do," he went on calmly, "I'll have to kill Ruth-Ann and Patty or Gloria or whoever the hell she is today, and I don't think you want that."

"Wait a minute," I gasped. "We can work this out." I plunked myself down on one of the chairs, gripping the sides tightly. If he wanted me, he was going to have to take the chair too. "Why'd you do it?"

"For money."

"The lottery money? You killed three people for my dad's lottery money?"

"They were scum. They were using me. I outsmarted them."

"Where's the real Jamie?"

"Dead."

"Who the hell are you? How do you know so much about him?"

"Same platoon. Let go of the chair."

I held on tighter. "Did you kill him too?"

I saw conflicting emotions pass quickly across his face. "No. Enough talk. Let go of the chair!"

But I kept talking, frantically trying to distract him as a

sudden thought exploded in my brain. "My dad's pills. Did you—"

"With him out of the way, the money would all have been Eve's. And by extension, mine."

"But you saved him."

"Temporary. Brodsky was asking questions."

The goose that laid the golden eggs. Ted had been right. My father was the goose, and Jamie had tried to kill him.

Rage enveloped me as bile rose in my throat. If I'd had the gun at that moment I think I could have shot him right through his treacherous heart. "You piece of shit! I took you into my home!"

"Let go of that chair!" And he jerked me to my feet and dragged me toward the door. I lost my grip on the chair, but as I slid past the coatrack, I locked both arms around it, briefly halting my journey to oblivion.

He grabbed me around the waist and pulled. "Let go, or I'll cut your goddamned arms off!"

This is the way the world ends, not with a bang, but a whimper.

My world was not going to end with a whimper! But if I didn't do something fast, I was pretty sure it was going to end with a very big bang.

He had my arms loose now, and he brought them around the rack and pinned them against him. As he did, I managed to hook my leg around the bottom of the pole. He gave it a hard smack with the butt of the gun and I let go, crying out in pain. But the coatrack started rocking, and as he dragged me toward the door, it came crashing down.

The door to my office flew open and Ruth-Ann rushed out, a cowering Patty on her heels. "What was that? What's happening?"

"Get back, Ruth-Ann," I screamed. "Lock the door. Call the police."

She stopped short, tried to back up, but Patty's bulk blocked her path.

Patty began whimpering. "Ms. Carlin. I'm scared."

"Doris," I yelled, a last-ditch idea forming. "Doris, come out!"

Jamie backed me up against the outside door and threw the bolt. "Okay, ladies," he said. "That's it." He shoved me over to the other two. "Lie down. Get your butts on the floor. Eat it."

Ruth-Ann stared at him in horror. "Jamie, what is this? What are you doing with that gun?"

I caught my breath. "Don't be crazy, Jamie—"

"Carl."

"Carl, then. You planning to kill all three of us? You'll never get away with it."

Patty started to wail. "K-kill us?"

My mind was racing, searching desperately for a way out. "Who will you blame this on? Eve's in jail."

"I won't be around to blame it on anyone."

But he had to realize that if he shot one of us, the other two would have a few seconds to rush him, to scream for help, and the gunshot itself would very likely bring people running from other offices.

Patty's wails grew louder.

"Shut up, bitch!" he shouted, swinging around and aiming the gun at her.

At this, Patty's wailing increased. I pushed her down on a chair and sat beside her, my brain in overdrive. "I can quiet her if I can get one of her other personalities to come out. I'll talk to her."

"Do whatever you have to do to shut her up. Just don't try anything funny."

I knelt in front of Patty, whose blubbering had continued

unabated. "Doris," I whispered very softly. "Patty's in trouble. She needs you. Come out."

Nothing.

"Doris," I hissed, putting all the urgency I could muster into the words. "Remember the guy in the subway who grabbed Patty? You came out and helped her. She's in terrible danger now. This guy is going to shoot us all. Come out."

I saw the blank stare, the shudder, the melting face, and suddenly Gloria was here. A silly grin spread over her face as her eyes lit on Carl. "Hiya, big boy," she yodeled. "What's doin'?" She heaved herself out of the chair and threw her arms around his neck. "Wanna fuck?"

"Jesus!" He reached up and tore her arms loose. "Get off me!"

"Doris," I yelled. "Come out!"

The melting face, the shudder again, and—Carl caught a rabbit punch in the kidney that knocked him to his knees, sending the gun skidding across the floor. I went for it, but he recovered quickly and pounced on me. As we grappled, the gun discharged, blasting the window and showering us with shattered glass. With one smack across my head he sent me reeling into Ruth-Ann, knocking us both to the floor in a tangle of chairs and broken shards.

But Doris had only just begun to fight. Letting loose a bloodcurdling war whoop, she closed in on him, going for his gun hand. Carl was taller than she was, but muscle for muscle they were pretty evenly matched.

"Gloria," he yelled. "You don't want to fight me. You want to help me so we can run off together."

"I'm not Gloria, that oversexed nitwit, you asshole!" Doris shouted, backing him up against the wall. "I didn't trust you from day one!"

With one enormous heave he shoved her off, knocking her down hard on her rear end.

The gun came up.

Both hands on the grip, Carl brought it level with her head. "You're dead, lady!"

"Don't!" I cried. Without thinking about the consequences, I scrambled to my feet, barreled into him—knocking him off balance—and flung myself across Doris.

Somewhere in the background I heard footsteps and banging on the door and a loud crack as heavy boots kicked it in, and I was grabbed off Doris and unceremoniously thrown aside.

I heard a shot and an answering barrage; I lifted my head to see crimson exploding from Carl's chest, a child's careless finger painting splashed onto the wall, as he slid to the floor.

Dizzy and disoriented, I managed to get to my knees. Vaguely, I could hear Doris spouting curses I'd heard only in X-rated films, as I crawled to where Carl lay drenched in blood, his breath coming in shallow gasps. Ruth-Ann, bleeding from her head, was leaning over him, mumbling the prayer for the dead in Hebrew. Nausea enveloped me, and for a minute I thought I was going to faint. I turned to shout for help, saw Ted's partner, Dan Murphy, kneeling over a tall, lanky body sprawled beside Doris, a body wearing shoes and pants that I recognized.

I have no recollection of how I covered the distance to that body—whether I got to my feet, or I crawled on my hands and knees, or if I sprouted wings and flew.

There was blood on his chest. I shoved Dan aside and threw myself over the prostrate form.

"Ted, oh, God, oh, God, please don't die, don't die."

He didn't move.

"Ted," I screamed. "Open your eyes. I love you. Oh, God, please don't die. I love you so much."

One eye fluttered open, and a pained smile lifted a corner of his mouth. "Christ almighty," he mumbled weakly. "I gotta get shot to hear you say that?"

"You're alive! Oh, thank you, God, thank you, thank you!" I pulled him into my arms and rocked him back and forth like a baby, taking in great gulps of air as tears of relief rained unheeded down my cheeks. "He's alive," I cried to Dan.

"It's only a flesh wound. He'll be okay." He got to his feet. "I gotta tend to the perp. He's in a lot worse shape than Ted."

Everything from that point on went by in a blur as I sat on the floor crooning to Ted, oblivious to the chaos around me. Dan came over and spoke to me, telling me something about Jamie's platoon leader, somebody named Heidelberg, clueing them in to Carl's identity, and I think I answered him, but I don't remember what I said. Dimly, I heard Doris cursing and Ruth-Ann praying as more police and medics arrived. In a haze I saw them put Carl on a litter and carry him out. It was Ted's voice that finally penetrated the fog.

"Carrie?" he whispered.

"What? What's the matter?"

"Please stop," he groaned.

"Stop what? Are you in pain?"

"Yeah. Pain. You're crushing me. Let go. I'm okay. It's over. Please, Carrie, you want me to live, I'm begging you. Let go."

Epilogue

J AMIE, A.K.A. CARL JORGENSON, died on the way
to the hospital. The bullet had struck a major artery and
he'd bled to death before they could get him to the emergency room. He was a true psychopath, an unregenerate
killer, totally lacking any concept of right or wrong. He'd
murdered three people, had attempted to kill my father,
and, but for Ted getting there when he did and taking the
bullet intended for me, he would have killed me and Ruth-
Ann and Elaine/Doris/Patty/Gloria. The cop who rode with
him to the hospital told us he'd remained conscious in the
ambulance and that he'd confessed to all three murders.

In his deathbed statement he'd said that Omar Kassel
had conceived the scam when he'd recognized Eve from
her television appearance. Omar had recruited Carl to im-
personate Jamie after an effort to locate Eve's real son re-
vealed that he had been killed in a plane crash while on a
training mission. Omar would have been content with the
twenty-five-thousand-dollar onetime payoff from Eve. Carl,

however, saw a chance for a lifetime sinecure, only possible if Omar was out of the way.

No one could quite figure out where Barbara Storey had fit into the picture, until the cops located Louise, who, fearing for her own life, had gone into hiding. She then had admitted that she'd known Barbara was living with Omar and that Barbara had probably been in on the scheme from the beginning. We could only surmise that Barbara had threatened to expose Carl after Omar's murder. As for Frank, evil as he was, he was no match for Carl in that department. Clearly he'd wanted in and had agreed to pretend that Carl was his son for a chunk of the take. Foolish man. No way would Carl have let him live. Louise, of course, knew immediately that Carl was an impostor, and her very sensible impulse had been to run. But she'd left the photographs for me and thus had been instrumental in his being exposed.

To the end Carl had insisted he'd rid the world of vermin. In his twisted mind he'd thought of his plan as a win–win situation. Eve would have had her son back, he—Carl—would be secure for life, and the bad guys were dead. His last words had been a message for me.

"Tell Carrie," he'd said, "the Cyclopes are all dead."

It made me wonder if, in his final moments, he'd included himself among them.

Two months later Ted and I were lying on a beautiful white-sand beach on the island of Maui. The trip was a gift from my father, who'd insisted that the lottery money, which had caused so much grief, should now be used to give pleasure. He and Eve were going ahead with their plans for a European trip in June. Dad felt that the best cure for the losses Eve had endured was to give her lots of love and keep her moving, and he was the man with the wherewithal to do both.

I finished rubbing suntan oil on Ted's back and handed him my bottle of Estée Lauder suntan lotion, number thirty. "I still can't believe that the distilled liquid from three or four cigarettes is enough to kill someone."

"Believe it," he said, squeezing the lotion onto his hands and starting on my back. "Frank Garrett died from cardiac arrest after ingesting only a few drops in his coffee."

"Could they really tell all that from the autopsy?"

"The postmortem indicated he died of nicotine poisoning. The lab tested the fibers from your carpet where the coffee had spilled and the tobacco dregs that you'd thrown in your garbage. That confirmed it."

"Those detectives went through my garbage the day they searched my house?"

"Standard procedure. You'd be surprised at what we find in people's trash. There are more ways to do somebody in with common household items than you could ever imagine in your wildest dreams. For example," he teased, "this lotion that I'm putting on your back could contain—"

Chills went up my spine. I kicked him away and grabbed the bottle from his hand. "Stop!"

I didn't ever again want to think about ways people do other people in. I wanted to lie here and soak up the sun and the beauty around me. I wanted to think about getting sand between my toes running along this magnificent beach and about drinking exotic drinks and eating grilled ahi tuna in tomato beurre blanc followed by chocolate Kona coffee mousse at Roy Yamaguchi's famous restaurant, and I wanted to think about making love on our hotel terrace, within sight and sound of the blue, blue ocean, to this man who'd taken a bullet to keep me alive and kicking. Even my old aversion to water couldn't diminish my enjoyment. I watched the palm fronds swaying and thought how I'd like to stay here in this paradise forever. And then I thought of a way I could. I traced the bandage around Ted's wound, leaned over, and kissed him.

"I've found a new safe place," I whispered.

"A what?"

"Eve keeps showing up in my tree house. She's rendered it unsafe. From now on this beach is where I'm coming in my mind whenever I'm stressed out."

He grinned. "You're beginning to sound like Elaine/Doris/Patty/Gloria," he joked. "You sure you're not developing a split personality?"

"There's a difference," I replied haughtily, "between having a mental illness and having an active fantasy life."

He moved in closer and began nibbling my ear. "I'm more interested in your active sex life."

"That's because I've never allowed you into my fantasy life."

"Ah, now you've piqued my curiosity."

But some things should remain up close and personal. I vowed I never would tell him quite everything that goes on in my dreams, and for sure I would never ever tell him about Apollo and the garden of the gods.

There's an old Yiddish proverb often quoted to me by my father: *If you have, hold on to it; if you know, be silent; if you can, do!*

Here and now I had Ted, and I intended to hold on to him; about my wildest dreams I would be silent; and as for the doing part—I jumped to my feet and grabbed his hand. "What say we go have another look at that fantastic view from the terrace?"